Mysterious America 1

SERPENT

Bill Thompson

Published by
Ascendente Books
Dallas, Texas

Serepent: Mysterious America 1
All Rights Reserved
Copyright © 2021
V.1.0

Published by Ascendente Books
ISBN 978-17355661-5-3
Printed in the United States of America

Books by Bill Thompson

Mysterious America Series
SERPENT

The Bayou Hauntings Series
CALLIE
FORGOTTEN MEN
THE NURSERY
BILLY WHISTLER
THE EXPERIMENTS
DIE AGAIN
THE PROCTOR HALL HORROR
THE ATONEMENT

Brian Sadler Archaeological Mystery Series
THE BETHLEHEM SCROLL
ANCIENT: A SEARCH FOR THE LOST CITY OF THE MAYAS
THE STRANGEST THING
THE BONES IN THE PIT
ORDER OF SUCCESSION
THE BLACK CROSS
TEMPLE

Apocalyptic Fiction
THE OUTCASTS

The Crypt Trilogy
THE RELIC OF THE KING
THE CRYPT OF THE ANCIENTS
GHOST TRAIN

Middle Grade Fiction
THE LEGEND OF GUNNERS COVE

THE LAST CHRISTMAS

CHAPTER ONE

I know this place. I've stood in this dark hallway another time. Perhaps more than once. The man beside me is gripping my arm. Not tightly, but enough so that I cannot escape his grasp. We are waiting to go...somewhere. Through a door, a flight of narrow stairs leads to an upper room. I know but cannot recall what is there.

The door at the head of the staircase opens, and I hear my name. The man gestures, and I climb the stairs slowly, somehow knowing but at the same time not knowing what is coming. I step into a room illuminated by gas lamps along its walls. As the flames sway, they cast dancing shadows everywhere, giving me an eerie, haunting feeling that I am in hell.

Somehow I know what to do. I walk across the cavernous room and stand at the left shoulder of a man seated in a large chair. He wears a black robe, and on the table before him rest an ancient sword and a black taper in a tall candlestick. I shudder as a memory slashes through my brain. Something my ancestors experienced will now happen to me. I gaze around the table at the others, all waiting in eager anticipation for what is coming. Something that involves me. Something evil and frightening and unearthly.

The robed man is called the Grand Master. When he speaks, his voice resounds in my brain like a hollow echo. Perhaps I have been drugged. That would explain why I cannot remember—why things are surreal—why the man's words sound as if they are far away, even though I am close enough to touch his sleeve.

"Let the ritual begin."

The words ring in my ears, triggering another memory. Others sat at this table, waiting in anticipation as a person is escorted into the room. Now it is my turn, and I am terrified. My legs tremble, and my captor tightens his grip to steady me.

I am aware of another figure standing in the shadows behind the Grand Master's seat. His clothing is of another time—a crested, brimmed helmet and full plate armor that protects his upper body, but he is transparent. Although he appears alive, I can see the wall behind him. It is this man—this phantom—who calls out an order in another language. "Treu la Serpent." Somehow I know what the words mean—Bring out the serpent. The Grand Master obeys.

He takes a box from the floor and sets it on the table beside the sword. It is no larger than a shoebox, and it is framed in wood with wire mesh forming its sides, top and bottom. There is a piece of wood on one end that slides up and down—a trapdoor. When I see it, I recollect what will happen next, and I shudder.

The Grand Master looks up. "Is she prepared?" he inquires, and my captor nods. I know what he is asking. Am I sufficiently sedated to endure the Ritual of the Envenoming?

"Then let us proceed." I am pushed to my knees beside the robed man. I place my hands on the table before me. Forcing down the terror that wells up inside my gut, I look into the cage that sits inches from my fingers. In the gloom, I can hear more than I see. There is a rustling, swishing sound as the creature picks up my scent. I see its body move easily along the wire as it prepares itself for

2

what is to come. Like the people seated at this table, the hideous, venomous reptile in this box is eager with anticipation.

My captor clasps my wrist firmly as the man in the robe slides the door up. In one deft motion my hand is plunged inside the box. I catch a glimpse of scarlet scales glowing in the candle's flame, and as the door is lowered to secure my hand, I feel the serpent slide easily across my flesh once, then again.

The horrid creature is savoring the moment. It will proceed slowly to make this experience more satisfying.

I fight the natural instinct to jerk my hand or fight the snake. I know if I move—or even cry out—the beast could react with fury, and everything will be over. I have but one chance, and that is to remain perfectly still and wait to learn if the serpent chooses me.

Time passes. Seconds that seem like hours as I and those at the table wait. The creature still strokes my skin with its awful scales, but it has not struck. Perhaps I will survive; somehow I know there is one more horrifying test—and only one of the Chosen could survive it.

The man in the robe raises his fist and brings it down sharply on the top of the box. It shudders violently, and through the wire mesh I watch the thing inside. Startled, it rises and prepares to defend itself. The only adversary it can attack is a human hand—my hand—that lies in the box with it. I stare mesmerized into the cage as my life hangs in the balance.

My fate rests in the hands of a creature that is coiled and poised to strike. Its forked tongue slips easily between two needle-sharp fangs. It raises its eerily beautiful head and seems to look into my eyes as it glides gracefully toward my hand.

CHAPTER TWO

Savannah, Georgia

"Dr. S, I have a question. Savannah must have a dozen or more ghost tours that take tourists around the city every night. Some say our city is America's most haunted. What do you think? Can a historian believe in the paranormal? Do ghosts really exist?"

Fletcher Skorza looked up from an ancient map, smiled and stretched. His shoulders ached from bending over a table, peering through a magnifier, and examining sixteenth-century Spanish inscriptions. He reached for his mug, took a swig of coffee, and grimaced.

"Damn stuff got cold on me."

"I'll fix a new one." His intern, a college freshman named Bexley Wolf, dodged stacks of books, drawings and rolled-up maps, started the Keurig, and waited for it to brew.

Even as a child Fletcher had found Georgia history fascinating. He loved this stuff, and back in his college days, he'd found few instructors who knew more than he. It was his passion, and Fletcher had aced every history course without cracking a textbook.

After graduate school, he'd moved to Savannah and landed a job as assistant director of the nonprofit Coastal

Center for Historic Preservation, or CCHIP. Today he couldn't imagine doing anything more rewarding. Even the place he worked was interesting—a twenty-thousand-square-foot house called the Parsonage that James Oglethorpe himself built in 1750 as a vicarage for Church of England ministers. In 1826, Albion Perryman came to Savannah, founded the Cotton Exchange Bank, and converted the Parsonage into a grand home befitting the city's newest banker. The house still belonged to the Perryman family, although none had lived there for decades. Today a museum occupied the first floor, and the historical society's offices, library and storerooms were on the second.

The Parsonage sat on two acres on Hull Street across from Savannah's Old Cemetery, where early citizens, including a signer of the Declaration of Independence, were buried. Today the graveyard was called Colonial Park, and it had been closed to burials for over a hundred and fifty years. Fletcher could see the lush grounds from his second-floor office, and he enjoyed looking out at a time capsule of Savannah history.

Bexley Wolf—Bex to her friends—was Fletcher's intern, an enthusiastic college student who had applied for a three-month summer slot and brought a fresh vitality and a keen interest to the society. Rather than offloading routine jobs, Fletcher cultivated his interns' passions for history and was rewarded with an extra pair of eyes and hands. Incredibly bright, Bex was shy and rarely initiated conversations, but as she handed Fletcher the mug, she said, "How about that opinion? Are any Savannah ghost stories true?"

He laughed. "You sound like me. We history majors are supposed to be interested in dates and facts and this war and that monument. But it's the people that fascinate me." He pointed to the window. "Each body buried across the street is a fragment of history. Their lives tell us things and give us clues about the past. But ghosts? That's a topic way outside the box. What makes you think I know anything about them?"

"Number one, you're not the stodgy professor type. I can tell you're interested in all sorts of things. Number two—your choice of reading material is a dead giveaway." She pointed to two books on a shelf behind him, *Haunted Savannah* and *Paranormal Activity in Georgia: 1800–1950.*

"Okay, you got me. I've always been curious about things that defy explanation, and reading about the supernatural expands my mind. So here's my answer about spooky places in Savannah. You live here, and you mentioned the ghost tours. There must be a dozen companies doing them, and hundreds of visitors a day ride around town, seeing old houses with eerie pasts. This is one of the most haunted cities in America, but one story's always been my favorite, because it has a basis in history. And it's not just about ghosts, but buried treasure too."

"De Soto's lost treasure? I first heard about that in middle school, but nobody ever proved it. It's a myth, right?"

"That's what I'm talking about, and you're right— no proof exists. Does that mean it's a myth? Perhaps, but I think there's enough truth in the story to make it worthwhile pursuing. I'll confess I even used a metal detector at a few locations I thought might be promising."

"No luck so far?"

Fletcher grinned. "You mean am I still assistant director of a nonprofit, instead of living on my yacht in the Mediterranean after finding de Soto's gold? Right, no luck so far. But I'm convinced his treasure's buried somewhere around Savannah. Now and then something I haven't read turns up—an old manuscript or a twist on the legend—that reveals another place where the loot might be."

Although she knew her boss was unconventional, it surprised Bex that he was an amateur treasure hunter. There was plenty of proof de Soto and his men were in this area in 1540, and records described a vast fortune in gold, silver and precious gems they'd brought from their expeditions in the Florida territory. Many believed that treasure trove was still around somewhere.

The basis for the legend lay in one indisputable fact. De Soto had had treasure when he arrived in what is now Georgia, but it disappeared. The loss would have been catastrophic, because de Soto had intended to take the spoils back to his king, proving that New Spain was filled with riches and deserved future expeditions and colonization.

"Sit down, and I'll tell you what I know," he said. She moved a stack of papers to the floor and sat, thinking his office needed a good cleaning and straightening, but so far he'd refused to let her tackle it.

"I heard about the missing treasure of Hernando de Soto as a kid, just like you did. People called it a fable loosely crafted around factual events. But I learned about a group who knows the treasure is real and where it's hidden, because they're entrusted with its safekeeping. Have you ever heard of *Orden de la Serpiente Roja*—the Order of the Red Serpent?"

Bex hadn't, and mentioned she hated snakes. Fletcher replied that the group's bizarre rituals would make herpetophobics cringe.

"You're using the present tense," Bex said. "Is it still around?"

"I'm certain of it. Lots of academics and historians claim the Order is a myth like the treasure, but I don't agree. If I were a professor or an archaeologist, I couldn't voice my opinion about something so controversial, but I'm blessed to work for an organization that encourages creative thinking. But hey, I'm getting way off the subject—this story isn't about me or snakes. You started all this by asking me what I thought was the most supernatural place in Savannah."

"And you threw me a curveball when you linked it to de Soto."

"Rightly so. The most haunted place in town is right across the street."

"Colonial Park Cemetery? That doesn't surprise me a bit. We took a field trip there in middle school. Talk about a history lesson! Revolutionary War veterans are buried there. Famous people too—politicians, civic leaders and businessmen—but also lots of regular folks. I saw the graves of yellow fever victims—moms, dads and kids who died within days of each other during the 1820 epidemic. I guess by definition cemeteries are the most haunted places; they have the ghosts, after all."

"That's true," Fletcher said. "I've researched dozens of alleged hauntings in that old cemetery. When you have over two hundred years of history crammed into a few blocks of graveyard, it makes perfect sense. I've never experienced anything myself, but when solid citizens with no reason to make up stories relate ghostly encounters, I believe them."

"But what does it have to do with de Soto? Didn't he die in present-day Arkansas? Are you saying you think he's buried across the street?"

"No, not at all. Historians believe he died in Arkansas, but there are lots of Spanish surnames on the markers over there. My PhD thesis focused on a hunch I came up with after years of research and theories, and when I get time, I plan to use our own archives to prove it. Every chance I get, I walk through the Old Cemetery and jot down notes about the Spanish buried there."

"I'd love to hear your hunch," she said as Fletcher looked past her toward the doorway, where his boss stood.

"Hey, Rob. What's up?"

Rob Taylor was a congenial man who seemed always happy, but today his face was twisted into an angry scowl. "The garden club is meeting here at five. Knock off the chitchat, and both of you come help get the parlor ready."

Wondering what had upset him, Fletcher followed Bex and Rob down the hall. As the second-in-command, Fletcher worked on administrative things like research and communication with state archaeologists and historians. Never before had he been asked to set up a room for an event. It wasn't as if the task was beneath his station, but Rob's assistant handled those responsibilities, and Bex lent a hand if she needed help.

9

BILL THOMPSON

How long had Rob been standing there listening, and why was he so upset? Was he trying to interrupt the story about de Soto? It felt that way, especially given his curt command. But why would he care about that?

CHAPTER THREE

Finn Perryman sat in his office behind the same antique partner's desk his grandfather had used. Founded by his ancestor, the Cotton Exchange Bank had stood in the same location on Bay Street for a hundred years, and Finn's tenth-floor office offered majestic views of the Savannah River and Hutchinson Island. This morning a huge container ship meandered up the river, dwarfing every vessel it passed. Finn loved this town, and it made him proud to think this bank played an integral role in Savannah's development, helping its customers start businesses, build homes, and create empires of their own.

To the public—customers of his bank, local business owners, and friends at the country club—Perryman was a walking historical encyclopedia. Whenever he spoke at the Rotary Club or gave a high school commencement, his remarks invariably focused on the heritage of his hometown. Founded by James Oglethorpe, the first city in the colony of Georgia had a unique Southern charm, dozens of old mansions, each with its own mysteries and legends, and a rich history that allowed Finn endless hours of research, enlightenment and pleasure.

Since bank examiners were due at ten this morning, Finn had arrived at eight, an hour earlier than usual. Some bankers regarded examiners with caution or fear, others with resignation or distrust, but Finn felt no emotion about the team of state bank examiners who would spend a week reviewing loans, deposits, assets and liabilities before issuing a report—a bill of health and a list of requirements or suggestions for improvement.

Perryman didn't like examiners; who would, when their job was to micromanage every decision the officers of your institution made? But he didn't fear them either. His bank had one major shortcoming—one perceived failure that examiners always noted—one "correction recommended." Cotton Exchange Bank was too conservative. With almost $192 million in deposits, another bank of its size would have loaned out well over $100 million. Instead, loans totaled only $51 million.

Every examination ended with another criticism over something that existed at Finn's bank and no other in the United States of America. The bank's equity base—the very foundation of its financial strength—consisted entirely of gold. There was no law against it, although for decades the state banking authorities had tried in vain to force more diversification of its assets. Banks were supposed to invest in things like securities, state and municipal bonds, and triple-A corporate obligations. But this little Georgia bank had more than $41 million in gold bars on its balance sheet.

They didn't keep the bullion on premises, of course. Finn was smarter than that. If unscrupulous characters learned the bank had a fortune in gold in its vault, there might be an *Ocean's Eleven*-style heist. Instead, the bullion sat deep in the secure vaults of Georgia's largest independent bank, Mercantile Guaranty of Atlanta.

Time and again, skeptical banking authorities had sent examiners to Atlanta to view and count the gold bars. Once they'd even hired Dillon Gage, a respected precious metals trading firm, to appraise them. Dillon's experts examined the bars and reported their markings were identical to others recovered from Spanish galleons. They were certified genuine, and the weight and current value of each bar was recorded. Back at the bank, the president and owner—always a Perryman—refused to explain where the gold came from. Perhaps he didn't know, they mused; the fact was that in 1971, the first time in decades that it was legal for US citizens to own gold, Finn's grandfather had brought the bars to the bank and transferred ownership from himself to the institution. Where they had been prior to that year, nobody knew.

Gold was worth a lot less back then, and as the price steadily rose to around two thousand dollars an ounce, the net worth of Cotton Exchange Bank rose as well. Even in times when the value declined, the bank was still fine, because it had far more equity than the regulators required. And should the need ever arise, there was plenty more gold where that came from.

This morning Finn looked out over his beloved Savannah, confident that no matter how hard the examiners questioned the unique assets, everything was completely legal and aboveboard, and the bars themselves and their value were real. This bank audit would go well, as every other one had. He'd accept the criticism that he needed to loan more, and he'd point out the numerous businesses and homeowners Cotton Exchange Bank financed. So he didn't make risky loans. Was that a crime? Finn believed not. On the contrary, it was a sign of good banking.

But there was something else. That controversial cache of gold bars was part of the dark side of Finn Perryman's life—another existence that would have astounded bank examiners and everyone else. That could never happen; Finn made sure no one saw behind the curtain. Nobody would discover who the conservative bank president really was or what dark secrets he kept hidden.

He left his office, drove the short distance to an antebellum mansion on Calhoun Square, and used a key to go inside. There were several things he needed to find, but after giving the rambling old house a thorough inspection, he came away empty-handed.

Where did Dixie Castile hide the objects? He'd give it some thought and return when he had more time.

CHAPTER FOUR

Grand old homes stood like soldiers around Calhoun Square, recognized as one of the most haunted venues in Savannah. Built in the eighteen hundreds by wealthy merchants, doctors and politicians, most of them received regular upkeep and maintenance to keep them pristine, but one—the Castile mansion—stood in stark contrast to the rest. Passersby on Abercorn Street stared at the once-beautiful home through a broken fence, past patches of weeds in the unmowed grass, and tsk-tsked, wondering why someone would let a property on one of Savannah's most-visited squares go untended.

This morning Dixie Castile's niece, Marcie Epperson, walked through the house, choosing a few things to keep. Technically, what she took wasn't hers. Dixie had willed the house itself to Marcie, her only relative, but everything else, including the furnishings and personal effects, went to the city library, where Dixie had worked for decades.

After going through the house, the estate's executor, a man named French who was an officer of the Cotton Exchange Bank, had called Marcie to come take whatever she wanted. He saw nothing among the furnishings and personal items that the library could have turned into cash.

What old furniture remained—tables, chairs, a breakfront, armoires in the bedrooms and the like—were in poor shape from lack of upkeep. They wouldn't bring anything in an estate sale, so they, like most everything else in the old house, would end up in the landfill.

Two days ago the executor had met her at the house and handed her a key. As she stepped inside, Marcie felt uneasy, and she declined his offer to let her spend the night if she wanted. "I only live twenty minutes from here," she said, thankful for that. The house was eerie as hell, and a chill ran down her spine after he left her there alone. She stood in the foyer, glancing into rooms filled with dusty furniture and bric-a-brac and feeling creepy about something she couldn't identify—memories from a long time ago, when she was a child staying here with her spinster librarian aunt.

Now that she was an heir, Marcie regretted not communicating with her aunt in fourteen years. Long ago there had been forced visits—a week every summer when her parents dropped her off and went on vacation. Having none of her own, Dixie was uncomfortable around children, and she dealt with it by ignoring her ward. Beginning when Marcie was eight, her aunt would go to work five days a week, leaving the child to traverse the town on foot or bicycle, and allowing her plenty of time to snoop around the drafty old mansion. She found nooks, crannies, hiding places and an attic crammed with mementos and relics that belonged to Castile family members long, long ago. She had found other things in the house too. Unexplainable things.

Back then the old house had scared her and made her wish her aunt wouldn't leave her there alone. Sometimes she'd think a person was behind her, but when she turned to look, nothing was there. She'd hear faint voices calling out, but she never understood what they said or if they were real. There were noises too—creaks and groans and movements like someone was walking in the upstairs hall.

Stop this! What the hell are you doing? Those

16

things never happened. They were products of a girl's overactive imagination stoked by being by herself all day in an ancient mansion. You're not a scared little kid anymore; you're twenty-seven years old. It's just a house—the home of someone you barely knew who's dead and gone. There's nothing to be scared about.

The pep talk didn't work. According to locals, the houses near Calhoun Square were hotbeds of paranormal activity, and ghost tour guides included Dixie Castile's house as one example of the most haunted places in a city filled with spirits.

Although Marcie didn't believe in ghosts, bad memories flooded her mind as she walked through the house. When she was little, every time she stepped inside she'd have a funny feeling, but then it became something else—a tangible foreboding that evil lurked in the shadows. Back then, as she explored the dusty rooms, picking up this piece or that and opening doors and drawers, she'd jerk around at the slightest noise. And she realized today was no different. Years had passed, but the house was the same forbidding, eerie place.

Standing perfectly still to listen, the first sound she heard was the tick-tock, tick-tock of an ornately carved clock that had stood in the foyer since Marcie was a kid. The echoing reverberation unnerved her then, but today it puzzled her. How could it still be running? It required winding, and her aunt had been dead for some time. The executor came, but why would he take the time to wind a clock?

Tick-tock. Tick-tock, just like the constant beating of a heart. That's what I thought back then. If you listen long enough, it will control your mind, becoming louder and louder until it rings through your head like a gong.

She walked away, searching for something else to concentrate on that might clear the cobwebs of dark memories. In a dusty bookshelf she scanned spines and titles, choosing two—an old family Bible and an unusual book bound in animal hide. It looked like some kind of journal, with spidery faded handwriting in a language she

17

didn't recognize. The latter part was in English, and maybe she'd learn some family history.

Startled by the tap-tapping of a branch against a windowpane, she decided to move to the next room. The faster she left, the better.

Thank God it's daytime. I wouldn't spend the night in this creepy place for a million bucks.

She raised a dusty sheet and found an old drop-front secretary desk. Pulling the cover away, she opened it and saw drawers and cubbyholes stuffed with papers, dried pressed flowers and scraps of ribbon. A tape dispenser, scissors and a roll of four-cent postage stamps sat to one side.

Aunt Dixie hadn't mailed any letters lately, she mused. Not only was Marcie not even born when stamps cost four cents, she also couldn't recall the last time she mailed a letter. Thinking she might go through them later, she raked everything from the slots and drawers into a box she'd brought along. Then she went upstairs to see the bedrooms.

With the exception of the master suite, the second-floor rooms were in the same grimy condition as the ones downstairs. Her shoes crunched in the grit as she walked along the hallway, looking into each room. Ghostly furniture draped in bedsheets. Faded, peeling wallpaper. Dust motes flying about everywhere. For some reason, Dixie Castile had closed down almost all of her house, leaving only the kitchen and her bedroom marginally habitable.

The flashbacks began in one of those dusty bedrooms. This had been her room when she visited in those summers long, long ago, and like then, now she felt goosebumps as she remembered how scared she'd been at night.

Her trembling legs gave way, and she fell onto a bed—the one she'd slept in as a child. The one where dreams once filled her mind with panic and fear. Remembering, she looked across the room. The rocking horse still stood in the corner. Back then she believed it watched her when she was sleeping. Afraid to look but somehow drawn to it, she'd peek from under the covers. Its lips were pulled back in a grin, and its eyes, glowing faintly in the darkness of her childhood room, looked in her direction. It was waiting—for what, she never learned, because the horse never moved. But she always thought someday it would come for her.

As she looked at the horse, she remembered an odd letter her aunt had written several years ago. They hadn't communicated in ages, and Marcie didn't understand what the letter meant. She tried the only phone number she had, but it no longer worked. She could have driven to Savannah, but as distant as the relationship was, it simply didn't interest her to learn anything more about the cryptic message. Although unaware of it then, she was Dixie Castile's only living relative, and the woman had reached out to her.

What did the note say? It was something about the rocking horse. I used to play on it as a child, and I broke it, but how? I remember! When I grabbed its head, it flew off and revealed a hole going down into the horse's neck. I screamed and cried as if I'd decapitated a real horse, but Aunt Dixie slipped it back into place and called it good as new.

Marcie recalled some of the letter. It read something like, "Remember what you did to the horse if something happens to me. It's important." Now it was time to learn what it meant. She walked across the room, pulled the head off, and looked down the hole. Something lay deep inside, but in the dim light she couldn't see what, so she wriggled her arm in until it was up to her elbow. Her fingers closed over something, and she brought it out. There was more, and in a moment she had collected everything she could feel.

She put three things on the bed—a cloth bag, a thick old envelope and a folded piece of paper. Not caring to spend any extra time in the old house, she gave each one a quick look. The bag held jewelry—three or four pieces—and the envelope was stuffed with twenty-dollar bills.

Cryptic symbols—some kind of code, perhaps—filled the paper.

Should I notify the bank that I found this stuff? No, the man had said take whatever you want, and she damn sure wanted the money. She put everything in her box to examine back at home.

There came a faint sound from somewhere outside the room. In another setting, she wouldn't have given it a thought. Here and now, in this dark, ancient house filled with someone else's belongings, the noise frightened her. It seemed to come from everywhere and nowhere, hanging in the dank air of the upstairs hallway. It happened again, louder and more distinct this time, and she stood quietly to listen.

There came a quiet, raspy, scratchy sort of sound that evoked a childhood memory of being at her grandfather's house. He'd let Marcie play old 78 rpm records on an ancient Victrola, and when the arm moved over and the needle hit the record, there was a faint whishing, clicking noise before the music began.

Ka-chee. Ka-chee. Ka-chee. This sound was like that old record player's needle scratching on the vinyl.

As quickly as it came, the sound stopped. She held her breath and listened for a moment longer, but there was nothing more, so she cautiously kept exploring. The hall closet was crammed with boxes, behind which hung a rack of moth-eaten dresses and coats that had surely been there for decades. Some of the boxes bore labels. Vacation souvenirs. Photographs. Winter clothing. Paperbacks. Nothing worth taking home. She doubted even Goodwill would take this stuff.

After two hours she called it quits. The box she'd brought along had only a few things inside—the papers from the secretary desk, the two books, and the things from inside the rocking horse. She carried the box to the stairs and turned to look back down the shadowy hallway, wondering what other secrets might rest within these walls.

As quiet as a whisper, it happened again.

Ka-chee. Ka-chee. Ka-chee. A scratchy needle on a

vinyl record, but different now—eerily unsettling. This time she heard more—a voice, like that of a nineteen forties crooner on that old Victrola. Scratchy and grainy and faint.

Hey! Hey! Hey!

The words hung in the air, and then it happened again. Marcie wondered if someone was calling to her, but decided the sounds were in her mind, triggered by memories and the spooky house.

Hey! Hey! Hey!

At last the unnerving voice stopped, but Marcie had had enough. The stairs groaned and rasped as she rushed down to the foyer and out the front door. Outside in the sunlight and away from the ghostly sounds, she paused to catch her breath. She turned to look back at the old mansion, wondering if that spine-tingling voice still echoed throughout the house. Or if it happened only because she was there.

She looked up at the dormer windows above the second floor. That was the attic, a secret, spooky place she'd discovered as a child while her aunt was off at work. She wondered if the raspy voice and scratching sounds came from up there. She didn't intend to find out; drained from what had happened today, all she wanted was to go home.

CHAPTER FIVE

Marcie unpacked the box at her apartment in Tybee Beach, a twenty-minute drive from Savannah. She added the money to a stash under her mattress, took four pieces of jewelry from the cloth bag, and unfolded the cryptic note. She put the Bible and the old leather-bound book aside and stacked the scraps of paper and other stuff from her aunt's desk on her kitchen table. Saving what she hoped was best—the jewelry—for last, she began with the pile from the desk, pulling a wastebasket close to discard as she went along.

She wondered if her aunt Dixie was a hoarder as she glanced at gasoline and restaurant receipts, landline phone bills, a parking ticket from 1973, paycheck stubs that revealed how little a librarian took home each week, and other useless scraps that provided a window into the life of an old woman she hardly remembered.

She found "While You Were Out" memos with names and phone numbers from long ago, slips with random first names and addresses, seven-digit numbers that might have been phone numbers without area codes, and appointment cards from hairdressers and doctors. Nothing seemed worth keeping, and soon everything lay in the wastebasket.

Next she looked at the folded note that came from inside the rocking horse. She opened it and saw bold words at the top in her aunt's easily recognizable handwriting. "Top Secret! Important! Don't Forget!" The remainder of the sheet, written in a different hand, contained row after row of random symbols, numbers and letters that reminded Marcie of video games containing secret codes that required deciphering.

As a pastime, Marcie solved puzzles and cryptograms online, and she wondered if this might be a simple letter-substitution code. Taking a pencil, she wasted a few minutes before deciding it was more complex than she thought. She felt certain her maiden aunt was no gamer. Whatever the words meant, Aunt Dixie had considered the document secret, important and something she shouldn't forget. But why?

She put it aside and took the jewelry from the cloth bag, arranging each piece in a row on the table and examining them one by one. There was a solitaire diamond ring in an outdated setting and a pair of diamond stud earrings. Both settings looked like silver, but the diamonds were dull and milky. Despite having a small stash of money hidden away, Aunt Dixie wasn't wealthy, and Marcie wondered if the stones were real.

Next she found a pin—a bronze medallion that commemorated forty years of service to the Savannah Public Library that was of sentimental value to her aunt, but not to Marcie.

She saved the most dramatic piece for last. Vastly different from the others, it was a stunning golden amulet around three inches by one inch in size. The top was a sword's hilt encrusted with a dozen small red, green and white stones. She held the piece closer, watching the stones shimmer as light hit their facets and wondering if they might be semiprecious.

Below the hilt lay the sword's silver blade, barely visible because of the snake whose scaly body twisted around it. The evil reptile's scales were made of red stones, its eyes glowed green, and from its mouth came a long, forked tongue. It was beautiful in an awful way—a finely crafted brooch that radiated evil—something that would never adorn an outfit unless the intent was to frighten away one's friends.

She held the amulet for a long time, turning it over and over in her hands. Gold and silver and hundreds of little colored stones danced in the light, and she wondered why her aunt would hide away something this beautiful. And why she had something so unusual in the first place.

Putting the jewelry and the coded note in the cloth bag, she tucked them under her mattress with the cash. Tomorrow she'd take the amulet to a jeweler and see what she could learn about it.

She walked a block to a beachfront restaurant, ordered pizza, and sat outdoors under an umbrella, enjoying the sea breeze. Three Coronas and two slices of pepperoni later, she stopped by her shop to be sure her clerk was holding the fort, then went home and crawled into bed. After two long days, she was asleep in no time.

CHAPTER SIX

Around midnight Marcie sat bolt upright in bed. She heard the usual, familiar sounds from the street below—people laughing, an occasional shout, and the thump-thump of bass tones as music blasted from cars going by. What woke her wasn't familiar. It was something else entirely.

What was it…perhaps a dream? She lay back down, drew the bedcovers up around her chin, and tried to sleep. She was still awake when it happened a second time, and she trembled, realizing it was the same cadence she'd heard at the mansion.

Ka-chee. Ka-chee. Ka-chee.

Marcieeeeeeeeeee. A soft whisper echoed throughout her apartment. She heard it a second time, then a third. Someone—something—called her name, drawing it out so long it faded away at the end.

Come back. Come back. Come back.

The voice compelled her to act, and she had no means to resist. Like a sleepwalker, she rose from her bed, donned clothes and shoes, went downstairs, and got in her car. Twenty-five minutes later she stepped through the foyer of her aunt's old house and closed the door. She waited for several minutes, but no voice spoke to her.

Suddenly Marcie emerged from the trancelike state and realized where she was.

What the hell's going on? She had no recollection of driving here, and her immediate thought was to get away—to run as fast as possible from the eerie old house. She trembled in fear as a drawn-out groan emitted from somewhere in the darkness.

Everything's okay. This is an old house, and old houses make strange noises. That's all it is.

Gathering her composure, she told herself she was here, so go upstairs and check things out. There was nothing to be afraid of. It was simply an old mansion and nothing more.

She was halfway up the stairs when she understood it wasn't the house making the noises.

Ka-chee. Ka-chee. Ka-chee. She stumbled, grabbed for the railing, missed, and tumbled down to the hardwood floor at the foot of the staircase.

Shit! Marcie tested her legs and arms, finding sore places but nothing serious. Chiding herself for tripping on the stairs, she got up and turned to leave. She'd spent enough time here. Checking out the upstairs was no longer on her agenda. Running away sounded better.

Come look. Come look. Come look.

Her hand on the doorknob, Marcie paused. *All I have to do is walk out. But dammit, I'm an adult, and everything that's going on in here can be explained. That's the way things work in the world. My brain's taking old-house sounds and making them into spine-tingling words. Stop being so damned scared. Go upstairs and look in the hall. Then you can leave.*

This time she made it all the way to the landing at the top of the stairs before it happened again.

Ka-chee. Ka-chee. Ka-chee.

Come here. Come here. Come here.

Not a request but a command, the words hung in the air. *Walk down the hall to me now,* it seemed to be saying, and the eerie voice frightened her.

28

"Aunt Dixie, is that you?" she murmured as tears streamed down her cheeks. "I know you wouldn't hurt me..."

Come here. Come here. Come here.

Marcie's legs gave way, and she collapsed on the dusty carpet. Afraid she might die, she curled into a fetal ball and waited. But nothing happened. There were no more sounds, no ghostly apparitions flew about, and after a long wait, she raised her head.

At the far end of the long hall, shrouded in darkness and barely visible, hung a wraith—a specter wearing a gauzy, flowing robe. The figure wafted in the air inches above the floor, its long, flowing hair moving slightly. Marcie forced herself to look into its face but saw only a cloudy haze. Then, in a swift move that caught Marcie by surprise, the specter lifted an arm and pointed an outstretched, bony finger at her.

That sent Marcie over the edge. *Go! Go! Go!* She screamed aloud, scrambling to her feet and darting down the stairs. She threw open the door, ran through the crisp night air, and clambered into her car. She gasped to catch her breath, hit the locks, and started the engine. Tires screaming, she raced around Calhoun Square, afraid to stop until she reached the brightly lit business district. Back in the real world at last, she pulled to the curb, put the car in park, and took several deep breaths to calm herself.

The damn place is haunted! Who the hell would have imagined?

Until tonight, Marcie didn't believe in the supernatural. Ghosts, zombies, witches and the like were fictional—the elements that made horror movies so delightfully scary. It was that stuff that made ghost-hunter TV shows like that guy Landry Drake's so popular. People enjoyed watching the clever camera tricks that made the paranormal seem real, but she wasn't fooled. She knew better. Until now.

She recalled going to horror flicks, feeling the tension build and anticipating the climax when the thing from beyond the grave confronted the terrified girl who'd stupidly gone into an old house.

That's me—a girl in an old house. And I can't deny what happened. This stuff is real. I saw an honest-to-God ghost in there. It floated off the floor and had no face and called my name. It scared the hell out of me and made me wonder if I was going to make it out alive.

But when she thought about it, she realized it hadn't been like that. Yes, it was eerie and frightening. How could it not be? To see and hear a supernatural being while standing upstairs in an old mansion in the middle of the night would be enough to terrify the most jaded skeptic.

As scary as the experience had been, she sensed the ghost at the end of the hall wouldn't hurt her. Yes, it was fearsome, but twenty years ago Aunt Dixie had been fearsome too—a tall, unsmiling, stern old woman who disliked keeping her niece as much as Marcie hated being there.

And she had this nagging feeling—an idea that the phantom had been trying to tell her something.

On the way back home, she decided on a course of action. She needed answers, and tonight she'd thought of someone who was in the business of providing answers to unexplained mysteries.

Tomorrow she'd call Landry Drake.

CHAPTER SEVEN

In New Orleans, you could expect rain almost every summer afternoon. Often it was brief and light, with the sun popping through gray clouds, but other times—like this afternoon—the dark, ominous sky hung over the French Quarter like a blanket. A sudden crisp breeze signaled pedestrians to seek refuge quickly, before the first fat drops hit the pavement. Within moments the rain was so heavy that anyone who missed the warning got a drenching. Strong gusts drove the rain sideways, and those XXXortunate at Mr. B's Bistro, or Felix's, or I Pontalba on Jackson Square ordered dessert or another glass of wine rather than a check. Hopefully the rain wouldn't last more than an hour, and if it did, people in the Big Easy would simply continue to Let the Good Times Roll.

In a TV production studio on the top floor of an ancient building on Toulouse Street, a crew filmed excerpts for a new cable show called *Mysterious America*. Famous paranormal investigator Landry Drake sat on a high stool in front of a green screen, reading from a teleprompter about supernatural places along America's eastern seaboard. From Maine to Florida, stories abounded of ghosts, unexplained phenomena and mysterious occurrences. Landry promised viewers plenty of fodder for the new show on his recently debuted Paranormal Network.

The director hoped to finish the segment before the storm hit, and he almost made it. Less than ten minutes remained when the first enormous thunderclap rattled the two-hundred-year-old windowpanes, and the electricity went off. A generator kicked in, but not quickly enough to salvage the interruption when cameras and audio equipment powered down. The storms were an unavoidable nuisance—the crew couldn't work when thunder and lightning threatened to disrupt hours of work.

When the director stopped the shoot, Landry stood and stretched. "Maybe we should use the storms to our advantage," he said. "Nothing like a badass thunderstorm to make a scary story even more creepy."

The director shook his head. "You know that doesn't work. Too damn noisy. I dub in thunder where I need it." He told everyone, "That's it for this afternoon. We'll finish up in the morning." Everyone filed down the narrow staircase to the second floor, where the network's offices shared space with Henri Duchamp's Louisiana Society for the Paranormal.

"Want to grab a late lunch?" Landry asked Cate Adams, his girlfriend and the office manager, who sat at a dining table-cum-desk loaded down with file folders and books. Still photos of paranormal sites were tacked on the wall behind the table, and hundreds of sticky notes covered everything. It was organized chaos, Cate told everyone. Even if no one else could find anything in the clutter, she could.

"Have you looked outside lately?" Cate laughed. "Unless Uber offers rowboats, I don't think we're going anywhere."

"This'll be out of here in thirty minutes," he said, and she laughed at his optimism. She offered Cafe Maspero, half a block away on Decatur Street, saying if they ran, they could be inside in under two minutes. Downstairs, they stood in the carriageway at the entrance to their building, hoping for a brief break but seeing none. At last she yelled, "Go!" and they scampered across Toulouse, ran down to the corner, and ducked inside.

The hostess told them there wasn't a seat left in the house, but a shout came from behind the bar. "Landry! Cate! Come on over!" A tall bartender in his twenties with a long red beard waved and pointed to two stools. They weren't side by side, but an obliging diner—a tourist dressed in a T-shirt that said "If found, return to Bourbon Street"—switched seats in exchange for an autograph from the well-known New Orleans ghost hunter. Cate wisely took the seat next to the tourist, potentially avoiding having him monopolize their dining experience.

"Francisco, you're a lifesaver," Landry said, shaking the bartender's hand. "I've never seen Maspero's this crowded."

"Nothing like a torrential downpour to bring in the drinkers. How have you guys been? Haven't seen you in a couple of weeks."

The proximity of their building to the historic restaurant meant they often stopped in for lunch, but typically armed with a reservation. The hostess at the front desk came over, tapped Landry on the shoulder and said, "Excuse me. When I heard Francisco call your names, I recognized you from your TV shows. I apologize I didn't know who you were, and I'm sorry I didn't have a table. Stay right here, and I'll give you the next available."

"Back away, girl," Francisco said with a grin. "They're mine now. You cast them off like drowned rats, and now they get treated to the finest service the French Quarter has to offer."

"We look like drowned rats," Cate said, stamping her sneakers on the floor. "We hit every puddle between the office and here." She ordered a Chardonnay, and when he held up two fingers, she said, "I guess the filming's done for today, since you're having wine for lunch. We don't want Landry Drake stumbling over his lines."

He shot her a look, and she understood. The man on the next barstool was listening to every word. He ordered his third Cajun Mary, and as Landry and Cate's food arrived, the man seized upon the break in conversation.

He leaned forward to see Landry. "Joe Parma, Pascagoula, Mississippi. Nice to meet ya. I've seen every *Bayou Hauntings* show, Mr. Drake. I'm a believer. I know the supernatural's real. My buddy and I had an experience of our own one time. We were in this haunted hotel, and…"

Cate turned to him. "I'm so sorry, but we're on a tight deadline. We're in the middle of a film shoot, and we're on a quick lunch break."

"Is your studio close by? I'd love to see it…you know, watch a filming or something. But I heard you say a minute ago you guys were done for today."

The eavesdropping and pushy attitude irked Landry. "Sir, I appreciate your moving so we could sit together, but we really are in a rush. The studio isn't open to the public, but eventually we may have live audiences. Jot your name on a napkin, and we'll put you on the list."

Satisfied, the tourist downed the last of his drink, tabbed out, and clumsily extricated himself from the corner bar stool. He slapped Landry on the back, said, "See ya in Hollywood, buddy," dodged tables and stumbled through the front door into the rain.

"I didn't know we were going to have live audiences." Cate laughed. "When hell freezes over, we might," Landry replied, asking the bartender to drop the napkin in the round file—the black trash bin behind the bar. After a second round of wine, Cate went over to the front window and returned with a weather report. All that was left of the storm was a few sprinkles, and they settled up and returned to work.

When they walked upstairs to their office, Henri Duchamp said, "I was hoping you'd return soon. I didn't want to disturb your lunch, but I took a tip-line call while you were out. Very interesting. Very interesting indeed."

CHAPTER EIGHT

When Landry, Henri Duchamp and Cate's father, Doc Adams, established the Paranormal Network, they set up a hotline so viewers could report unusual phenomena. As the fledgling channel debuted on more and more cable outlets, Landry's face appeared several times a day, promoting the hotline and offering a thousand-dollar reward to anyone whose suggestion became an episode of the new *Mysterious America* series.

"Are you planning to send the lead to Harry?" Cate asked Henri. Harry was a private investigator with an office just around the corner. He was also a friend and a participant in several *Bayou Hauntings* investigations.

"Not at the moment. There's something different about this call, and I wanted us to discuss it before involving others. This caller wasn't your run-of-the-mill tipster; she was so scared, her voice trembled as she spoke. Her story is she was clearing out a deceased relative's house in Savannah and discovered things that made her very nervous. She called it 'frightening and inexplicable.'"

"Why us? Why not call the cops?" Landry asked.

"I asked her the same thing. She claims to want no publicity. She recalled hearing we had a paranormal hotline on one of our shows. This isn't a tip—it's not about getting a thousand-dollar reward or being on TV. It's just the opposite; the woman's afraid of something she found, and she wants our help."

Landry said, "I'll call her and get enough information to turn Harry loose. We'll caution him to play it low-key, and if he digs up something interesting, I'll take a look at it."

Cate disagreed. "Helping people is great, but it's not our mission. We can't take our eyes off the ball when we're focused on building a new network. Running on a tight budget with a minimum of employees keeps the company lean and mean, but it means more effort's required from the three of us. We hold the future of the Paranormal Network in our hands, and we can't allow anything to change our focus. We don't have the luxury of considering new storylines right now."

"Right as usual," Landry conceded. "But Harry's not an employee; he's a contractor working for time and expenses. First thing he'll do is call her, and then he might decide there's nothing worth our time. Even if he takes the next step, a Southwest flight to Savannah and a few hours of investigation can't cost us more than a couple of thousand dollars. I say it's worth spending the money to see what's up."

"Of course you do," she snorted, only half serious. "You're the adventurer, and I'm the one who has to figure out where the money to pay Harry comes from. But then again, you're the star of the network, and your vote counts just as much as mine. And FYI, I still love you even if I think you're a foolish spendthrift." She asked Henri to cast the tie-breaking vote, hoping their conservative partner would agree.

He surprised them. "I'm afraid I have to side with Landry on this one," their typically conservative friend said. "I heard the tone of the woman's voice, and one couldn't miss the fear. She paused once, gasped for breath, and sounded as if she were about to break down. If I were a betting man, I'd say Harry Kanter's going to find this is a story worth our pursuit."

Cate said, "Yes, but even if it's the biggest supernatural event since Amityville, we can't use it. No publicity—that was her requirement. I'm sorry, guys, but this one's not for us. If we discover this is a great ghost story, we still have to let it go. So we're doing it for what? Charity? Curiosity? Come on, guys. That's simply not what we do, and it takes our focus off the ball at a critical time."

Landry got down on one knee. "How about I do it only at night or on weekends, and only after I've eaten all my greens and finished my homework?"

"Very funny. Someday when you grow up, you'll understand my side of this. Meanwhile, we have two votes in favor, so that means you win. Henri, since you took the call and can describe the situation firsthand, it's best for you to contact Harry. Just let him know I'll be watching his expenses like a hawk!"

CHAPTER NINE

Former Louisiana state police detective and current private investigator Harry Kanter had worked several *Bayou Hauntings* cases with Landry while on the police force. Skeptical at first, he became a believer when he experienced one supernatural phenomenon after another. After decades of service, his vindictive boss fired Harry for disobeying an order to stay away from Landry and his cases. Faced with the loss of his pension, Harry won an appeal, received his retirement benefits and a hefty settlement, and had the satisfaction of seeing his superior ignominiously booted from the force.

Harry moved to New Orleans, hanging out his PI shingle on Decatur Street just around the corner from Landry's building. Like many retired cops, his background proved valuable to clients, allowing him to open doors and gather information others couldn't. He also had a knack for research, and future plans called for the new Paranormal Network to let Harry vet its hotline tips.

After Henri explained what the girl had said, Harry returned her call without identifying himself as a PI, which sometimes intimidated people. She hesitated, stammering that she shouldn't have called, then repeated that she wanted help, not publicity. Before she'd say anything, she wanted a confidentiality agreement signed by Landry Drake himself.

Harry told her it didn't work that way. "The network's mission is to uncover and report on paranormal events. Right now they're working on episodes for the new *Mysterious America* series. You've told me nothing about your experience, but I can vouch for Landry and the team. I've personally witnessed seances, exorcisms, spirits and demons—and it's all real. How about this—I listen to your story and pass it along. If the team agrees to work with you, it won't cost you anything, but if Landry Drake wants to turn it into a show, you'll have to agree. That's how it works."

"I can't do that. It wouldn't be right…"

"I don't understand. Who are you protecting? You experienced something in a deceased relative's house, right? Why can't you talk about it?"

"Because she's…my aunt was a respected member of the community. I don't want people to think she's a kook or something."

Harry understood and explained he had felt the same way the first time he interacted with Landry Drake. He walked her through his own thought process as in time he realized the paranormal isn't something crazy. It exists—perhaps in a parallel dimension or in the energy forces of dead people who can't or won't leave their houses. Maybe it's something else entirely, he added, but one thing he could promise. Landry would treat her, her deceased aunt and the house with respect.

"If he experiences the same things I did, do you promise he won't put it on TV without my permission?"

"Yes. He'll go over everything with you, but out of fairness to Landry and his people, and the time they might spend on your case, please keep an open mind."

She agreed, and at last she revealed who she was—Marcie Epperson, a shop owner from Tybee Beach, Georgia. Her maiden aunt, Dixie Castile, had retired a few years ago after serving as Savannah's city librarian for forty-something years.

"After she died, I drove over to her house. It's less than half an hour away, but I was too late. I'd missed everything."

"Missed everything?"

Marcie said she and her aunt weren't close, although Marcie was her only living relative. After Marcie's mother—Dixie Castile's sister—died twelve years ago, Marcie didn't stay in touch. "Maybe I should have," she admitted, "but after those summer visits when I was a kid, we never talked to her again. Just let the connection die, I guess. Sad."

Harry asked again what she had missed.

"Everything. Her death, her funeral—things like that. I only learned she died when some guy from a bank called and said they were ready for me to come go through her belongings to see if I wanted anything, and said she had left me the house. That was a shocker."

"My condolences," Harry said. "If you don't mind, in the interest of time let's fast-forward to the reason you called the hotline. Then I can decide if I need to come that way. Are you in Savannah now?"

"No. I finished up there, and I'm back at my place in Tybee. It's very close though. I can be in Savannah in twenty minutes. Her will said I get the house, and the library gets the rest. There wasn't much—an old car, junky furniture and personal things—and the executor told me to take what I wanted from in the house. The banker said when one of his people started boxing things up, they found my mother's address and phone number, but it was disconnected. They found me on Google. I inherited an old house, but I might be better off having never known she died."

"Why? Because you didn't inherit everything?"

"No. I don't care about that. Like I said, I never even knew she died. We weren't close, obviously. I just wish I hadn't gone to the house. I can't sleep for thinking about it."

"Did you spend the night?"

"Spend the night? Are you kidding? I'd stay under a

bridge before I'd be caught there after dark."

Harry wasn't a patient man, and he sensed her evasiveness. "Okay, Miss Epperson. You called the network. They asked me to return the call. Can we talk about what's going on?"

She told him what she knew, and ten minutes later, Harry assembled Landry and the crew in their conference room. After recounting her experiences, he got the green light to fly to Georgia.

CHAPTER TEN

Bank examiners always arrived precisely on time, and today the four at Cotton Exchange Bank were busy setting up shop in a second-floor conference room. In the president's office eight floors above them, a wisp of smoke from Finn's pipe curled toward the ceiling as his second-in-command, a woman named Fielding, awaited orders.

In addition to being executive vice president, the tough female was also the bank's compliance officer. That meant she dealt with examiners, answered questions or found someone who could, argued for favorable treatment, and represented Cotton Exchange Bank in disputes with the audit team over any negative findings. If she had a first name, nobody at the bank knew it. Everyone simply called her Fielding.

After getting the examiners settled, she had come directly to the president's office to let him know where their efforts would be concentrated during their visit. They always began by reviewing the loan portfolio, and last week they'd requested a list of all the bank's loans. Bank examiners always requested every nonperforming loan and spent hours poring over the files, the creditworthiness of the borrower, and the chance of repayment. It was different in this case because of Cotton Exchange's ultraconservative lending policies. The bank had only a handful of nonperforming loans and had experienced an almost unbelievably low number of defaults. Today the lead examiner requested seventy-five loan files; of those, just three percent were nonperforming. The others were randomly selected by the audit team to ensure the bank wasn't understating its bad loan numbers.

When Fielding told her boss what the examiners started with, he waved his hand dismissively. They both knew the auditors would find nothing, because the loans were as solid and well-documented as any bank's in Georgia.

"That should take an hour," Perryman smirked. "What else is on their agenda?"

"The usual. I expect they'll write us up again for not loaning enough, but the lead examiner has already threatened to lower our A+ rating if we don't change. They want to see more loans to small business, low-income housing, community redevelopment—all the buzzwords we've heard before."

"Loans that will increase our likelihood of write-offs. That's what I call the kind of stuff they want. None of these jokers could run a bank. Not even a CPA firm would hire them. That's why they work for the government and come harass people like me."

Fielding knew that wasn't true. Examiners were well-trained, well-respected accountants who made good salaries and took their jobs seriously. But she let her boss rant, as he did every time these people showed up. It did no good to challenge him.

"And they want to see the gold this time."

Finn scowled. "Why? How many times…"

"You know why, Mr. Perryman. Just because they saw it a few years ago doesn't mean it still exists."

"That's ridiculous. Every single year the custodial bank in Atlanta certifies that the gold bars are there. Biggest damn independent bank in Georgia says we have the assets we claim to have. Why the hell do they pester me? It's the damned government. I contribute to every damned campaign that comes along—the governor, senators, representatives, hell, even the dogcatcher. And what do I get for it? Unmitigated harassment from these civil servant bastards."

Fielding frowned at so much wasted energy over something he couldn't control. "When they ask, we must provide what they want. You can rant and rave, but these guys have you by the balls, pardon my French, and you know it."

Perryman slammed a fist on his desk and glared. "How dare you lecture me? Do your job, Fielding. Do what you're hired to do and let me worry about things that don't concern you. Now get out of my office and get to work."

Other subordinates would have left in tears or complained or resigned or filed a lawsuit with EEOC. But Fielding wasn't another subordinate. She knew where the skeletons were buried, and that made her the most valuable asset Finn Perryman had inside the Cotton Exchange Bank. He knew it, so did she, and that was enough.

CHAPTER ELEVEN

The local jeweler Marcie selected at random stood on the opposite side of a glass showcase, peering through a loupe at the diamond solitaire ring. "Poor-quality cubic zirconia in a sterling silver setting," he proclaimed, and the earrings were the same. "The silver's worth maybe fifteen dollars," he added with a dismissive wave. "Anything else I can do for you?"

She had saved the red serpent amulet for last, and the man raised his eyebrows when she dumped it out of the cloth bag. "My, my, what have we here? Where on earth did you find this?"

"Among a deceased relative's things. Isn't it beautiful?"

"Indeed. It's fascinating. I've never seen anything like it." He examined the back and said, "I wonder what it is. A brooch, perhaps, although there's no fastener, and it would be quite heavy hanging from one's lapel. No, it's not a brooch. What then is it?" He turned the object around and around, pausing several times to use the loupe. "Do you mind if I dip it in a cleaning solution? It'll brighten it up, and perhaps we can find a mark."

He took the piece to the back and returned a couple of minutes later. "Look how it shines now," he said, handing it to her.

"Is it worth anything, or are those little stones all glass?"

The jeweler smiled broadly. "This is a treasure, my dear. I only wish I knew its story, because the piece is amazing. Although the back bears no marks, I'd bet it's twenty-four-karat gold and pure silver. We can test for that if you wish. And the stones…oh my goodness, yes, they're real. Diamonds, rubies for the snake's skin, emeralds for its eyes, and sapphires too. The stones and metal contribute to its value, of course, but the real worth of this piece lies in its age and superb craftsmanship. It's very, very old. Sixteenth or seventeenth century, I'd guess. Whoever made this was likely a renowned European artisan. This is one of the most beautiful objects I've ever seen. Did you find it here in Savannah?"

"No," Marcie lied. There was no need to tell this stranger anything.

He smiled when she asked what it was worth. The heirs always wanted to get to the bottom line. Even if it had been a relic from Jesus Himself, they always wanted to know how much cash they could get for it.

"It would take further examination to give you a precise number, and I'd love to make you an offer, but in my professional opinion, you'll be better served consigning this to an auction house like Heritage or Sotheby's. It's exquisite, and its value is whatever a willing buyer would pay. I wouldn't be surprised if it brings three-quarters of a million dollars, and that estimate may be far too low. If you're interested, I'd be happy to act as your agent to facilitate the sale and simplify the process for you."

She was stunned at the estimate and took a moment before replying. "I'm not going to sell it. The valuation amazes me, and the money would be nice, but now isn't the time. I believe this object is a clue to solving a puzzle I've stumbled upon. Thank you for your time. How much do I owe you?"

"Nothing, miss. I was privileged to be able to hold something so beautiful, and should you ever decide to sell, please keep me in mind."

She walked out with the cloth bag clutched tightly in her hand. As she stood on the sidewalk in downtown Savannah, suddenly everyone passing by represented a danger. Her eyes darted here and there. What if the man coming her way knew what she had? What if those teenagers driving by planned to jump out and steal it? What if...

She considered getting a safety-deposit box. Since she'd never had anything nice before, she didn't know how to get one, but she decided to keep it close. When the man from the Paranormal Network came, she'd show it to him.

CHAPTER TWELVE

Marcie owned a T-shirt shop on the Strand just across from Tybee Beach. Situated among the area's most popular beachfront venues, Marcie's shop enjoyed a steady stream of tourist shoppers. In the summer she hired a college student to assist with increased traffic, and right now that allowed Marcie a little free time to handle the enigmatic situation about her aunt's house.

The Dixie Castile Marcie thought she knew was turning out to be anything but a simple spinster librarian in her eighties. For one thing, she lived in a haunted house. For another, she owned a piece of jewelry worth three-quarters of a million dollars. What other secrets remained to be discovered?

Three days after her harrowing experience, Marcie still had the key to the house and was surprised the trustee hadn't called to request she return it. Now, as she drove over to meet the investigator from New Orleans, she wondered if she'd have the courage to set foot in that old mansion again.

These past few days she hadn't slept well, couldn't concentrate on work, and wasn't eating. She'd spent her life as a paranormal skeptic, but there was no denying what had happened up there on the second floor. The eerie scratching sound and the faraway voice calling to Marcie had shaken her, but seeing a ghost for herself was something else entirely. It was still hard to believe, and she would never forget the dread that swept through her body as the specter floated in the half-darkness just down the hallway from her. This was real, and something in her gut told her she couldn't simply walk away, because somehow, in some incomprehensible way, she was a part of it.

Harry Kanter was waiting on the porch when she arrived, and she confessed she was afraid to walk across that threshold today. When they'd spoken earlier, Harry admitted he hadn't believed in the supernatural, but working with Landry Drake changed his mind. There were just too many things that defied explanation, he said again today.

"So I'm not crazy?"

"Not at all. You'd be crazy not to wonder what's going on in there. Our minds are conditioned to deal with rational situations. When something radical happens—like seeing a ghost, for example—everything we're supposed to believe goes out the window. We use our database of life experiences to explain an event, but a unique circumstance short-circuits our processes. That's an explanation I concocted to convince *myself* I'm not crazy." He laughed and so did Marcie.

"Before we go inside, let me ask you one more thing," Harry said. "What vibes did you get from the spirit? Did you sense it was friendly or hostile?"

"That's an interesting question. It scared me out of my wits. It was at one end of a long hall, and I was at the other. The moment I saw it, I had an overwhelming sense of dread. I began shaking and thought if I didn't get away from the house, that thing would come after me. Somehow I got out; the first thing I remember is driving away like a maniac. Then I calmed down. I was back in the real world, and what just happened felt like a dream. I even thought maybe it was trying to communicate with me somehow—to tell me something important." She looked at Harry. "I guess I'm rambling too much. Does any of that make sense?"

"It makes complete sense, and I appreciate your willingness to meet me here today."

Marcie shivered. "I may not get further than the hallway, but I'll try. Let's do this before I chicken out." She led the way to the door, inserted the key, and turned the knob. The door swung open noiselessly, and they stepped inside.

Putting her finger over her lips, she cocked her head, listened closely for sounds, and looked around the wide foyer and up to the top of the staircase. The house was quiet, and everything appeared unchanged from her last visit.

She pointed to the stairs and asked Harry to go first. He started up with Marcie close behind, and when they reached the hallway, she pointed to where a large mirror hung on the far wall. Oversized wooden chairs stood on each side.

"I'm going to take a look," Harry said, walking down the hallway alone. Marcie stood in the light that filtered through large dirt-encrusted windows, but the far end lay shrouded in darkness. He tried a set of switches by the stairs and another halfway down the hall. When nothing happened, he wondered if the bank had shut off the power after Dixie Castile's death. Harry took out a compact LED flashlight, turned it on, and played the beam around the walls and floor. He knelt and looked closely; a thin layer of undisturbed dust covered every surface, confirming no one—at least no inhabitant of this world—had been at this end of the hall in a while.

Ka-chee. Ka-chee. Ka-chee. He cocked his head and listened. Marcie had described the sound, and Harry agreed it was like an old-fashioned record player's needle hitting the vinyl.

Leave. Leave. Leave. Words as soft as a breeze hung in the air, faint words bearing an overwhelming sense of malice. Then Harry heard another sound—a scuffling noise from somewhere at the other end of the hall—and he sprang to his feet and ran. Even as he began his sprint, he could see that she was gone.

"Marcie! Marcie, where are you?" He shouted her name over and over, and he examined the stairway, seeing their footprints in the dust. She hadn't gone downstairs, so why didn't she answer?

He raced through open doorways into long-abandoned bedrooms, seeing carefully made beds bearing raveled, decaying coverlets. He jerked frayed white sheets off chairs, tables and nightstands, threw open closet doors, and searched behind racks of moth-eaten clothes. He went prone on the floor to look under the beds, but he found no sign of the girl he'd left behind moments earlier.

Ka-chee. Ka-chee. Ka-chee.

"Where is she? What have you done with her?" he yelled, angry at himself. He'd been in enough of these situations with Landry to know not to assume anything. The girl was scared, and he'd left her alone. Helpless, he realized he was dealing with the supernatural—forces beyond human understanding that could have snatched Marcie from under his very nose. Harry had to work fast—the more time that passed, the more danger she could be in. But where could he look? She had vanished.

Leave. Leave. Leave. Whispers hanging in the air, so faint as to be nothing, really. Not even words.

Except they *were* words—eerie, hauntingly malicious, ethereal warnings meant for him.

CHAPTER THIRTEEN

Harry went out to the street where the rented SUV was parked and called Landry, his conscience dishing out guilt as he saw Marcie's car. He brought Landry up to speed and asked if he should call the police.

Landry nixed the idea, asking Harry what he'd tell the cops if he called. That Marcie disappeared after Harry left her at one end of the hall to go ghost-hunting at the other? Calling the police wouldn't help things, because so far there were no answers to the secrets the house held. Marcie was somewhere inside the mansion. They just had to figure out where.

"I'm coming to Savannah. I'll check the airline schedules and call you back." Shortly he called with flight information and said he was on the way to the airport.

That afternoon they stood outside the gates of the Castile mansion. As they maneuvered through brambles and tall weeds in the front yard, Landry said, "The place couldn't have gotten this overgrown in the short time Dixie Castile's been dead. Looks like she didn't care much for yard work."

Harry turned the knob and pushed on the door, but it wouldn't budge. He rattled the knob again. "That's odd; it's locked. I left it unlocked, because Marcie had the only key. Somebody's been here since I left to go to the airport."

"Let's find another way in," Landry said, trying windows around one side of the house. Harry went in the opposite direction, meeting up with Landry in back. Careful to avoid tripping on the rickety wooden steps, they walked across a porch and looked through the dirty panes of a locked door. "This is as good a place as any," Harry said as he took out a compact flashlight and tapped on a glass pane a few times until it broke. He removed the shards, reached his hand through, and unlocked the door. They were in.

He and Marcie hadn't been in this part of the house, and Harry made a couple of wrong turns before finding the front hallway. "That's where it all happened," he said, pointing up. They climbed the stairs, and Harry took him to the spot where Marcie had stood just before she disappeared. "She said she saw the phantom down there at the far end of the hall, right in front of that big mirror. With no windows on that end, you can't see much from here."

They were startled when a nearby bedroom door opened, and a neatly dressed young man stepped into the hall. He appeared as surprised as they to find others in the house.

"What are you doing here? How did you get in?"

Harry said, "I was wondering the same thing. Who are you?"

"I'm Carter French, the executor of Dixie Castile's estate, and this is her house. I have every right to be here. When I arrived, the door was unlocked. How did you get in, and where is Marcie Epperson? Did she give you a key?"

Ignoring the question, Harry introduced himself as a private investigator who was working with Marcie.

The man raised his eyebrows. "A private investigator? Who did she hire you to investigate? She inherited this house. I invited her to come go through her aunt's things before we dispose of them. I don't understand..." He had glanced Landry's way a couple of times, but now a flash of recognition lit his eyes.

After years of television appearances dealing with

56

supernatural and paranormal events, Landry had achieved national celebrity. Like the hapless tourist in that New Orleans restaurant, everywhere he went, well-wishers interrupted for selfies or autographs, and he understood the banker had just realized his identity.

"You're Landry Drake, aren't you?" French asked, visibly unnerved as he pulled a cellphone from his jacket pocket. "Both of you stay right here. I'm calling the bank."

Landry raised a finger. "Hold on a moment. Marcie Epperson inherited this house, correct?" The man nodded.

"Then there's no problem. She called our office and asked for help. Harry came up yesterday, and I just arrived. We're here at her invitation, so everything's fine."

The young banker hesitated, unsure what to do next. His boss, Finn Perryman, had sent h over to keep an eye on Marcie and report what she found in the house. When he arrived, he'd found the house unlocked and empty. He'd been doing an upstairs walkthrough when he heard Landry and Harry outside in the hall.

If Landry was telling the truth, he had every right to be here, but where was Marcie, and why did she call a legendary ghost hunter for help? He knew Mr. Perryman would be very interested to learn about this.

"Where's Miss Epperson?"

Harry answered truthfully if not completely. "I don't know. She brought me here earlier today, and I haven't seen her since I left a couple of hours ago."

"That settles it. If she isn't here, then you must leave. I have to confirm she wanted you in here and find out why she called you."

Landry shook his head. "With all due respect, you're Dixie Castile's executor with well-defined and very limited responsibilities. As Dixie's heir, what Marcie Epperson does is none of your business. She doesn't answer to you or your bank. Am I right?"

"The bank doesn't want anybody poking around..."

"Oh really? Why is that? Why does the bank care about Dixie Castile's house? It's not theirs—or yours. It belongs to Marcie now. Your comment intrigues me, Mr....what was it...French? Why exactly does the bank not want anybody 'poking around,' as you put it?"

He backtracked awkwardly, apologized, and moved toward the staircase. "If you see Miss Epperson, please ask her to call me," he said as he descended and strode across the foyer to the front door. They watched him stare at the locked deadbolt a moment, then look up at them, obviously wondering why he hadn't heard them arrive if they came through that door. He locked it behind him, and through the window they watched him cross the yard and go out the gate.

Harry said, "Did you see how nervous that guy was? Hard to tell if he was the one who got caught snooping around, or if we did. Once he realized who you were, he looked like he was about to throw up his lunch!"

They laughed, but the banker's offhand remark about keeping people out was curious. "Once we figure out where Marcie is, I hope she can answer some questions about the Cotton Exchange Bank's interest in this house. One thing's certain—this isn't your typical executor-and-heir relationship. We've wasted enough time with that guy; we have to find her. Let's retrace every step you took when you went down the hall and she disappeared."

Four miles away from the old mansion, the president of the bank listened to his young employee describe his encounter with a private investigator and the famous ghost hunter Landry Drake at the Castile mansion. Finn wished the kid hadn't met up with them, but from what he related, there was nothing to worry about. He'd handpicked Carter French to serve as Dixie Castile's executor precisely because of his naivety. The young man knew nothing about what was really going on, nor would Finn enlighten him.

Once his underling left, Finn pondered the impact of Landry Drake's coming to Savannah. Why would Dixie's niece have called a ghost hunter? He made a mental note to find out.

CHAPTER FOURTEEN

By the time the executor left, it was almost five, and the sun had dipped behind the ancient live oaks in the front yard. Marcie had been gone seven hours, and they had to keep searching. As they walked through the foyer, they heard the loud *tick-tock, tick-tock* from a beautiful old clock near the stairs. As it solemnly chimed the hour, Landry asked if that thing had been working when they first came in. Neither had heard it, and they knew the executor didn't wind it, because they'd watched him leave. He wouldn't have done that anyway, so maybe they just hadn't heard it.

After hearing Harry's description of the scratchy record-player noises and faint words, Landry hoped to hear them too, but the typical creaks and groans were all they got as they went room by room, beginning with the ones nearest where she vanished. They knocked on panels, emptied junk-filled closets to check the walls and floors, and on hands and knees, Landry crawled around the far end of the hall, knocking on floorboards.

"Is the electricity on?" Landry asked as deep shadows crept along the walls of the upstairs hallway. "I don't want to leave yet; we have to find her as quickly as we can."

"Power's off, but it may be the breaker. Dixie

Castile hasn't been dead very long; why would the bank turn off the power before Marcie could come look around? I don't get it. I'll go look for the box." He went downstairs, and Landry heard him opening and shutting doors. Landry's next place to look was a hall closet; he opened the door and pushed aside dusty winter coats. When it was empty, he saw the breaker box cover on the wall and yelled to Harry.

He flipped a large switch at the top of the box, and chandeliers hanging at opposite ends of the hallway flickered to life, casting spears into the shadows. He turned on lights in the bedrooms, and soon they had enough illumination to keep looking.

Landry took Harry to the hall closet and pointed up. "I just saw this; it's a pull-down attic stairway, right?" Harry directed his flashlight up and looked at all four corners. "I think so. There's the little hole at one end where a chain would hang down to open it."

An old wooden stepladder stood in the back of the closet; Landry brought it up, leaned it against the wall, and tried the first rung, which snapped in two under his weight. "That might have worked fifty years ago," Harry said, "but we're going to have to find something else."

Landry got a step stool he'd seen in a closet and climbed to have a closer look. The stool was short, even on the top rung Landry could just touch the ceiling, but it was close enough to check things out.

A rectangle made of wooden slats snugly framed the piece of plywood they presumed was a door, but without the pull cord or tools, Landry couldn't budge it. Pushing up didn't work either, and Harry went downstairs to get some tools he'd found in a kitchen closet while looking for the breaker.

Landry kept at it, running his fingers around the sides of the rectangle. On one side he felt something different—a tiny metal latch. Standing on the top of the stool, he raised himself up on tiptoe, teetering as he struggled to maintain his balance, but he couldn't get close enough to see it. He moved the latch back and forth, but nothing happened. He eased a finger under the object and pushed up, losing his balance and tumbling to the floor as the stool crashed down beside him.

Hoping Harry hadn't heard his clumsy fall, Landry picked himself up. Fine white lint littered the floor, and he looked up to see a dark hole. His finger had been under the metal object when he fell, and the extra pressure must have caused it to open. He saw that it wasn't a pull-down stair, but instead a door on brackets that rose and slid to one side.

The white lint on the floor and hanging in the air was cotton, used for insulating houses two hundred years ago, and he assumed the door opened into an attic. Since the stool was too short, he decided to give the rickety ladder another try, and after climbing carefully, he got high enough to put his head and upper torso through the hole. He picked up the musty odor of old clothes and long-forgotten discards, but he could see nothing in the darkness.

He pulled himself up into the attic, tested the floor to be sure it would support him, and slid to one side. As he reached into his back pocket to get his phone for light, he heard a noise. Behind him, the door slid back over the hole, moved downward, and sealed the entry.

He sprang to the opening to stop it, but he was too late, and in the process he dropped his phone. The door had swung shut in seconds, and in the absolute blackness he couldn't see if it could be opened from where he sat.

He heard Harry's muffled cry from below. "Landry, where are you?"

"Harry! Harry, I'm up here in the attic! There's a latch that opens the door!"

He slid over to the wooden door, intending to kick it with his shoe. Before he could get into position, he heard a rustling noise and sensed something was right beside him. He felt around on the floor for his phone, but just as his fingers wrapped around it, a light blinded him. He shouted in alarm and jerked backwards as something hard connected with the side of his head. After a moment of pain, there was nothing.

CHAPTER FIFTEEN

"Landry! Where are you?" Harry went from room to room, calling out, unable to imagine what had happened in the brief time he'd been downstairs. He'd left Landry trying to access the pull-down stairs, but now the step stool and ladder lay on the floor, and Landry was gone.

He assumed whatever had happened involved the rectangular door in the closet ceiling. It looked as though it had snowed—the floor was covered in tiny white puffs of insulation. He positioned the ladder against the wall and raised his foot to the second rung, but it snapped under his weight. He outweighed Landry, who might have climbed the ladder, but he couldn't. He went back to the cabinet downstairs where he'd found the tools, got an eight-foot ladder, and carried it through the kitchen and dining room into the foyer, where he found a middle-aged man wearing a pinstriped three-piece suit. His air of superiority might have cowed another, but after decades in law enforcement, Harry didn't bend to pressure.

"Just what do you think you're doing?"

"I think I'm carrying this ladder," Harry replied. "Just what do you think *you're* doing?"

"Who are you?"

"Want to play Twenty Questions all day or cut to

the chase? I'm Harry Kanter. I'm here at the request of Marcie Epperson. She owns this house."

"Not yet, she doesn't. I'm afraid you're a bit premature, Mr. Kanter. Until a judge proclaims it settled, the house belongs to Dixie Castile's estate. Miss Castile's trust appointed Cotton Exchange Bank as executor. As president of the bank, I have ultimate say over the property for now. I invited Miss Epperson to go through the house and take whatever she wanted. In due course, she will inherit the house, but for now, you're trespassing, and you must leave immediately."

"I didn't get your name," Harry replied without blinking an eye.

"Finn Perryman," came the haughty response. "Earlier you met one of my officers, Carter French. He asked you to leave, and you failed to comply. I came to insist you do so. You and your friend Landry Drake."

"Glad you brought that up," Harry replied. "Your man Carter French said the bank didn't want people poking around in the house. What did he mean by that? Are you hiding something?"

Perryman flashed a condescending smile. "Not at all. Why on earth would you jump to that conclusion? We have a trust relationship with the estate of Dixie Castile. As such, we are obligated to protect her property until the heir receives it. I don't want strangers in a house filled with personal belongings and antique furnishings. Sometimes things have a way of disappearing, if you know what I mean. Where is Mr. Drake, by the way?"

"He's upstairs stealing things. I was carrying the ladder up so we could take down the chandeliers. I told you Marcie Epperson invited me here. What the hell do you think we are, robbers?"

The banker interrupted. "I don't *think* anything, Mr. Kanter. My bank has rules that govern estates, and the trespassing rule applies to everyone but specific invitees— the *bank's* invitees. I don't know who you are, nor do I care. I do know Landry Drake by reputation, and I am deeply offended that Miss Epperson would desecrate the

Castile family home by inviting a charlatan inside these walls. Poor Miss Dixie Castile is turning over in her grave, I imagine."

That was it for Harry. "Wait just a minute…" He paused, fearing if he unleashed his fury, he'd be banned, making finding Landry impossible. "Landry Drake deals in a controversial field—the paranormal—and I was also a skeptic once, but I promise you it's all real."

"Whatever you say, Mr. Kanter. Perhaps you're his employee. Whatever you are, you follow the party line very well. This discussion is over. I have more important things to do, and I'm sure you must have something else as well. Where is your friend?"

"He's gone." Harry's answer was truthful yet evasive.

"And Miss Epperson? Is she here?"

"No. She's gone too."

"Then I'll walk you out. Inform your friends none of you may return without my express permission. We were generous in allowing Miss Epperson access although the house doesn't yet belong to her, and it seems she abused the privilege. If you show up here again, you'll be arrested for trespassing. I do have one question out of curiosity— what *were* you going to do with that ladder?"

"Climb it, Mr. Perryman. That's what people do with ladders, you know." He walked out the front door, climbed into his rental car, and called Landry. After several rings, the call went to voicemail.

Marcie is missing, and now Landry is too. I'm persona non grata at the house where they disappeared. What do I do next? Harry's law enforcement training told him to get the authorities involved. Call the police, explain the situation, and enter the premises with them. Do this by the books and force the banker to let them inside.

But he asked himself what Landry would do if the situation were reversed. Would he call the cops or avoid the red tape and questions by handling it himself? Harry knew the answer.

As he left, he asked Siri to guide him to the nearest

hotel, and he got several results within a few blocks. He chose one—a B&B called the Azalea Inn—and he was there in under five minutes. He met Teresa, the innkeeper, who rented him a beautiful courtyard room.

CHAPTER SIXTEEN

A massive oak dining table that could easily sit thirty stood in the middle of a darkened room, its only light coming from the dancing flames of gas lamps mounted along the walls. Heavy curtains covered the windows; anyone outside the old house who glanced up at the top floor would never suspect people were up there tonight.

The house, named the Parsonage in 1750 by its builder, General James Oglethorpe himself, had been owned by the Perryman banking family since 1826. Today it housed a museum and historical society on its lower floors. The third, where four people assembled tonight, was private; only members of the Order were privy to its secrets.

Each walked to the house after parking some distance away. Arriving at staggered times to avoid attention, they entered a code into a numerical keypad that unlocked the front door. Each ascended the staircase alone, walked through a small door that stood open along the second-floor hallway, and climbed a last narrow flight. At the top was another door; after a single rap, they entered. Now the assemblage—two men and two women—sat at one end of the scarred old table.

Finn Perryman occupied the tall chair at the head of

the table. A descendant of the banker who bought this old house in 1826, Finn lifted an ancient sword in one hand, a tall candlestick in the other, and recited a sentence in Spanish that called the meeting to order.

Nos unimos como la Orden de la Serpiente Roja.
We join as the Order of the Red Serpent.

In English he said, "As the ranking member of this group, I propose to serve as Grand Master until we elect Dixie Castile's successor. A member of her family has led the Order since its founding, but our dearly departed member had no offspring. Her only living heir is a niece named Marcie Epperson, who lives in Tybee Beach. According to custom, Miss Epperson must be recruited, initiated, and become chairperson of this group. That will take time; until then, a temporary Grand Master must be elected. I am the eldest and most experienced, and I place my own name up for consideration."

"That comes as no surprise," snapped Rudy Falco, who sat on Perryman's left. A slim man in his mid-forties, he was dressed in a black tracksuit and wore designer sunglasses despite sitting in a shadowy room at midnight. Perryman tolerated him because it was required, but his ostentatious behavior rankled the prim banker. He ignored the comment and called for a vote.

There were three ayes, and Rudy raised his hand as well. "It's only temporary," he muttered, "but I still wonder how much damage you can do, Finn."

"No one wants my tenure to be short more than I," he replied evenly. "Now if we're finished with the backbiting, we have business to consider. First off, the amulet and the sheet are missing."

"Have you looked for them?" Rudy asked.

"Of course, Rudy. My bank is her estate's executor, and after Dixie's demise, I went over to search her house. Given her age and declining mental acuity, I was impressed that she left nothing about the Order for anyone to stumble upon. In fact, she did such a good job that I couldn't find the two items I went to collect."

In its nearly two hundred years in business, Cotton

Exchange Bank had served as executor for many a deceased Savannah resident. Families trusted the bank's officers to prudently and efficiently handle their affairs. Everyone present tonight had granted the same power to Finn Perryman's bank, for a very important reason.

As executor, a bank representative was permitted to enter a deceased person's house before the family. When a member of the Order died, a few things had to be tidied up before heirs were allowed in to sort through personal possessions. If a member died, Finn Perryman—both a banker and member of the Order—collected anything that could link the decedent to their society. Since Dixie Castile had been Grand Master, she had two important things—an ancient amulet and a coded sheet. During his first visit, Finn found neither, which meant another trip very soon. It was critical the items be removed before others found them.

"What about this Marcie Epperson person?" Falco snapped. Succession was a major hurdle and one the Order rarely faced, since their number was few and the appointment ended only at death. "Has she gone to Dixie's house yet?"

"Yes, because I gave her a key. Refusing it would have raised questions. She is Dixie's heir, after all."

"You gave her a key even though you can't find the amulet and the sheet? What if she finds them first?"

"What if she does? The sheet's so carefully coded it will tell her nothing. And the amulet will be hers soon anyway, when she assumes her position as Grand Master of the Order. In the meantime, I can explain it away."

There was a bit of bad news he debated revealing, before deciding it best they hear it from him. "The niece has brought someone else into the picture," he said. "For some reason, she's spoken with Landry Drake. He and an associate have already been inside Dixie's mansion." Finn chose not to stir the fire by mentioning that the associate was a private investigator.

Rudy shouted, "She invited Landry Drake there? You say that like it's no big deal. I can't figure out if you're crazy or senile. Presumably the amulet and the sheet are still in there somewhere. Landry Drake's a trained investigator. People like him turn up things other people don't want them to know. If he starts uncovering our little secrets, it could get nasty very quickly. *Comprende?*"

Even though Falco was right, Finn Perryman refused to agree with the arrogant bastard. "Drake's a paranormal investigator—a ghost hunter. He's not law enforcement, and he's not formally trained. He does seances and such, as far as I know. And if he finds the missing items, he won't know what they represent."

Rudy pressed on. "He uncovers secrets about people and houses and old buildings. Cover-ups and hidden things and unexplainable deaths and garbage like that. His viewers eat that stuff up, right, Finn? But what if he starts looking closely at *you*? You're a pillar of the community. Fifth-generation banker. Chamber of Commerce. All that blah, blah, blah. But if he peels back the veneer, what else might he learn about Finn Perryman, civic leader? What lies beneath the surface?" Rudy sat back, crossed his arms, and smiled.

Everything Rudy said was correct, and Finn squirmed uncomfortably. The man voiced things he hadn't allowed himself to think about. Tonight, with the Order assembled before him, he would continue to hide his true feelings—that knot in his stomach since he'd learned Marcie had invited Landry Drake and an ex-state policeman to her aunt's house in Savannah.

Abby Wright, a sassy girl in her mid-thirties, asked, "You said there were two of them. Who did Landry Drake bring with him?"

Members were bound by a number of oaths, and the Grand Master had to answer every question honestly, withholding nothing. "Harry Kanter. He's an ex-cop and a private investigator in New Orleans."

Each seemed stunned by the revelation, and Rudy said, "Does that send waves of terror through you, Finn? Because it should. Think what we could lose if our secrets were uncovered."

CHAPTER SEVENTEEN

After a period of uncomfortable silence, the fourth member, a man named Rob Taylor, said, "How about we move along and discuss what to do next? It's well after midnight, and unlike most of you, I have to get up in the morning and go to work."

Taylor, the director of CCHIP—the Coastal Center for Historic Preservation—joined the Order in 2000 after the death of his father. It was Finn Perryman who had come to Rob's office after the funeral to explain about the Order, what Rob's dad had been involved in, and that he was required to take his father's seat at the table.

Rob's father had invented a medical device that simplified a rare type of neurosurgery. He'd sold the patent to a British healthcare company for almost a hundred million dollars and turned to charitable works, including creating and managing CCHIP as a museum and research center. Today his son Rob filled that same role, running the historical society from offices just one floor below where they sat tonight.

Years earlier, when Rob's father had inherited his seat at this table, he'd maintained secrecy so well that his son never had an inkling about it. The responsibility of being a member of the Order of the Red Serpent had significant benefits. Those who served never worried for money again, although they were cautioned to maintain a conservative lifestyle to avoid questions. In Dixie Castile's case, for instance, the townspeople never knew that the matronly librarian who sometimes shushed them with a stern look had access to all the cash she wanted—millions for the asking—whenever she wished.

A heavy responsibility accompanied membership. Once there had been a noble goal, but over the centuries the Order became a cauldron of dark secrets so sinister no member could ever be allowed to quit. One gave up his or her seat around the table only by dying. If the member embraced everything the Order required, they served until their natural demise. But if someone resisted or threatened or broke the oaths, there were means in place to hasten the termination process. Fortunately it happened rarely, but members had employed those means several times over the centuries.

Rob Taylor's request to continue the meeting wrenched Finn from the concerns coursing through his mind. Something must be done, and the decision belonged to the group. If everyone voted, Finn would get no accolades if everything went right, but likewise no blame should a disaster happen. But if he acted alone, he would be held accountable, and that terrified the banker.

Finn said, "Marcie Epperson is in line to succeed Dixie Castile as our newest member. I have already had a confrontation with Mr. Drake's associate at the Castile mansion, and it might be best if someone else approached Miss Epperson to explain her new obligations."

Abby Wright's hand went up. "I'm the closest of us to her age, and that might help in persuading her, but I've never done it before."

Rob said, "I'll help you, Abby. I agree you're the best one to approach Miss Epperson, and I'll come with you if you wish. Either way, I can guide you. I've explained the ritual once before. You're likely to encounter resistance at first, but you can make her understand. It wasn't that long ago you received the approach yourself, right? Don't you remember?"

"The approach, yes. But not the initiation. That was all a blur."

Rob nodded. "Of course it was. That's how it works."

"What if I don't convince her? What if she refuses to join?"

"She can't refuse; you know that," Finn replied. "If it comes down to that, there are ways to convince her she must join. She absolutely has no choice." He handed her a card, saying, "Here's the girl's cell number and the name of her shop in Tybee." That subject concluded, he asked if there was any other business.

Rudy had to get the last punch in. "The only business on your personal agenda should be getting Landry Drake and that private investigator out of the picture. I don't care what it takes, but we're all in danger if they dig up anything interesting. You might lose everything, Finn, including your precious reputation. I think it best that I take care of Mr. Drake myself."

The banker could scarcely contain himself. He resented the man's brash attitude and wanted nothing more than for this meeting to end.

"No, Rudy. I'll handle him. Stay out of it."

The next agenda item always came last. "Does anyone need support?" he asked the others.

Falco raised his hand casually. "Sure, boss. I'll always take a little support."

Perryman raised his eyebrows, thankful he only had to deal with the man's impertinence during these rarely called meetings. Falco lived ostentatiously—ordinarily a taboo for members of the Order—but everyone in town knew the onetime software whiz kid had made millions selling out to Microsoft. His vulgar display of wealth was accepted as part of his personality. As such it cast nothing negative on the Order, and none of them chose to call his hand, because he wouldn't have changed anyway.

Finn couldn't resist needling the guy. "You're

requesting support again? Of our group, I'd think you were among the best-situated financially. Have you run through your windfall so soon?"

There was a collective gasp, and Rob said, "Finn, that's out of line. You have no right to question him about support. He gets it whenever he wants. We all do."

"No problem," Rudy said dismissively. "Finn's a petty man who wears his jealousy on his sleeve. I have forty million dollars deposited in his bank, and of all people, he knows I'm still keeping my head above water. Since you asked, I'm thinking about taking a trip to Africa, and a little support might just about pay the tab. Maybe I'll pick up a twenty-something chick who's footloose and looking for a good time."

"With a sugar daddy twice her age," Abby snorted. Falco grinned and shrugged.

It was any member's prerogative to request support, and there was no shortage of it. With a sigh of resignation, the Grand Master asked how many he wanted.

"Two should be plenty. When will they be ready?"

Finn replied, "Thursday afternoon. Be in my office at two."

With that, the conclave adjourned, and the members departed one by one. Rob Taylor stayed behind to lock up the door that concealed the third-floor stairway. He gave things a last look to ensure the employees who worked on the second floor would see nothing unusual, and left the building.

CHAPTER EIGHTEEN

Landry opened first one eye, then the other. He lay on a wood floor, and his first sensation was pain—a pulsating beat in his right temple so intense it threatened to overwhelm his senses. He gripped his phone and turned on the flashlight to survey his surroundings, a room cluttered with boxes, furniture and racks of old clothes. He could see up to the roof through exposed wood rafters and beams. It appeared to be an attic.

Fighting a searing headache, he forced himself to remember. Earlier—how long ago he didn't know—there had been no light. He climbed up...to where? Then it came to him. He recalled a dark room where the door closed behind him, leaving him in the blackness of a space—this attic—that lay above a closet. But where? What house was this? Memories re-formed; he was in Dixie Castile's house, the place where Marcie went missing. Harry had been there too, but not at the time Landry climbed up the ladder while Harry left to...to do something. *Think, Landry.* Okay, Harry went to fetch tools.

Piece by piece, things came together. *Harry went downstairs; I climbed the old wooden ladder, opened the door, and hoisted myself up into the space above the closet. The door closed behind me, and I dropped my phone, trying to get a light. When I swung around, I hit my head on something—a rafter, maybe. The blow knocked me out, but where am I now?*

"Harry! Harry, are you here?"

A whisper came from someplace close by. "Be quiet! He'll hear you!" With considerable difficulty, he propped himself up on one elbow and maneuvered until he was sitting on his butt. He played the light around but didn't see anyone.

"I *want* him to hear me. That's why I'm yelling. Who's there?"

"Shh! Keep it down!" A woman around his age emerged from behind a tall stack of cardboard boxes. She turned on the powerful LED flashlight that had blinded him a few minutes ago. "How do you feel?"

"I feel like shit, if you want to know the truth. Who are you?"

"I'm Marcie. Marcie Epperson. I'm so sorry, but you were yelling, and I can't risk having them find me."

Landry stared at her, his headache preventing him from processing all the information at once. "Who are you afraid of? Harry? He won't hurt you. He's an ex-cop."

"Not Harry. Someone else. I should never have called you. They know you're here. The bank president came and made Harry leave. I heard them talking through the air vents. For some reason they want to get me."

"Okay, okay. Slow it down a little so I can understand. First off, I'm Landry Drake…"

She interrupted. "I know who you are. I watch your shows. That's why I called your hotline. I'm sorry I hit you…"

"*You* hit me? I thought I bumped into something in the dark. Why did you do that?"

"I said I'm sorry. It was a knee-jerk reaction. You started yelling, and I had to stop you. I grabbed a piece of wood—that one—" she pointed to a short piece of two-by-two "—and gave you a rap on the head. I didn't mean to hurt you, but I had to shut you up."

"I'll live," he said, wincing as he touched the spot. "I sent Harry Kanter here to interview you. When he told me you disappeared after seeing a ghost, I came to town to learn what was up. What's going on here?"

"This was my aunt Dixie's house. I learned the secret entrances to the third floor a long, long time ago. As a child, I played up here when I visited in the summer. There are two ways in. You found the hidden door that swings up. It's easier to get up here through the other one, but it's very cleverly concealed. It's a stairway behind a panel, and I guess the Castile family—my ancestors—had their reasons for keeping the attic a secret."

More concerned for their safety than a description of the attic, Landry asked again who she was afraid of.

"The scary part is, I don't even know if it's a *who*. I ran away from Harry because I was scared. When he started down the hall to investigate, something happened. I saw a cloudy mist form around him. He seemed not to notice, but it was gray, and something about it felt wrong, like it was coming for me next. And in the darkness down there, I saw it again. The ghost was hovering above Harry, floating just below the ceiling, and my heart jumped.

"At that moment I believed something awful was going to happen to me. I had to get away, and I thought of the hidden hall panel. While Harry's back was to me, I ran over, opened it, and closed it behind me. Then I hid in the attic. I feel bad that I abandoned him, but seeing the ghost overwhelmed me. I felt danger everywhere, and I had to get away."

"Speaking of Harry, I need to let him know we're both okay. Can we get out of this place now?"

"Sure. And I'll show you something interesting downstairs. It's the least I can do since I coldcocked you and deserted Harry." She led him through a maze of boxes and crates to the end of the attic, pointed to a wooden staircase, and cautioned him to watch his step. "And be quiet downstairs until we make sure we're alone," she added.

A panel stood at the bottom of the stairs. Marcie felt

for a catch and twisted it sideways, and it swung open. They stepped out into the bright end of the hallway, and she pointed the other way, showing him where she had seen the phantom.

Once the panel slid into place, it became just another in a long series framed in ornamental molding. Only a tiny hole on one side indicated this one was different, and it explained how she'd quickly and noiselessly disappeared.

Landry called Harry, who was relieved to hear from him and surprised to learn they were still in the house. He wanted to come back, but wondered if the banker had hired security guards to watch the premises. He suggested sneaking in through the side hedges, and Landry laughed.

"This is the twenty-first century, not the Middle Ages. I don't know what's going on, but I can't believe a respected banker has some ulterior motive for keeping Marcie out of the house she inherited. We're her invited guests; as long as she's with us, they can't keep us out. But look, Harry. It's almost nine. It's been a long day, and I've got a splitting headache from where she clubbed me with a stick. Where are you staying?"

Harry told him, and Landry said, "Book me a room, and I'll see you shortly."

When he finished, Marcie apologized again for hitting him, led him into a bedroom, and pointed to a rocking horse in the corner. "I found some interesting things inside there," she said. "Look at this." Removing its head, she showed Landry the hole running down inside. "There was jewelry and a coded note in there." She didn't mention the cash.

"Stuff your aunt hid?"

"I'm sure. I broke the horse's head when I was a kid. I haven't been back in ages, and at some point she apparently started using it for a hiding place. If you want, I'll show you the things I found inside it. They're at my house in Tybee."

"I'm bushed. Right now I just want to go to the hotel and get some rest. Can you give me a ride?"

They arranged a time and place to meet tomorrow, and as she drove him to the Azalea Inn, Landry fell fast asleep in the front seat next to her.

CHAPTER NINETEEN

Bone-tired, Landry waved as Marcie pulled away. Struggling to put one foot in front of the other, he clomped up the front stairs, shoulders slumped and eyelids drooping. Through the window Harry watched Landry collapse into a chair on the veranda and ran out to help. He saw a knot and matted blood in Landry's hair. "Hey, man. You don't look so good. Maybe I should run you over to a minute clinic."

Landry collapsed into a chair. "I'm exhausted. I even fell asleep riding over here in Marcie's car. I don't want to go anywhere except bed."

"Well, let me tell you a little problem. This B&B is small and fully rented. I'll give you my room and go stay in a hotel for tonight. The innkeeper says she'll have one for you tomorrow."

Landry asked if Harry's room had two beds. Harry nodded, and he said, "Great. Now you have a roommate. I won't keep you up—no worries about that. Lead the way."

When they got to the room, Landry dropped his backpack, stripped down to T-shirt and shorts, and crawled into bed. He fell asleep within minutes, and Harry worried he might have a concussion. He was up often, listening to Landry's steady breathing, and around three he slept at last.

He awoke to the sound of the shower. Sunlight

flooded the room, and the muted TV was tuned to WJCL, the local ABC affiliate. Harry cracked the bathroom door, yelled that he was going into the dining room to get coffee, and when he returned with two steaming cups, Landry was getting dressed.

The story of the rocking horse's head intrigued Harry, and Landry texted Marcie, reminding her to bring the objects she'd found there when she came back this morning. "Ready to go over for breakfast?" Harry asked, and Landry said he was starving. They walked into the inn's main building as tantalizing aromas wafted from the kitchen.

Teresa, the innkeeper and owner, introduced herself to Landry, saying she was a fan of his paranormal shows and hoped he'd come to research a story. Noncommittal as usual while things were still developing, Landry said at this point it was more helping out a friend, but in a spooky city like Savannah, one never knew what might turn up.

The innkeeper herself presided over the dining room, ensuring coffee cups were filled, pouring mimosas for guests, and watching as her servers delivered breakfast. Landry's stomach growled when his plate arrived. There was a beautiful omelet that had been cooked in a jelly-roll pan, French toast and link sausage. It smelled like heaven, he proclaimed, and a moment later he told Teresa it tasted like heaven too.

With an hour to kill until they were supposed to meet Marcie at the house, they lingered over coffee after the other guests left the dining room. Teresa asked if they'd like to hear about the hand-painted murals that covered the walls. Very old scenes were next to modern ones, each featuring people engaged in various activities. She started in a corner and worked her way around, explaining this piece of Savannah's history and that battle, and even a scene showing previous owners of the B&B. On the third wall she pointed out a man wearing a steel helmet and carrying a sword.

"Want to hazard a guess who this is?" she asked, and Landry wondered if it might be de Soto. "Was he ever in this area?" he asked.

"He certainly was. Hernando de Soto came here in 1540. That part of history is accurate, although the man who painted this mural claims the scene is fictional. Next to de Soto are two men dressed in armor and prepared for battle. The one on his right has paper and a quill; that's his scribe. The other man holds something in his hand, and on the ground beside him are several wooden chests. The muralist calls him the banker because he was in charge of the treasure. And there really was treasure; many accounts describe the vast hoard of valuables de Soto picked up as he explored the Florida territory. His goal was to take it back to Spain, but it didn't happen. Some say he lost it in a battle; others say he hid it before continuing his expedition. Nobody knows for sure."

Landry stood, looked closely at the scene, and pointed. "What's going on there?"

"De Soto's handing an object over to another man who's dressed like a civilian."

"What's that thing wrapped around his sword?"

"A red snake. The muralist is depicting an ancient legend that's been around here for centuries. I mentioned it a minute ago—de Soto had so much treasure it was cumbersome, so he left a contingency of troops here to guard it. Supposedly they built a hiding place, but de Soto died without ever returning for it."

"Is there anything to the story?" Harry asked, and Teresa replied it was like all legends. Maybe it had a grain of truth and maybe not. How much of each, nobody knew. No one had ever found the treasure cache, but for decades people had spent time and money searching for it.

After their lively and entertaining history lesson, they drove the short distance to Dixie Castile's house and found a police car sitting out front. "Wonder what happened after I left last night?" Landry said. They pulled to the curb behind the cruiser, and Harry asked Landry to stay in the car. Being an ex-cop himself, the unspoken kinship among officers should get them inside.

Except this time it didn't.

Landry watched for several minutes as the men walked. Harry returned and said, "He says we're not getting in. I forgot to mention that yesterday while I was here looking for you and Marcie, a banker named Perryman confronted me. He said I had no right to be here and threatened to have me arrested if I came back."

"Now he's posted a guard." Landry laughed. "What do we do?"

"The guy's an off-duty cop the bank hired to protect the property. I talked with him cop-to-cop and tried to explain that Marcie was the heir and had permission to enter. He said he'd like to help, but he has his orders. Nobody goes in unless Finn Perryman says so. Perryman's the president of the bank, by the way."

Landry wondered why the bank was going to extremes. If there had been a family feud over the property, or someone to challenge Dixie Castile's mental state when she wrote her will, that might make sense. But this one was cut and dried. Why then wouldn't Perryman allow Dixie Castile's niece and sole heir—and anyone else she wished—to enter the house that would soon be hers anyway? Maybe something lay hidden in the house Marcie shouldn't find.

When Marcie arrived, they were standing outside the fence. The news enraged her; she jabbed at the keypad on her phone, reached the bank's main number, and got Perryman's assistant, who said the banker wasn't available.

She snapped, "This is Marcie Epperson, and I'm at my aunt Dixie Castile's house right now. Mr. Perryman hired a damned cop to keep me out of the house I inherited. Tell that son of a bitch to call me back in ten minutes, or I'm going to file the biggest lawsuit your bank has ever seen."

They waited in Harry's rented SUV, the men in front and Marcie in the back. "I brought the things I found inside the rocking horse," she said, handing the valueless jewelry and coded sheet up to Landry. He snapped a photo of the paper to examine later and handed them back.

"You said you found interesting things inside the

horse," he commented. "Is this it?" Without speaking, she passed the small cloth bag over.

He untied the drawstring and let the amulet fall into his hand. "My God, it's stunning," he murmured, turning it over and over. "Unnerving too, in a way. Scary, almost. What is it? And is it real?"

"I have no idea what it is. I took it to a jeweler downtown. The stones are diamonds and rubies, emeralds and sapphires. He thinks it's pure gold and silver. It's worth…" She hesitated, suddenly reminded she was sitting in an unlocked car with two men she barely knew, showing them an amulet worth a fortune. No matter that Landry had a great reputation. Awful things sometimes happened when a lot of money was involved. "The jeweler said it's valuable because of the stones and all, but also because it could be hundreds of years old."

"I've never seen anything like it," Landry said as goosebumps rose on his arms. "It's eerily beautiful and ominous too."

She replied, "That says a lot, coming from you. How can we find out what it is?"

Engrossed as they were in studying the amulet, a sharp rap on Marcie's car window startled them. She saw Finn Perryman's face peering through the glass, slipped the amulet into her pocket, and they all got out.

Marcie made no attempt at civility. "Mr. Perryman, how nice of you to come by. Maybe you can explain why the hell you hired a cop to keep me and my friends out of my aunt's house—the house I inherited, by the way. Is there something you want to find before you let me in? It feels that way to me. Care to explain what's going on?"

Uncharacteristically ebullient, Finn forced a smile and offered what appeared to be sincere apologies. "I've attempted to explain our fiduciary relationship with your aunt's estate to you and your friends. After your call, my assistant relayed your frustration, and I realized I've taken the bank's responsibility a step too far. You are the heir, as you correctly pointed out to my assistant, and there's no reason to deny you access to the house that will soon be yours. I came right over to remove the policeman. His job was to keep out trespassers, but that doesn't include you and your guests."

This is a bit too easy, Landry thought, shooting Harry a raised eyebrow. But Perryman did as he promised. Five minutes later he and the cop left, and the three of them entered Dixie Castile's house.

CHAPTER TWENTY

At half past three on Thursday afternoon, an irritated Finn Perryman sat behind his desk as his assistant ushered Rudy Falco into the office.

"Our appointment was at two p.m. You're an hour and a half late," the banker snapped as Rudy treated him to that disdainful shrug Finn detested.

"You might have been ready at two, but I was having a three-martini lunch at the club and having too much fun to stop. I figure as your biggest depositor, I can see the president whenever I want. Who's more important than Rudy Falco?"

A lot of my customers who work for a living, Finn thought as he came around his desk. "Let's get this over with."

Rudy took a chair. "Sit down, Finn. We need to have a little chat first. There's something on my mind that's bugging me."

Finn was surprised. This had never happened before. Other than meetings of the Order, he'd spent almost no time with this detestable individual. He sat behind his desk and waited.

"Sending Abby Wright to talk to Marcie is a mistake. Abby's too young, too inexperienced, and she has no idea what a dangerous situation we're facing. I don't think you do either. It's tricky; someone must reveal just enough about the Order to Marcie that she'll agree to join. If she refuses, we have a ticking time bomb on our hands— an outsider who knows too much and who's aligned herself with a television ghost hunter. This situation requires delicate handling."

"Perhaps you're right. I'll speak with her myself…" Finn began, but Rudy shook his head.

"I'm going to do it, and here's why. We don't know how Marcie's going to react. Revulsion, anger, understanding, acceptance, resignation—there's no way to gauge what she'll do when she learns the magnitude of what her old lady aunt was involved in. Plus the fact she now has to do it herself.

"Despite the grief I give you, I think you're the right man to lead the Order—a respected banker without a blemish on your reputation. If you broke the news to Marcie Epperson and she went ballistic, she could reveal your involvement and blow up the Order itself. If I go and she balks, I can deny every accusation she throws my way because I have nothing to lose. I can also be more persuasive than you. It's in my genes: Type A on steroids. Total extrovert. If I can't convince her to come along with us, nobody can."

Once again, the cocky bastard is right, Finn acknowledged silently. But he wouldn't give the man that grudging respect. Instead, he said he'd convene the Order, and everyone could vote on Rudy's suggestion.

"Not gonna happen that way, buddy. You call Abby, tell her she's off the hook, and I approach Dixie's niece. Simple as that."

"But that's not how we've always done it…"

"Listen to yourself. You're a stuffy old banker who's set in his ways. I like to stir the pot now and then. 'Subject to change without notice' is Rudy Falco's motto." He stood and asked Finn to give him what he came for.

Finn spun the dial on a safe behind his desk and removed a cloth bag. He put it on his desk, and Rudy removed two shiny bars. After a quick glance, he nodded his approval, unzipped his backpack, and put the bars inside. As he turned to leave, the banker said, "You know to be careful with those."

"Seriously, Finn? You know how many times we've done this? You worry too much, buddy. You need to take a vacation sometime. Maybe get out of that suit and tie and go sit on a beach with a hooker and a margarita." He grinned, slapped Finn on the shoulder, casually slung the pack on his back, and walked out with over a hundred thousand dollars in gold.

CHAPTER TWENTY-ONE

Not only had Marcie never been to the Oglethorpe Club, she'd never even heard of it. Uncomfortable wearing "church clothes" as Rudy insisted, she tugged at her pantsuit—the only dressy outfit she owned—as the valet opened her door. Her late-model sedan looked out of place among a row of expensive cars—Jags, a Ferrari, Mercedes, Range Rovers and some kind of racing car that made her wonder if James Bond had come for lunch.

Maybe he's here, she thought with a smile. *Maybe he's in the bar having a martini—shaken, not stirred.*

Growing up in a middle-class family, she'd lacked for nothing, but this place was something different. It was a world people like Marcie rarely experienced. She was captivated the moment she drove onto the grounds through ancient oaks bedecked with Spanish moss, beds overflowing with brilliant azaleas and camellias, and perfectly manicured lawns. In the midst of a vast acreage of beauty stood the clubhouse, a fifteen-thousand-square-foot nineteenth-century mansion that exuded Southern sophistication and opulence. She felt a little giddy as she walked inside to the hostess stand. When Marcie said she was meeting Rudy Falco, the young lady smiled as if at an inside joke.

"Mr. Falco's predictably late," she stage-whispered. "At least he made a reservation this time. Come on, I'll show you to the lounge, and you can enjoy the view while you wait." She seated Marcie at a high-top next to the windows and left a piece of paper on the table with Falco's name on it. Marcie ordered a glass of sauvignon blanc from a list of wines with no prices attached and settled back to wait for what promised to be an interesting lunch.

Two days earlier, when Rudy had walked into her T-shirt shop, her immediate reaction was that he was one of the most handsome, dashing people she'd ever laid eyes on. Designer jeans, expensive long-sleeved shirt—untucked, of course—and shades even indoors projected him as a wealthy man who could have whatever he wanted.

How quickly that first impression changed, she recalled. They had spoken only a few minutes before the arrogant cockiness that she'd misread as self-confidence reared its head.

He can't help it, she realized as she listened. *It's how he is, and if you plan to hang around with Rudy Falco, get ready for a heaping portion of narcissism.*

That conversation had been brief and mostly one-sided. She listened as he told her about a society in Savannah dedicated to preserving certain aspects of local history. Her aunt had been a member, Rudy said, but he declined to say much more. He used words like *sworn to secrecy* and *ensuring the future of history* and *many people wouldn't understand,* and Marcie hoped it wasn't something akin to the Ku Klux Klan.

"Exactly what does this society have to do with me?" she had asked, and he explained that the society had been around for hundreds of years. Membership was passed down through families, and as Dixie Castile's only relative, it fell upon her to take her aunt's place.

"What if I say no? You haven't told me anything substantive about this society and what it does. If this is some kind of segregationist crap, I'm not interested. I hardly knew my aunt, and whatever club she belonged to isn't my affair. I'm a little younger, and I'm sure my ideas about things are totally different than hers were."

"I hear you," Rudy had purred, leaning in. "I knew your aunt, and you're certainly nothing like her. Let me assure you she wouldn't have been involved with a racist organization. I'd like to tell you more, but it's a secret society. Nothing nefarious—think of it like the Freemasons or the Elks. Those are exclusive, and they have secrets. This one's the same. Like I said, it's about preserving history."

That was when Rudy had asked her to join him for lunch at his club. Intrigued enough to learn more, she accepted, and he pulled out a three-page single-spaced document. "Look this over. It's a confidentiality agreement, and if you're willing to sign it and abide by it, I'll tell you much, much more when we meet." He paused, looked her up and down a moment, and added, "Wear your church clothes. The place we're having lunch is upscale." He was almost out the door when he looked back and said, "Don't discuss this matter with anyone else. Period. I'll explain why when we meet."

Now she waited in a room surrounded by people who exuded power and superiority, halfway through a glass of wine and reluctant to order another. She wanted to be on her toes to learn about this mysterious club her aunt had belonged to. According to Rudy, lots of her ancestors were members. She had the document with her but didn't know yet if she would sign it. If she didn't like what she heard, she'd simply turn Rudy down and not discuss the society with anyone else. Pretty simple.

She would like to have confided in Landry Drake, telling him about Rudy's visit, the cryptic conversation and the enigmatic agreement. Landry would know about such things and give her good advice. But Rudy insisted everything be kept secret, and she told herself she'd learned nothing worth revealing so far anyway. She could talk to Landry after today's lunch.

"Good morning, Mr. Falco," she heard from across the room as he made an entrance, wearing his sunglasses and a sport jacket draped Italian-style over his shoulders.

He waved to the bartender, planted a big kiss on the cheek of a young female server, and stopped to chat with a group of men, ending up at last at her table. By the time he arrived, a martini in an ice-chilled glass sat across from Marcie, along with a small carafe holding a refill of her wine.

"Thanks for coming." He moved in for a smooch as she deftly pulled back and made it an air-kiss instead. He raised the martini, touched it to her glass, and said, "Cheers. To knowledge and understanding." He took a drink, set it down, and said, "Did you bring the agreement?"

She handed it over, and he flipped to the last page. "You've neglected to sign it," he said, bringing out a gold fountain pen, removing its top, and placing it beside the document.

This pen's probably worth more than my car, she thought as she picked it up. "Before I sign, I'd like to ask what happens if I learn about this society, and then I decide it's not for me. I've never been much of a joiner, and I doubt I'm going to be interested."

"I caution you against preconceived notions," he said, placing his hand over hers and giving it a slight squeeze. "There are vast benefits to joining this organization, but if you have any hesitancy at all, then don't sign the document. You'll enjoy one of the best lunches you've ever had, and we will go our separate ways."

Admitting she was intrigued, Marcie asked to hear more. "I can sign, get the spiel from you, and then just never mention it again if I'm not interested, right?" She took the opportunity to rescue her hand from beneath his.

He leaned back and took another drink. "It's not as simple as that. If you learn about our group and then refuse to accept membership, there would be consequences."

She didn't understand.

"That and many other things will become clear once you've agreed to join us. Let me see if I can make this simple. If you sign the document and I tell you everything, you *must* join, and you must take a solemn oath to keep its secrets safe from outsiders, just as your aunt did. If you don't want to make that commitment, then don't sign the document, because once you hear what I have to tell you— once you learn the secrets—there's no going back."

He saw her suppress a shudder and said, "I'm sorry I've made you uncomfortable. How about this? Let's set this aside for now and order lunch. You can tell me about yourself. There's nothing more I'd rather do than while away the afternoon with a beautiful lady." He downed the last of his drink, but before the empty glass hit the table, another appeared, along with another refill for Marcie. Rudy lifted his glass, took a long sip, and withdrew her menu.

"I'll order for you," he said, which sounded more like a command than a request. "The fish here is excellent."

"Whatever you think. Excuse me a moment." As she began to rise, he pulled out her chair. A waiter appeared, gave her directions to the restroom, and put a new folded napkin on her plate.

"Pull yourself together, girl," she said to the reflection in the mirror as she applied lipstick and splashed a little water on her forehead. "You're already on your third glass of wine. Slow down and relax." She returned to the table, allowed a server to seat her, and listened drowsily to Rudy drone on about Savannah history.

Five hours later, at almost nine p.m., Marcie awoke in her apartment, lying fully clothed on the covers of her bed. Her head throbbed like a million hammers were banging away, and she struggled to recall what had happened.

They had been at the Oglethorpe Club. Their main course arrived and so did more wine, which she declined because she was feeling light-headed. But why? Three glasses of sauvignon blanc? Piece of cake. Done it a million times. What was different?

Disjointed memories flashed through her mind. Holding Rudy's gold fountain pen as his hand guided her. Something about a red serpent. Her giggling acceptance of a ride home since she was feeling a little tipsy. Then more, as bits and pieces melded to form disturbing memories.

Rudy Falco's high-rise apartment with the stunning views of Savannah. The silk sheets on his bed and her clothes strewn about the room. Just one more drink. How he took his time to strip her naked before…before he started doing anything he wanted. His promise to repeat everything about the Order of the Red Serpent when her mind was clear. There would be plenty of time; after all, she'd made a lifetime commitment. Those were his words, and even in the alcoholic fog of memories, they were etched in her mind.

Oh God, what have I done? What happened this afternoon?

CHAPTER TWENTY-TWO

Something's going on. She seems cold and distant compared to yesterday, Landry thought after calling Marcie. He'd asked to meet her at the Castile mansion on Saturday, but today the person who'd sought his help was strangely aloof and distant.

She had refused to come to the mansion, saying she was busy. Only two days earlier she'd vowed to spend as much time with Landry and Harry as it took to solve the mysteries surrounding her aunt and the house. She'd offered to work with them all weekend, but suddenly she had a commitment both days.

After Landry's call, Marcie took another swig of Bud Light, emptying the can and tossing it on the floor, where it joined a growing stack of others. She hadn't left the apartment since Rudy had brought her home the afternoon—or evening, who the hell knew—before last. Her shop was closed, since she didn't call her clerk to fill in. Instead, she sat in her living room with the shades drawn tight to keep out the harsh light of day that forced a person to face her shortcomings. It was less painful to hide and drink away the memories.

What the hell happened? I'm not aggressive, especially with guys. And casual sex? Maybe in high school once or twice, but never as an adult. I've got my head on straight...or at least I had it on straight until he turned on the magic charm machine. Damn, damn, damn! I hate myself!

She remembered Rudy taking her to his apartment in a high-rise downtown building. She signed the document, and he handed her another drink. *To knowledge,* he toasted, and they drank. They talked about the Order and somehow ended up in the bedroom, where he explained some more until she stopped listening, giggled like a teenager, and gave herself to him like a whore.

No, not a whore. Whores get money. I didn't get anything but a bunch of crazy information, most of which I don't remember. Now I have to call that bastard up and have him tell me that stuff again. Or maybe not. Perhaps I'll just walk away. Quit while I'm ahead. Or while he's ahead.

More memories floated about in her mind—disjointed, convoluted phrases.

Safeguard the treasure...afraid of snakes...trust each other and nobody else...I'll take those off for you. That last one was her panties, she recalled. And they were the last thing she'd been wearing at the time.

Marcie wanted to blame Rudy—to accuse him of drugging her before committing rape—but as drunk as she was, she couldn't be certain, so she had to be quiet. She knew friends who got themselves into a situation and accused a man to shift the blame, and she'd be the first to report a guy for rape if she knew it was true. In the meantime, she'd signed a document that...that did *what*?

More wisps of conversation flowed through her mind. She recalled him talking about joining the Order. How it was a commitment for life. The only way out was death. And the penalty for violating the oath of secrecy. And the horrifying part about the snake.

I can't quit. I'm not allowed to walk away and forget it ever happened. That realization struck her hard: an innocent lunch, too many drinks, a signature on a document and a lifetime pass to the Order of the Red Serpent.

Whatever that meant, it gave her cold chills.

Since she couldn't remember most of the things he'd said, she'd have to go back for another lesson. She vowed to keep her wits about her—and her panties on—the next time. For now, she had to return Landry's call. She owed him more than a curt dismissal, although she'd have to couch her words carefully.

Her phone vibrated on the table beside her. She'd muted it after Landry called, and now she saw two more calls from him. She had to fix this—it wasn't his fault, and he had come here to help her. It wasn't fair.

Her doorbell rang. *Landry's come to check on me! Now I can explain.* She jumped up, pushed her hair back, and wished she weren't wearing yesterday's sweatshirt. She unchained the door and opened it.

"Landry!" she began, then paused as she saw Rudy standing there.

"Do I need to explain again how dangerous Landry is? I thought we went over this…"

"We didn't go over anything! At least I didn't get anything. What the hell did you do to me?"

He looked to the right and left to see if neighbors heard her shouting. "Would you mind if I come inside so we can talk about this in private?"

She turned, walked back to the recliner, sat down, and popped another beer. He paused a moment, then stepped inside and closed the door. He dodged dirty clothes, a stack of mail and beer cans to get to a couch.

"I'm sorry you're upset. At the time, everything seemed fine with you. When I brought you home, you thanked me for a wonderful afternoon."

"Did you put something in my drinks?"

Rudy locked eyes with hers. "Absolutely not. I don't need drugs to get women. Mature women who know themselves and what they want. I thought you were one of those. Perhaps you're not. But it's neither here nor there. I came to see if you had any questions about the Order and what's going to happen next."

"Yes, I have questions," she snapped. "It's a shame you didn't record your presentation. You could just play it back, since I missed the entire spiel. I don't know what happened, but I've never gotten shit-faced on three glasses of wine."

He stood and went to the door. "Having never met you before, I had no idea that so few glasses of wine would hit you like that. I wondered if you might be popping pills. My goal was to convince you the Order is something you must do. You willingly signed the confidentiality agreement. Do you remember that?"

She nodded.

"Then you're forever bound by the oath of secrecy that it protects. There's no turning back, Marcie. You'll be initiated into the Order of the Red Serpent very soon. I'm going to leave you now. Remember you can't speak about this to anyone. My suggestion is to send Landry Drake and his investigator away. They're dangerous to have nosing around. When you want to talk more and feel up to it, call me." He tossed a card on a table and opened the door.

"One question, Rudy. You told me your goal was to get me to join the Order. Was it also to get me naked in your bed?"

"Of course not. That simply happened, as these things sometimes do. A natural, fortuitous event between two consenting adults. Fun and games with no commitment. Afternoon delight. Don't spend too much time dwelling on it. It may be new to you, but I can't remember how many Marcies there have been." He gave her a wink and closed the door.

She threw her almost-full can of Bud Light across the room. It slammed into the back of the door and spewed beer everywhere.

"That's going to be a bitch to clean up," she thought idly as she popped another one.

CHAPTER TWENTY-THREE

She glanced at the clock beside her bed. 5:20 a.m. Way too early to go to work, and she felt like shit anyway. Tiny hammers still pounded in her brain, and plodding through the front room on the way to the coffee pot, she grimaced at the pile of beer cans on the floor.

What have I become? I've got backbone, dammit. I'm strong enough to overcome some asshole who raped me. I won't go to the police, but he'll pay, by God. Sometime, someday an opportunity will arise, and Rudy Falco will get his.

The pep talk—and two cups of strong black coffee—invigorated her. As her mind cleared, she realized it was Sunday, and she didn't have to worry about her store until tomorrow. She showered, dressed and called Uber to take her to the Oglethorpe Club to get her car, but it wasn't there. The night watchman said nonmember vehicles were towed after twenty-four hours. She Ubered to the impound lot, paid two hundred and forty bucks for the three days it had been there, and left more pissed than before. Damn that bastard. This was all his fault.

But it wasn't, and deep inside she knew it. Deceiving herself to shift the blame wouldn't help her work through this. Everything about Rudy mesmerized her—the fancy club, his clothes and shades, and the way the waiters fawned over him, the gold ink pen, the Maserati…she just remembered that part, riding in his red Maserati from the club to his building.

Marcie considered herself a well-grounded girl, not one prone to foolish, gushy fawning over materialism or men. She figured Rudy was twice her age, but for some reason that was a big plus—he had all the things guys her age wished for. Everything about him radiated wealth, self-confidence, worldliness and excitement. He was handsome, dashing, smooth…

Jesus, Marcie. What the hell are you doing? The guy raped you, for God's sake. You have but one motive in life with this asshole—to get even. His money and power and good looks will make it harder to do, but there will come a time down the road when the opportunity arises.

I won't let that opportunity pass me by. I promise Rudy Falco will pay for what he did to me.

She smiled, thinking that was a good little talk. As she pulled into her spot in the building's parking garage, she began to formulate plans. First off, she wanted to call Landry. She owed him an explanation, even if it might not be the whole truth. Then she had to figure out the consequences of signing that confidentiality document. All that mumbo jumbo about secrecy and the Order of the Red Serpent and penalty of death was mind-numbing. This was the twenty-first century, not the Middle Ages. People didn't die for violating an oath, did they?

Marcie spent the morning cleaning up, hauling trash bags down to the dumpster, and opening the windows to remove the stink of stale beer and pizza that had sat on the counter for three days. She changed the sheets, made her bed, scrubbed the bathroom fixtures, straightened the furniture, and proclaimed the job well done at half past eleven.

It was a gorgeous Sunday, and she treated herself to lunch, walking along the Strand to Fanny's two blocks away. She chose a sidewalk table with an umbrella and looked at the menu. She wasn't ready to face a beer just yet, and she swore she'd never drink another sauvignon blanc. She ordered a Dr Pepper and a BLT, picked up her phone, and dialed Landry's number.

Apologizing for her behavior, she asked if he'd like to meet in a couple of hours and spend the afternoon at the mansion. Landry said that wasn't possible; after she'd declined to meet them yesterday, he and Harry had returned to New Orleans. He had come to Georgia to help, and now it was time to get back to work. He doubted he'd be back any time soon.

"Are you saying you're quitting?"

"We are, and from the tone of our conversation, I thought that would be fine with you. We have way more leads than we can handle. The promising ones deserve our time and effort—ones where the victims cooperate. Find someone else."

"I get that you're mad I wouldn't meet you yesterday, but I have an explanation. I went to lunch with this guy who told me some interesting things about my aunt Dixie. She was mixed up in a secret..." She caught herself before saying more.

"What kind of secret?"

"I...I signed some document, and I can't tell you anything else. Maybe I shouldn't even have said that. There's so much going on that I don't understand, and I have no one else to talk to. You and Harry were going to help me, and there's a ghost in the house. I saw it floating in the hallway. That's what you do—ghosts and stuff. So please help me."

"Marcie, you refused to meet us. Look at my side of it. Harry claims to have heard something, but I experienced nothing at all—no ghost or paranormal activity. Now you say you signed some document and can't tell me anything more, so that's it for us. I hope things work out well for you. Good luck and stay safe."

With that, Marcie was on her own with no idea what to do next.

CHAPTER TWENTY-FOUR

After lunch Marcie drove over to Savannah. If Landry Drake wouldn't help, then she'd have to figure things out by herself. Since she had to return to work tomorrow morning, this afternoon was the only time off she could afford to devote to whatever was going on there.

She couldn't blame Landry. She'd asked for help, and he responded. Now she couldn't tell him anything, at least until she learned more herself. But he wouldn't listen now anyway, because he'd gone back to New Orleans.

Even in daylight the Castile mansion stood dark and forbidding, its gables in stark contrast to the puffy white clouds above. She unlocked the front door, stepped inside, gave a shout, and she saw no signs of activity. And thank God no eerie voices played on a Victrola.

She went straight to the upstairs hall panel, pressed the pinhole, stepped inside, and pulled it shut behind her, and climbed the narrow stairs to the attic. She pulled the chain to turn on an overhead bulb and looked around. Her goal today was to gain understanding—to sift through boxes of memories and see what things her forebears considered important enough to store up here in recesses between the rafters. Overwhelmed by the sheer volume, she randomly selected one ragged cardboard box that lay behind some others. A faded sticker on the side read "Andrew and Robert."

Keeping her hand on the bottom so the flimsy box wouldn't collapse, she placed it under the light and opened it. She took out stacks of letters tied with strings, childhood toys, two sports pennants—Georgia and South Carolina—and two wooden boxes, each with a name engraved on a gold plate.

The first one bore the name Andrew Evan Castile. She opened it and saw a beautiful medal nested in blue satin. Beneath it was a document—a letter from the Secretary of the Navy that issued Lieutenant Andrew Evan Castile the Navy Cross for extraordinary heroism in the Battle of Okinawa. As she read the citation, she imagined the sadness and grief this family experienced.

After shooting down two Japanese war planes during a fierce battle on April 1, 1945, Lieutenant Castile's aircraft was struck by enemy fire. He went down off Okinawa. The officer is missing in action, the letter said, but this soldier's heroic deeds will never be forgotten.

The plate on the second box read Robert Charles Castile. Inside was a similar medal—this one a Purple Heart—and a commendation issuing the award for wounds received in action that led to Captain Castile's death at Salerno, Italy, on September 13, 1943. It was signed by the Secretary of the Army and the Adjutant General.

Two brave young men—her ancestors—who gave their lives for their country. Now the other things in the box—the letters mailed home from the two soldiers, the playthings, souvenirs of the teams they liked—were all that remained of two boys who grew up, went off to war, and never returned. She said a prayer for each of them and thanked them for their service. Then she closed the box and returned it.

If I take that long with every box, I'll be here until I'm seventy, she thought as she chose another one. Six boxes later, she called it quits for the day. The things were vaguely interesting and sentimental, but they were memories of people she never knew. Perhaps there were answers up in the attic, but digging through a hundred more boxes wouldn't necessarily find them. There had to be better things to do with her time.

Earlier Marcie had noticed another old secretary desk sitting in a corner with boxes stacked all around it. She moved a few, and when she opened the pull-down front, its old hinges snapped, and the piece of wood crashed to the floor, sending dust motes flying through the air. Whereas the crannies of the desk downstairs had been stuffed with notes, this one was empty, and she wondered why someone decided to keep it.

Ready to quit after hours in the dusty attic, she noticed something odd as she prepared to leave. There were six little drawers in the secretary. She had pulled each out to see if anything was inside, then closed them again. But two drawers didn't quite shut all the way. Certain she'd pushed them in, she tried again, but these two stuck out just a little.

She removed one and peered inside, but it was too dark. When she stuck her hand in, she pulled something out—a wad of money rolled into a tube with remnants of a rubber band on the outside. She unfolded the money, carried it into the light, and was surprised to see money she didn't know existed.

Are thousand-dollar bills real? They looked like today's currency, with serial numbers, a green seal and the date 1928, signatures and the picture of President Grover Cleveland. On the back it said United States of America, and they certainly looked authentic, although she figured nobody used them anymore.

Sixteen of the bills were hidden back behind that drawer, and now she took out the other one that wouldn't close. Behind it lay the same thing—another rolled stack of thousand-dollar bills, nineteen in all.

She had thirty-five old, brittle banknotes and another enigma. *Was this Aunt Dixie's money? If so, why did she hide it away for all these years?*

Is this money what Finn Perryman's been looking for?

107

She carried them to the kitchen, found a plastic food storage bag in the pantry, and put the money inside. She locked up and drove home, where she searched the internet for clues about the old money. An exciting tenseness grew in her belly as she surfed websites, discovering that not only were the bills still legal tender in the USA, they were extremely rare. The government had stopped using them in the 1960s, and the few that remained were in the hands of collectors or museums. The bills—especially the ones in the middle of each stash, which had less decay and tears— were worth thousands more than face value.

Her aunt apparently lived modestly on a librarian's salary while a stash of bills lay hidden inside the rocking horse. Now a whole lot more money turned up in an old desk. Did the house have more secrets to reveal? And would she ever learn where the cash came from?

Desperate to share her questions with someone, she berated herself for getting in a funk and running off Landry Drake, the one person who might have helped her figure all this out.

CHAPTER TWENTY-FIVE

Finn called Marcie first thing Monday morning but got her voicemail. Many people didn't answer calls from numbers they didn't recognize, and Finn left a message he hoped would elicit a prompt response.

And it did. She wanted to know what new information Finn had about her aunt's death. He said the issue of interment needed to be dealt with. As executor, the bank would normally abide by the decedent's wishes, but Dixie Castile had left no instructions.

"As you are her only living relative, may I offer a suggestion? Mr. French, our officer who's serving as executor, advises there is a Castile family plot in Bonaventure Cemetery. Your family members have been buried there since the mid-nineteenth century. I went there yesterday and found a nice area bounded by a low chain fence. There's a crypt that contains the remains of six family members and spaces for two more. I saw two other gravestones in the plot, but there are likely more of your relatives there. Bonaventure opened before the Civil War, and many of the early stones have become illegible or disappeared completely. But I digress. Cremation is always the least expensive option, but if you wish, Dixie may be interred in the family crypt. What do you think?"

Everything he'd said until now was a charade to mask the one answer he wanted. He knew Marcie wasn't close to her aunt; Dixie Castile had never mentioned her once in all the years Finn had known her. He assumed Marcie would agree to the executor's suggestion, and she did.

"Good. I'll let Mr. French know. Do you want a service? You choose the day; we can arrange it to fit your schedule."

Marcie thought about it. She couldn't care less about a service, but her aunt had left her the house, and even in poor condition it was worth something because of its historic neighborhood. She would end up with money when it sold, and the secret stashes she'd found inside the mansion made things even better. Aunt Dixie deserved a service, and she would come to pay her respects.

"Uh, Miss Epperson, are you there?"

"Yes, sorry. I had to think a minute. I'm back in Tybee Beach now, and after being out all last week, there are things I need to take care of. How about Saturday afternoon? I'll get someone to cover for me."

"Absolutely," Finn replied with a smile. "I'll ask Mr. French to get with you on a convenient time."

Now he knew what he needed—she wouldn't be at the mansion today. Once the call ended, he spoke with Carter French, then left the office to search the house.

When he arrived, he found a yard crew hard at work trimming hedges, mowing, raking, and picking up litter. He'd instructed Carter French to hire the workers because the place was looking shoddy and run-down. Old Dixie hadn't cared, but Finn believed a home on such a historic square should be properly maintained.

He crossed the yard, pausing to look at the house. *It needs paint and repairs, but Miss Epperson can deal with that. Presuming she passes initiation, she'll have enough resources to do whatever she wants.* He wondered if she'd move from Tybee, sell her little shop, and live in the old house, but he decided this ancient place wasn't something a young woman would want. *It'd be a pity to sell it, given the part it played in her family's history, but such is life.*

The last time he came, Finn had found nothing. Today his goal was to locate the note and amulet, and to look for a fortune the old lady must have hidden somewhere. Dixie had received support numerous times over the years. No one could challenge a member's request—a case in point was Rudy Falco's recent one. The man had a vast fortune, much of it sitting in Finn's bank, earning almost nothing in interest, but he periodically asked for support because it was his prerogative. He probably pissed it away, Finn thought, but he could do nothing about it, so it wasn't worth further consideration.

Dixie Castile wouldn't have pissed hers away. Over the decades, her standard of living never changed. She drove a 1982 Oldsmobile, spent little maintaining the house and grounds, and her kitchen appliances and clothes washer and dryer were more than twenty years old. She wore off-the-rack clothes, no jewelry and little makeup. In short, she was the consummate librarian—matronly, conservative to the hilt and never prone to excess. Yet she had received a fortune.

"Where'd you hide them, Dixie?" he wondered aloud as he went from room to room, opening drawers, looking behind books and draperies, and tapping on mahogany wall panels. The money and the note had to be here, she had no safety-deposit box at his bank, and she knew better than to open one somewhere else. Any outsider who saw that amulet would surely ask difficult questions.

Finn had just completed searching the master bedroom—a likely hiding place but yielding nothing—and stepped into the hallway when he heard an odd noise. *Ka-chee. Ka-chee. Ka-chee.* A scratchy, tinny sound that reminded him of the Al Jolson records his grandfather had played when Finn was a kid.

He perked up and listened as it happened again, followed by faint but unmistakable words.

Ka-chee. Ka-chee. Ka-chee.

Leave her alone. Leave her alone.

"I'm sorry to intrude, Dixie dear," he said to the

empty hallway. "I'm looking for something. I'll be out of the way quickly if you'll just point me to where you hid your support and the other things." It seemed obvious she didn't spend it, so where did Dixie hide gold bullion worth one million, three hundred ninety-four thousand dollars?

LEAVE. HER. ALONE! The words boomed throughout the house, frightening Finn for a moment before he recovered his composure. He had no idea if it was Dixie Castile's ghost making those scratchy sounds and words, but he was no stranger to the paranormal.

"Is that you, Dixie? I don't understand. Are you asking me to leave?"

LEAVE. MARCIE. ALONE! Followed by an eerie scream, the words emanated from the gloom at the other end of the long hall, where a wispy figure floated before a mirror, its arm outstretched and its bony finger pointing directly at him.

Unafraid to face the spirit, Finn said, "Aha, so you're worried about your family member joining the Order? Don't worry; you know it has to be this way. She'll either prove herself worthy or...well, you know what happens to those who fail. Now, Dixie, I'm here to help your niece. You asked for support several times over the years, and I don't think you spent that money. Where did you hide the gold bars? They must be returned to the Order now. Your niece can request support once she takes your place at the table."

A roar reminiscent of a jetliner's takeoff startled Finn. He covered his ears, realizing he'd taken things too far. Reeling, he fell to his knees as the phantom swept down the hall toward him, its finger aimed directly at his heart and its eyes blazing with fire. He lowered his head, covered his eyes, and cowered in fright.

Instantly the roar stopped, and the house was quiet. Finn raised his head and slowly removed his hands to see the spirit floating two feet away. He could see a dark, swirling void where its face should have been, and the bright, fiery glow of her eyes.

"I'm...I'm sorry, Dixie," he mumbled as he tried to

push himself backwards and away from the horrifying figure. "I'll do whatever you want. I'm not trying to take your family's place. I'm Grand Master now, but only because you...because of your passing. Each of us knows the Grand Master is always a Castile. If I've done anything to offend, forgive me. The moment we can initiate your niece, she will become the new Grand Master of the Order."

Noooooooooooooooooo! The horrifying scream echoed throughout the house, its intensity causing a dizzying ringing in Finn's ears.

A split second later, beams of light brighter than the sun flashed from the spirit's eyes. Aimed directly at Finn, the white-hot rays burned into his eyeballs; he screamed and collapsed on the floor, writhing in pain and clawing at his eyes.

Mercifully within seconds the pain vanished, and now his only goal was to leave this house quickly, fleeing its secrets and the vengeful spirit of Dixie Castile. He sat up, opened his eyes, and realized what horror the phantom had inflicted upon him.

Sitting on the floor in the upstairs hallway, blinking his eyes and looking from one side to another and seeing nothing but utter darkness, he began to sob quietly.

Finn Perryman was blind.

CHAPTER TWENTY-SIX

Finn was thankful for two things—he felt no pain, and the house was quiet again. No scratchy sounds or jet-engine roars, no eerie words hanging in the air, and he hoped no spirit hovered inches from his face.

He needed help, and quickly. He took out his phone and debated which of three people—the other members of the Order—to call. They were his only choices, because he could tell them the truth about why he went to the Castile mansion.

He couldn't call his assistant or Fielding or his golfing partners at the country club, because he'd have to concoct a reason for how he went blind in a dark old house. He couldn't risk betraying the Order. The consequences would be more severe than blindness. This was preferable to death, at least for the present.

Rob Taylor at the historical society was his first choice to ask for help. One of the others—Abby, the youngest member, or Rudy, whom Finn detested—would be a last resort.

Eyes wide open and staring into darkness, he commanded Siri to call Rob, explained his situation, and asked him to come to the mansion. Then he waited, acutely aware of even the faintest sound. Totally disoriented, he dared not move for fear of running into something or tumbling down the stairs. Sometime later he heard the front door open and Rob call his name.

"Up here! I'm in the upstairs hall!"

Amazed to find the banker in his rumpled three-piece suit sitting on the floor, he was more astounded to discover the man had lost his eyesight. He held his phone flashlight in front of Finn's face, but the man saw not even a glimmer of light. Finn gave Rob the address of his ophthalmologist and phoned him as they drove to his office. He'd already decided to tell his doctor he accidentally stared at a welder's torch for too long, but Rob heard the real story.

"Dixie Castile's ghost was in the hallway," he explained as the hairs on his arms prickled. "She came at me and told me to leave her niece alone. I looked into her face; everything except her eyes was a gray mist. They blazed like fire, and they shot a laser beam into my eyes. It hurt like hell, and I fell. Next thing I knew, I was blind, and she was gone."

Rob asked if Abby had contacted Marcie to explain about the Order, and Finn told him no. Insisting Abby was too young and inexperienced, Rudy had demanded to meet with her himself. Reluctantly, Finn had agreed he was right.

"Has he contacted her yet?"

"I haven't heard. I spoke with Miss Epperson myself this morning to make sure she wouldn't interrupt me while I was at the mansion, but she didn't mention meeting with Rudy. She's back in Tybee, and she intends to stay there until her aunt's memorial service on Saturday."

Rob waited in the reception area of the doctor's office as a nurse took Finn by the arm and guided him away. Thirty minutes later she came out and escorted him back to an office where the two men sat.

"Take a seat," the doctor said. "Mr. Perryman has asked me to share my findings with you. He has the most severe case of solar retinopathy I have ever encountered. It occurs when the light-sensing cells in one's retina are subject to so much illumination they release certain chemicals that can damage retinal tissue. The condition derives its name from the effect of looking directly at the sun. Even a few seconds can irreparably affect the retina, causing blurred vision or temporary blindness. Other ultrabright lights, such as the welder's torch Mr. Perryman says he looked at, can do the same."

"So this blindness will go away soon?" Finn asked.

"There's no assurance of that."

"But what's your opinion? Surely you have an idea..."

"Your retinal tissue is severely damaged. As I said, it's the worst case I've come across, and I'd give you a one percent chance of regaining full sight. Things may improve over time—you may see indistinct shapes, but I wouldn't expect anything more than that."

Finn felt for the chair next to him, found Rob's arm, and gripped it tightly. "Are you saying I'm going to be blind for the rest of my life?"

"In my opinion, yes, but physicians can be wrong. The Cole Eye Institute at Cleveland Clinic is one of the world's most advanced eye treatment facilities. I suggest you visit them for a second opinion. But before you leave, Mr. Perryman, I'm going to ask a favor. I've been straightforward with you. Will you grant me the same courtesy?"

"What do you mean?"

"Tell me what really happened. With all respect, you didn't get damage this severe looking at a welder's torch. Your eyes would have begun burning long before you got to this point, and you couldn't have endured the pain. So please, for my professional edification and to satisfy my curiosity, tell me what really caused this. I'm guessing you stared into the sun, but how did it happen?"

Finn moved both hands to the chair arms, pushed himself up, and took Rob's arm. "Come on," he said. "Take me home."

CHAPTER TWENTY-SEVEN

The seconds pass like hours as the serpent prepares itself, then backs away only to caress my hand with its scaly body and move into position once more. I struggle to be still although the man beside me holds my wrist in a viselike grip.

I know the others in this room. The women and the men, including the one in the robe and the man who grips my wrist. I know that one intimately. He is as much a reptile as the red serpent in the box, for he violated me against my will. Soon the snake will do the same.

A soft moan—a plaintive cry for help—escapes my lips, and I fight to suppress the sobs that would rack my body and jerk the arm that lies halfway inside the box. Help me, I plead, but only in my mind. It would do no good to speak; as the others watch, they appear as aroused as the snake by the ritual. They have seen this before, and somehow I know what is coming also, even though I have never watched the ceremony.

These memories are not my own, I realize as I wait for the serpent. Another person—my relative—sat at this table once. It is her memories that play out in my mind like scenes from a horror movie, yet I am the one who will live or die as the snake decides.

BILL THOMPSON

Five people stare in morbid fascination—five living ones, that is. I am aware that the tall figure who stands behind the others belongs to a different time centuries ago. Somehow I know him—a man who traveled with Hernando de Soto and founded this Order. Thanks to him, this awful legacy survives today.

It seems like hours have passed, although I know it has been only a minute or two. Some in the past have chosen to remain still, only to have their lives snatched away by one lunge of the reptile. Others flexed their hands but found the snake disinterested and unresponsive. That is the purpose of the ritual. The serpent decides who will take a place at the table.

I can endure the suspense no longer. As the serpent glides across my hand once more, I turn my hand palm-up and caress its repulsive, scaly body. I have surprised it, for it glides more quickly than before, extricating enough of its body to raise its head and glare at me through the wire mesh.

"Do you dare me to bite you?" it seems to be asking, and I whisper, "If it shall be, then end it now." Everyone in the room sees my hand move and hears my words, and a collective gasp issues forth as the snake slowly moves its head to the right and left, performing some grisly dance at my expense. I flex my fingers, and it raises itself to the top of the box and draws back. I see its fangs glistening in the candlelight. I sense it pondering its next move. And I wait.

CHAPTER TWENTY-EIGHT

Gathering the members on a stormy night posed challenges. Each had an appointed arrival time, but wet streets, traffic signal outages and mud puddles in the yard made for slow going. One by one they stomped through the hallways and stairwells, shook off mud and water, and put aside coats, hats and umbrellas before they ascended to the meeting room.

As Finn sat in the Grand Master's tall chair, each member cast sidelong glances, watching him fidget with his hands and shift uncomfortably in his chair. Although Savannah residents wondered about the prominent bank president who mysteriously went blind, Finn had called each person at this table to explain Dixie Castile's fury about involving her niece.

Finn wore dark glasses, prompting a comment from Rudy, who was never without them. "Nice shades, buddy. You're finally becoming a fashionista." He laughed, but the attempted joke at Finn's expense fell flat. Rob sat to Finn's left and whispered, "They're all seated. We're ready to go."

The moment Finn called the meeting to order, Rudy raised his hand, and when Finn ignored him and began speaking, Rudy remembered the man couldn't see. So he interrupted. "Finn, I move that you be relieved of your duties as Grand Master until such time as you regain your sight. Whatever trauma you've endured must be taking a mental toll, not to mention the physical incapacity of being blind."

"Now just a minute," Finn shouted as Abby seconded the motion. "This isn't fair. No one knows how long my...uh, my affliction will last. I could be cured by tomorrow."

"And if so, you may request your Grand Mastership back," Rudy said. "For now, there's a motion and a second on the table. Do you want to call the roll, or shall I?"

It was clear Rudy had done his homework. Abby voted with him, and Rob abstained, knowing Finn couldn't fulfill his duty in his condition, but unwilling to take sides against him. That left only Finn to vote against the motion. Shredding the poor man of any remaining dignity, Rudy dismissively told him to vacate the Grand Master's seat and offered to give him a hand to find another chair.

"He doesn't need your help," Rob snapped, taking Finn's arm to steady him as he stood, pushed the massive chair back, and moved to an empty place. Rob sat beside him, glad that Finn couldn't see Rudy's smug grin as he settled into the Grand Master's place and called on Finn to explain what had happened.

Flustered from the humiliation of defeat at the hands of those he thought were friends, Finn stumbled to describe the eerie sounds, the faint words and the ghost he believed was Dixie Castile.

"Why did you go back there?" Rudy asked.

"To retrieve the support Dixie has taken over the years. I doubt from her lifestyle she ever spent any of it. Did she even convert the gold to cash? I don't know. But she received more than $1.3 million total. If it's hidden somewhere, it was incumbent upon me as a steward of the Order to get it back."

"For yourself?"

"No, Rudy," he sneered. "I have plenty, and each of us can always request support, so stealing it would be asinine. When it's located, it will return to the coffers under our protection, which as you might recall is the mission of our Order."

"You're blind, so how do you intend to find it?" Several of them gasped at Rudy's insensitivity.

"Rob will help me..." The once-proud banker's voice was weak and hollow, the voice of a man desperately attempting to cling to one strand of normalcy.

"Sorry, Finn. This is too important to leave in your hands. As Grand Master, I hereby appoint myself to explore Dixie's house, see what I can find, and report back to the Order."

A passive man by nature, Rob Taylor was fuming now. "Hey, Rudy, how about giving Finn a break? Got any empathy behind those Hollywood sunglasses?" Rob cared no more for Finn Perryman than anyone else, but the man was suffering, and Rudy's words stung.

Abby changed the subject. "Rudy, you appointed yourself to contact Marcie about joining. Do you think that's wise in light of Finn's encounter with her aunt's ghost? Are you worried about Dixie Castile?"

"Am I worried about the ghost of a librarian?" he sneered. "Seriously? She might have scared old Finn here, but I have a hard time believing his story about what happened." He turned and said, "Sorry, man. No offense."

"But what if it's real? What if Dixie stops you?"

"Too late for that. Marcie Epperson and I have already met. He leaned back and tented his fingers. "Ah, where do I begin? She had the usual hesitation—why me? What's it all about? Why must I join, and what happens if I don't? All that stuff, which I handled with my usual aplomb. She's not quite there, but she'll come around. One more meeting and she'll willingly join. There will be no more Landry Drake in her life, and our secrets will be her secrets. One more dose of the Rudy Falco charm, and she will be putty in my hands...*our* hands, that is. She will willingly submit to the initiation."

"Aren't you making this sound a little too simple?" snorted Rob. "Nobody submits willingly once they learn what it involves."

"Leave it to me."

"Don't screw things up," Finn said, staring straight ahead as he spoke. "One of these days someone's going to burst your balloon, Rudy. It can't come too soon, and I hope to be around when it happens, and you'd better be careful. You think you're hot stuff, but you're on dangerous ground with Dixie Castile's spirit. I agree she must be recruited, but until we have her in the fold, she's a threat to everyone at this table. Get it done, and don't screw things up."

CHAPTER TWENTY-NINE

First to arrive at the Parsonage the next morning, Fletcher was surprised to find muddy footprints leading across the porch, into the house and up the stairs. It seemed several people had come here during last night's rainstorm, but why? He followed the tracks along the upstairs hallway to a narrow door that was locked as always. Although he'd never found it open, he knew it led to the top because he found an eighteenth-century floor plan in the archives.

The third floor originally was an enormous ballroom that ran the width and breadth of the house. His boss had said it was used for occasional board meetings and storage of the museum's surplus relics, memorabilia and files. If records were stored there, it stood to reason Fletcher would have been allowed access, but he got a clear message to stay out. It was none of his business, he told himself, although he couldn't help but be curious.

If a hankering to trespass had hit him, it wouldn't have been difficult. Not long ago Rob had asked for help moving a file cabinet in his office. They had maneuvered it into a closet where a board on the wall held dozens of keys hanging on hooks. Some were labeled—back door, A/V room, museum lighting room and the like—but others weren't. Today, in front of the locked door through which a number of people went inside last night, Fletcher decided to find that key.

Bex called out a "Good morning" from downstairs, thwarting his plans. He enlisted her to help mop the floors and stairway before the museum opened for visitors. "What happened here last night?" she asked, and he said he didn't know. The third floor was a boardroom, and maybe there had been an impromptu, special-called meeting that took place during a driving rainstorm. It made no sense, but it was off-limits, and that was that.

Rob arrived, seeming irritated at them once again. "What are you doing?"

"We're cleaning up. The floors were muddy—lots of footprints leading up to the boardroom stairway. That was a hell of a thunderstorm. That meeting must have been something special to bring people out on a night like that."

"Nothing, really. Committee meeting or something like that."

On the third floor? On a stormy night? Something's wrong with all this.

"Bex and I will clean everything up. We can do the upstairs too; it shouldn't take long to knock it out."

"No, you all have other things to do. The housekeeping crew comes tonight. They can handle it."

He's lying. The cleaners never went through that door, and Fletcher knew it. A couple of hours later he noticed Rob walk down the hall, and he heard a door open and shut. Fletcher crept out to the door and saw the key inserted in the lock. He quickly removed it, memorized a three-digit number stamped on it, and put it back. Now if he got the chance to be in front of that key board in Rob's closet, he'd be able to identify it.

Thirty minutes later Bex came in, advising she'd finished the archives work. She asked if he could spare a few minutes. "Can you tell me your theory about Hernando de Soto and the Old Cemetery? We kind of got interrupted the other day."

That's an understatement, he thought. "Okay, this requires thinking way out of the box, but here goes."

He'd barely begun when Rob strode into his office. "Fletcher, sorry to interrupt. Can I see you in my office?" He walked away, leaving Fletcher wondering if there were cameras in his office or if, by an amazing coincidence, Rob had just stopped the de Soto story a second time.

Fletcher didn't believe in coincidences.

CHAPTER THIRTY

Two days before her aunt's memorial service, Marcie visited Bonaventure Cemetery for the first time. Opened in 1846 as Evergreen Cemetery, Bonaventure's moss-covered trees shaded the final resting places of men, women and children who were veterans, victims of epidemics and disasters, and ordinary citizens. Some stones bore more than one name—one caught her eye, and she said a little prayer for a mother and her daughters, aged two and five, who died within six days of each other from a tragic outbreak of yellow fever in 1876. She must have seen a hundred more from that year as she walked among the memorials.

A statue of a young girl marked the grave of Gracie Watson, who died in 1889 at age six. Marcie paused to search the web and learned why toys, coins and stuffed animals lay beside her marker. Gracie had died of pneumonia, and her heartbroken parents had moved north, leaving the child all alone. Today hers was Savannah's most visited—and most haunted—burial site. Many visitors recounted stories of the young girl's ghost running among the markers, laughing and singing.

From an online search Marcie knew the Castile family plot lay near the back of the hundred-acre cemetery.

The fence the banker had described consisted of low concrete posts every few feet with a rusty chain strung in between. Mr. Perryman had mentioned two stone markers, and she found them close to the crypt—Andrew Evan Castile and Robert Charles Castile—the World War II casualties whose mementos she'd found in boxes in the attic. Chunks of marble and stone lay strewn about, a grim testimony that the names of others buried in this family plot had been erased by time and the elements.

A large crypt like those in New Orleans stood in the center of the plot. Across the top was an etched marble slab with the name "Castile." Eight doors made up the front of the vault, six bearing names and dates. None was familiar—Abraham, his wife Elizabeth, Reuben, Jacob, Noah and wife Mary. *All we need is Joseph and Jesus to round out the Bible story,* she thought.

She wondered which was her aunt's father. Since Dixie had died at eighty-one, she'd have been born around 1940. The only dates that fit were Noah's, who lived from 1918 to 1966. Next to his resting place someone had scrawled "Dixie Castile" in chalk on the front of an empty crypt. Tomorrow her aunt—or at least her earthly remains—would be laid in that rectangular hole to spend eternity.

The executor had suggested cremation, explaining that since her aunt had left no instructions, it was the least expensive option. But Marcie refused to consider it, instructing him to buy her an inexpensive casket and put her with the rest of the family. Marcie had an aversion to burning up someone's body, likening it to passing judgment and damning them to Hell. She knew it was irrational, but still she'd never be cremated.

Once she set the date for the service, Marcie had made two important decisions. First off, she contacted Landry Drake. Unsure what to expect, she left a voicemail and was pleased when he returned the call that same morning. She apologized for her earlier behavior, saying if he gave her a chance, she would explain everything. She'd found a lot of old currency in the house, and she had information about the mysterious cult. In a nutshell, she needed his help.

"I'm also having strange dreams," she confided. "I don't know what to make of them, but it's like I'm replaying someone else's life in my mind. They're awful—some kind of ritual involving a poisonous snake—and I don't know who else to turn to."

Landry gave her two reasons why he still wouldn't help. First, he wasn't a dream interpreter, and second, his team had withdrawn their support. After her rebuff, they'd written this one off. He wouldn't be back.

She played her last card. "I'm going to spend tomorrow night—the night before my aunt's funeral—inside her mansion. Just the thought terrifies me, but I've told myself there's nothing to be afraid of. Except her ghost, I guess. I know it's there because I saw it myself." She chuckled nervously and blurted, "You can come too if you want."

Damn, I sound like a teenaged girl trying to get a boy to like her.

"What I mean is, it might be a good opportunity to get footage of whatever is happening there. She'll be buried the next day. Maybe her spirit has something to say about that. I don't know. I'm new to all this, but you're not. Please help me, Landry. I have nobody else but you."

He sympathized with Marcie. She'd gotten involved in things that defied explanation. He said he'd ask the others, and to her surprise, he called back and agreed to bring his girlfriend, Cate Adams, and they would spend a night in the mansion with her.

They flew in the next morning, and as Marcie drove them to the house, she hoped the famous ghost hunter would experience the paranormal. At the same time she prayed nothing would happen. The scratchy noises, the faint, old-fashioned words and the wraith at the end of the hall had scared the daylights out of her. Tonight she would face her fears, and thank God she'd have reinforcements.

CHAPTER THIRTY-ONE

Marcie poured wine as Cate and Landry sat in the living room. She and Cate hit it off from the moment they met, and after half an hour touring the mansion, Cate had said the place certainly seemed spooky enough for a paranormal event. In this room, Marcie had removed the sheet covers from a few pieces of furniture and vacuumed the dusty rug in a vain attempt to spiff it up. Unfortunately the ravages of time had taken their toll, and what light filtered through the heavy curtains and gauze sheers revealed crumbling plaster and peeling wallpaper instead of cozy warmth. The room was trapped in a time warp—a museum of a bygone era's furnishings and knickknacks, and completely inconsistent with cocktail hour in the twenty-first century.

"There's a certain…uh, charm about the place," Cate said, eliciting a laugh from Marcie, who said thanks, but the place was anything but charming.

"I don't know what'll happen to it once the estate is settled. I get the house, but everything else of my aunt's, including the furniture in here, goes to the city library where she worked. I don't plan to move to Savannah, so I guess I'll sell the place. It's a historic landmark, but who knows what a new owner would do to it."

"Would that be sad for you?" Landry asked, and she shook her head.

"I hardly knew Aunt Dixie, and I hadn't seen her in fourteen years. I spent some time here as a child, but those are ancient memories now. I have my own life to live…"

"Look! Did you see that?" Cate interrupted, pointing to the hallway. The others saw nothing.

"A shadow passed across the doorway."

"The ghost?" Landry asked as he sprinted through the door to have a look.

"I can't say because it happened so quickly. I saw a gray shadow move down the hall past the door."

"When I saw her, she pointed a bony finger at me," Marcie said. "Did she do that?"

"No. You think it's your aunt, don't you?"

"I'm sure of it. And as scared as I was when I saw her, I don't think she's out to hurt me. Everyone else maybe, but not me. She floated upstairs at the far end of the hall, and I decided she was trying to tell me something. Perhaps a clue or a secret. It was just a feeling, but if we see her tonight, I'm going to ask her what she wants."

"It's her house," Landry said. "Many times spirits get trapped and can't leave for some reason. Other times they come back to seek retribution or revenge, or even because they lived there for so many years they don't want to give it up. I've seen it go a number of ways."

"Are you suggesting I don't try to communicate?"

"You can try. If we're lucky enough to see the spirit, I want to get a feeling about its intentions. If you think it intends to harm you, the safest thing to do is get the hell out."

They ordered pizza, unpacked paper goods Marcie had brought to avoid using her aunt's long-unwashed dishes, and uncorked another bottle of white wine. Landry asked if there was firewood, and Marcie directed him to the back porch. The logs were brittle and old, but soon they had a roaring fire in the living room's massive fireplace, and when the pizza arrived, they sat on the floor in front of it and ate.

Marcie had much to tell, and while she had Landry's undivided attention, she intended to reveal everything. She began with her lunch with Rudy Falco and left out nothing about that afternoon, including her belief that he drugged her and then raped her in his apartment. She told them as much as she could recall about the secret society her aunt belonged to and how she was required to join to keep the family tie going. A lot of what Rudy had revealed got lost in a fog of alcohol, drugs, or both.

She told them about finding a significant amount of money, some inside the rocking horse but far more hidden in a piece of furniture. She handed Landry one of the thousand-dollar bills and said they were very rare and worth a lot of money. They couldn't imagine who would hide so much cash in an old desk, or how long it might have been there.

After dinner Marcie told them about her nightmares. "I'm having what I call dream sequences—like a novel that I'm dreaming in chapters. You know how sometimes you dream the same thing over and over? This is just the opposite. Every dream continues the story, and they scare me so badly I wake up in a cold sweat and can't sleep with the lights off anymore." She described the horror of a serpent in a box and having her hand forced inside so the reptile could attack if it chose.

"Any idea where the dream takes place?" Landry asked, and she described walking into a house, ascending a flight of stairs, going down a hall and up another flight into a large, dark room with a massive table. She said there were other people—she didn't recall how many—but one sat in a tall chair, and they all wore robes. Behind the leader stood an ethereal figure dressed in period costume from centuries earlier. And beside her, a man gripped her arm, holding her hand inside the box.

"Something about the dream just came to me. The man gripping my arm and holding it in the box is Rudy Falco. In my dream I say this man violated me before, and now he's doing it again."

135

"Allegorical?" Cate wondered. "Perhaps you're projecting your rapist into the dream where he forces you to do something against your will."

"I think it's really him. What I mean is, the person I see in the dream is Rudy."

Landry said, "But you admit it's a dream, right? Rudy Falco has never stuck your hand in a snake's cage. You've never been to that large, dark room or seen the other people."

"I do know one of the other people. The man in the robe who sat in a tall chair is Mr. Perryman, the president of the bank."

Landry raised his eyebrows. "You're projecting people you know into a dream sequence. Happens to everybody, and it doesn't mean anything."

Cate scolded him. "You don't know that! None of us knows why she's dreaming about this ritual. She's trying to explain something that scared her. You could have a little empathy."

Landry apologized, saying he sometimes jumped to conclusions too quickly. Then he asked more about the secret society her aunt belonged to. "Did Rudy say you have no choice but to join, and that membership passes down through family lineage?"

"Yes. After...after he raped me, he said I'd already made a lifetime commitment, and he'd explain everything again about the society—he called it the Order of the Red Serpent—when my mind was clear."

Landry nodded. "Don't you both see the pattern? Here's another example of something real that ended up in Marcie's dream. Rudy told you about a red serpent, and in your nightmare, he forces your hand into a reptile's cage.

"Marcie, I'm not discounting what Rudy did to you. Whether or not he put something in your drink, he raped you while you were unable to defend yourself, and there's no excuse for what he did. But I really believe your dream sequence is a hodgepodge of bad things and bad people. You don't like the banker or Rudy. You heard a scary story about a secret society and a red snake. It's just a dream, and as real as it may seem to you, it isn't."

"I'll never believe that," she whispered. "You could never understand what it was like."

"You may be right," he conceded. "Let's talk about something else. Why did you say you made a never-ending commitment? You haven't joined anything yet, right?"

"No, but he made me sign some kind of legal document. It was several pages long, and I only gave it a quick glance, thinking I'd read it later. He kept bringing it up at lunch and after, telling me I needed to sign it. Then I lost control, and we ended up at his place, and I did what he wanted. He said he wanted to tell me everything about Aunt Dixie, the society and my responsibility, but he couldn't unless I signed it. I hardly knew what I was doing."

"I wouldn't worry about that," Landry said. "I'll bet he has the only copy, so we can't read it. You can't be forced to sign something under duress, and from how it sounds, he doped you to get that paper signed."

She flashed a rueful grin. "And I guess afterwards I took off my clothes and climbed into his bed to celebrate the signing."

"Don't keep beating yourself up," Cate said. "None of this is your fault. We just need to figure out what it all means."

They helped Marcie take the trash into the kitchen and went upstairs. She showed them to a guest bedroom and pointed across the hall. "That's the master, where I'll be sleeping." Landry got permission to set up some basic cameras in the hallway where the ghost had appeared, and he and Cate settled in under a down comforter between clean sheets Marcie had bought for their arrival.

"You were too hard on her," Cate said, and Landry reminded her they had to be realistic. There was no use creating false expectations or fears when the dreams could be explained by events that really happened.

"I'm more convinced than ever there's no supernatural angle to this story," he continued. "Maybe she's telling the truth, but you never know. Some people

137

will do anything for attention, even saying they saw a ghost. She seems sincere enough, but unless I see something myself, we're leaving tomorrow and closing the file on this one. I'd like to know more about this Order, but if nothing paranormal turns up tonight, I'm done."

With no TV and no internet, it was lights out at ten and bedtime for them.

CHAPTER THIRTY-TWO

A quiet ding awoke Landry. There was a faint glow coming from the screen on his phone. He picked it up, saw it was fourteen minutes after one, and smiled at the one-line notification. MOTION – CAMERA TWO. Cate was snoring lightly; he carefully put on sweatpants and shoes and tiptoed across the room.

He had mounted cameras at either end of the hallway to capture activity. Camera two was on their end, aimed toward the dark, windowless part where Marcie claimed the ghost had appeared. He looked at the video on his phone, but the camera's light filter couldn't fully penetrate the darkness. The audio feed was a different story; it came through perfectly.

Ka-chee. Ka-chee. Ka-chee.

So as not to disturb Cate, he slipped out into the hall, rewound the footage from four minutes earlier, and turned up the volume.

Ka-chee. Ka-chee. Ka-chee.

The scratchy, ancient record-player sound Harry Kanter had reported hearing in this hallway the day Marcie disappeared. And words too—eerie sounds floating in the air.

Danger. Danger. Danger. Then silence, as if

someone turned off the record player.

Sensing movement behind him, he leapt back and saw Cate standing in the doorway. She whispered, "What are you doing out here? I thought I heard someone talking."

"I heard words too—they came from out here in the hallway. I got a ding on the camera and stepped out to see what was up. I didn't want to wake you when I replayed the video."

"The words I heard came from inside the bedroom. I woke up and heard whispers, and I thought you were talking to somebody. Then I realized you weren't there, and I came to look for you."

"Did they sound like this?" He rewound the recording and played it for her.

"The scratching sound was the same, but not the words. I heard *Help her. Help her. Help her.* Landry, look!" she cried, clutching his arm and pointing down the hallway. "Look down there!"

In the darkness at the far end of the hall, a spirit shimmered, the hem of its robe just a few inches off the floor. Its wispy black hair hung almost to its waist, and the face was a gray void. They could easily see the mirror through the figure, proving it was not of this world.

Ka-chee. Ka-chee. Ka-chee. The scratching sound, followed by a moment of silence.

Help her. Help her. Help her.

The bedroom door across the hall flew open, and Marcie stepped out. "What...what's going on? I heard something..." She saw their faces and turned to see what they were looking at. Again the words came, as quiet as a lilting breeze rustling leaves.

Marcie raised a hand to her face and stared. "It's her. It's my aunt Dixie."

Cate asked how she knew, and Marcie said who else would it be, here in the mansion that had been her home? Besides, when she looked at the spirit now, she felt an odd sense of protection, as if her relative had her back.

Shrugging off a sudden chill, Cate whispered, "She

said *help her*. Is she talking about you?"

Marcie walked halfway down the hall. "Aunt Dixie, are you trying to help me? What should I do?"

As the ethereal figure swayed to and fro, it slowly raised an arm. A bony finger appeared from beneath the figure's cloak, and the odd sound began.

Ka-chee. Ka-chee. Ka-chee. A moment of silence, then *Find it. Find it. Find it.*

Its finger outstretched, the figure slowly turned from side to side. Its head looked up to the ceiling and down to the floor, and then it looked at Marcie again. In the dark void that was its face appeared two bright, pulsating lights. They were its eyes, glowing like embers.

Find it. Find it. Find it.

"Aunt Dixie, it is you, isn't it? What are you trying to help me find?" The instant Marcie uttered the words, the specter's eyes went dark, and it vanished. Landry pulled up the app on his phone and checked to see what the camera had recorded. Marcie and Cate looked over his shoulder and listened to the eerie sounds and words, but when the spirit appeared, the only thing the camera captured was its glowing eyes.

Landry checked the camera for malfunctions, but it was fine. The failure to capture the ghostly figure rested not in the equipment, but in the supernatural. Finally they returned to bed, hoping to rest but doubting it would happen.

At six thirty, Landry left Cate asleep and went downstairs. Grateful that Marcie had prepped a Keurig last night, he fixed a cup of coffee and carried it back up. He went to the dark end of the hallway and set out to examine every square inch of the area where the phantom had appeared. He knocked on panels, ran his hands over surfaces to detect anomalies, and looked behind the heavy curtains. On his hands and knees, intently tapping the floorboards one by one, he jumped when something touched his shoulder.

Marcie stood in pajamas, stifling a yawn. "You're up early. What are you doing?"

"I think the ghost might have been giving us a clue. It floated right in front of this mirror, and it gazed and pointed all around. I'm wondering if there's a secret recess somewhere."

"Coffee first, thinking later," she said, stretching and yawning. "I didn't get a lot of sleep after the wake-up call. See you in a bit." She plodded off down the hall toward the staircase. By the time she returned, Landry was back in his room. Half an hour later they gathered downstairs.

Landry wanted to talk about what had happened during the night—the words and sounds both he and Cate experienced. "I never felt uneasy," he said, and neither did she. Quite the contrary—they thought the phantom was trying to help somehow. "It said *danger* and *help her* and *find it*. Nothing malevolent about that," Cate added.

"The ghost has said other things. When I first came here, I heard the scratchy noise, and it said, *Hey. Hey. Hey.* Then it called my name very slowly. *Marcieeeeeee.* Like that. And it said *come here* and raised that finger at me. Scared the living hell out of me, to be honest. I was here all by myself, and it was the eeriest thing I'd ever seen. I had a feeling something really bad was going to happen. But last night was just the opposite. With you all here, it didn't seem so scary, even though it's something I'd never reveal. If I told someone a ghost spoke to me, they'd think I was nuts. And right now, here in the daylight, I'm not sure myself if it really happened or I dreamed it."

Cate smiled. "Lots of people feel that way. We're programmed from childhood to think the paranormal—you know, ghosts, the undead, vampires, goblins and that sort of thing—is imaginary. Ghosts and ghoulies are fun to hear about around a campfire, but they don't exist."

"But I know differently," Marcie interjected, and Cate nodded. "That's my point. Landry has proven some of those things exist. It doesn't mean they all do. I've never seen a goblin or a vampire, and I hope I never do. But ghosts and the undead are as much a part of the world as we are. Why and how, I don't know. But I've seen them.

142

We all saw the figure in the hall last night. That was a ghost, not a trick of light or a figment of our imaginations or a story we all made up."

"You can count me as a believer," Marcie said. "And it *was* Aunt Dixie. Don't ask me how I know, because nothing about that phantom resembles the woman I once knew, but I have this feeling. Does that make sense?"

Landry nodded. "Gut instinct is rarely wrong. I can't count the times I've gotten out of a bad situation by heeding my gut."

"And how many times you got in trouble when you didn't listen to mine," Cate said with a smirk.

Marcie asked if Landry had changed his mind. After what he saw last night, would he help her figure out what was happening and why?

Glancing Cate's way, Landry replied, "Three people have to give a unanimous thumbs-up to any project I accept. It's nothing to do with you or the importance of all this. It's strictly business—there are only so many hours in the day, and we have a network to build. That said, two of the three people are in this room. Cate, how do you vote?"

"I say we give it more time. Rudy Falco's as much an enigma as the ghost. I want to know what he's up to."

Landry agreed, and Marcie asked who else had a vote. Cate explained that their partner Henri Duchamp was the head of the Louisiana Society for the Paranormal. Once he saw the footage from last night—the eerie sounds and the glowing eyes—they'd have his vote.

"I have an idea," Landry said. He hadn't mentioned it to Cate, and he wondered how she and Marcie would respond. There was risk involved, although Landry thought he had a way to ensure Marcie would be in no danger. After discussion and questions, they were in agreement. Marcie would call Rudy and request another meeting.

Before they left, Marcie pulled a key from her pocket and handed it to Landry. "I made a copy, just in case you need to get in the house when I'm not around. You never know." That key would come in handy soon when Marcie disappeared.

CHAPTER THIRTY-THREE

Rudy faced a dilemma. After bragging to the other members, he had to deliver Marcie Epperson ready and willing to be initiated into the Order. It wasn't likely to be easy—back when they'd submitted to initiation—a rite called the Ritual of the Envenoming—both Abby Wright and Rob Taylor had had to be sedated so heavily they couldn't walk into the room under their own power. Rudy didn't believe in doing it that way. He'd faced the serpent like a man, and when it came someone's time, either they accepted the inevitability of their lot, or they refused and accepted the consequences.

Marcie called Rudy before he could invite her to lunch again. It surprised him to hear from her after the encounter at her apartment, but his narcissism kicked in. Obviously she'd thought things over and realized she'd enjoyed their afternoon tryst. Now she wanted to learn about the Order with a clear head so she could understand everything.

Rudy, you devil. No matter how hard they try, they simply can't resist.

He reminded her about the confidentiality document and laughed when she asked for a copy. "Just don't say anything about anything and you'll be fine," he replied, but agreed when she insisted.

"Let's meet at the club for lunch tomorrow," he suggested. "One glass of wine, I promise."

"Since you brought it up, there's something I want to know. What did you put in my drink?"

He laughed. "What on earth are you talking about? You relaxed and got comfortable, that's all. Don't go getting paranoid on me."

Yeah, you jerk. You drugged me until I felt uninhibited enough to drop my drawers.

"I don't want to go back to your club. Blame it on bad karma. Choose a restaurant instead."

"Fine. I'll pick you up at your store at noon tomorrow."

"Where are we going?"

"I'll surprise you—it's a nice place on the river, a proper restaurant with plenty of other people around, so don't worry about a thing. I know you regret what you did the other day, but it's already forgotten."

I regret what you *did the other day, you asshole. And I'll never forget it.*

When the call ended, she turned to Landry, who had heard it all, and said, "I'm afraid to go with him."

"Don't worry, you'll be covered. Wherever he takes you, you'll have company. Harry Kanter's an ex-cop, and he'll be watching your every move."

Finn Perryman called Rudy around eight that evening. The banker, emasculated by blindness and stripped of his Grand Mastership, hardly deserved an update, but Rudy was in a conciliatory mood.

"Hello, Finn. Any progress on your vision? I can't imagine how helpless and weak you must feel."

"Your compassion is touching, and I'm certain my infirmity has buoyed your spirits. You've wanted to run the Order for some time, but I have news for you. Your arrogance and impertinence will be your downfall."

Rudy laughed. "You're a wealthy man, Finn, but I've pissed away more money in the last five years than you'll ever make, including support from the Order, which an honorable man in your shoes shouldn't accept. Your family took far more than its share of the gold to start the bank. The Perrymans have been leeches since the eighteen hundreds, and it's time for new blood at the helm. That would be me. Now what the hell did you call about? You interrupted a perfectly good martini."

"I called about Marcie Epperson. Have you brought her around yet?"

"Working on it. When she's ready, you'll be among the first to know."

"How much have you told her?"

"Some, but she was too drunk to remember. She called me today to say she's ready to learn everything. We're meeting tomorrow. She's already signed the document, so she can't reveal any of it…"

Finn interrupted. "You're a fool. This is your project, and you don't even know how to keep an eye on your initiate. Do you know where she was last night?"

"You tell me. Where was she?"

"At the Castile mansion."

"You gave her a key. Why wouldn't she go? How'd you find out?"

"I saw them go inside."

"Them?"

"Marcie and Landry Drake and another girl. And after they spent the night, Marcie happened to call you, wanting to get together and talk about the Order. Coincidence? Of course not. They have a plan."

Rudy concealed his surprise. "Finn, you spend too much time dwelling on the negatives. Marcie's curious, that's all. She wants to know what dear old Aunt Dixie was mixed up in, but trust me, she realizes the penalty for spilling our secrets." As he spoke, Rudy thought it unlikely she'd told the ghost hunter anything important. She was so dopey the other afternoon she couldn't have remembered much.

"Leave it to me. Marcie's putty in my hands." He

hung up and altered his idea for revealing the Order's secrets at lunch. Instead of friendly banter and instruction, he would come down hard. Before he was finished with her, she'd be terrified to defy the Order.

Marcie Epperson would understand the penalty for betraying her heritage.

CHAPTER THIRTY-FOUR

A bell above the door tinkled as Rudy walked in. "Back in your quaint little shop once again," he commented as he glanced at the merchandise. "Do people actually buy this stuff? I passed a dozen stores just like yours on the way in. How do you make a living?"

"I manage just fine, but thanks for your concern."

"That's what people always say when they can barely make ends meet. I used to worry about them, but then I decided if all they want out of life is to *manage*, then so be it. I just had a little more ambition, I guess."

And a hell of a lot more ego, you insensitive asshole. He asked if she was ready for a great lunch.

It was time to initiate the plan. She nodded, punched a button on her phone, and came around the counter with her backpack. "Where are we going?"

"Vic's on the River. It's a beautiful setting, and the food can be outstanding. If the right waitresses are working, the scenery inside isn't bad either." He gave her a wink, and she forced a tight smile, hoping the time would pass quickly.

Telling her clerk she'd be back later, she saw a thumbs-up emoji on the phone. Now Harry knew where they were going. She clicked it off and walked to the curb where Rudy held the passenger door of his Maserati convertible. She got in without a word.

He made small talk about the beautiful day, her little shop and the information he had for her. "Maybe you should go easy on the wine," he began, but she cut him off.

"We both know what happened the other day."

"Yet here you are, going to lunch with me again. I guess you just couldn't resist." He flashed a big grin her way.

"I want to know what my aunt was involved in and why you made me sign a confidentiality document. Which reminds me, did you bring my copy?"

"In the glove box." She opened it, took out the sheets, and put them in her backpack. She avoided further conversation, which was difficult anyway as he sped along in the open-top car. In a few minutes they arrived, a valet opened Marcie's door, and Rudy tossed him the keys with a thumbs-up.

The hostess greeted Rudy by name and escorted them to a table by the window. On the Savannah River below, watercraft of all sizes meandered along, providing a spectacular view. Soon after they arrived, Marcie noticed the hostess seat Harry at a nearby table. He put his napkin in his lap, opened the menu, caught her eye for a moment, and looked away.

When Landry had convinced her to go to lunch with Rudy again, he had to ensure she would be safe. When she'd insisted on going to a restaurant, her demand hadn't surprised Rudy. He agreed but wouldn't name the venue. When he'd picked her up at the store today, she speed-dialed Harry's phone and kept the call open until Rudy told her the name of the restaurant. It had happened smoothly, and Harry had headed to Vic's the minute he got the information.

Once they were seated, Harry requested a particular table close enough to hear the conversation and to protect Marcie. She wore a bracelet with a tiny microphone inside, and every word would be heard by Landry, Cate and Henri Duchamp in New Orleans.

It didn't surprise Marcie when a waiter arrived unannounced with a chilled bottle of wine and two glasses. "None for me, thanks," she said, holding her palm over the glass.

"Please try a little. It's not on the menu, I have them special-order it for me, and it's one of the best vintages in decades."

Part of the plan was to string him along, and for that she had to play her part. *Be careful,* she reminded herself for the hundredth time today as the waiter uncorked the bottle, poured a taste for Rudy, and filled their glasses.

"All right, I'll try it. Switch glasses with me," she said, holding hers across the table. He laughed, traded with her, raised his, and said, "Cheers. To a wonderful afternoon."

"It won't be an afternoon. I have to get back to my little store and manage to make a living, remember? Can we get menus now?"

Landry texted Harry, saying the audio feed was coming through loud and clear. Harry donned AirPods and listened too as Rudy started with a sixteenth-century history lesson.

The story was about the Spanish explorer Hernando de Soto, who spent time in Georgia in 1540. One of many legends described how de Soto and six hundred men came to a mighty river and camped on its banks. "That river was the Savannah, and de Soto's camp is presumed to be along present-day River Street," he said, pointing out the window. "De Soto could have camped right below where we're sitting at this very moment. Fascinating, isn't it?"

Harry noticed that as Rudy talked, Marcie never looked at him. She picked at her salad, ignored the wine, and kept her eyes averted. As important as this lunch was, it was obvious she hated pretending to like this bastard after what he'd done to her.

Rudy continued, "For months de Soto and his men had explored the colony of Florida, and along the way they accumulated a massive treasure. By the time they got to Savannah, porters and horses were laden down with gold, silver and precious jewels. De Soto intended to take the booty back to Spain as proof of the vast riches in the New World, but carrying a huge weight in valuable cargo through unexplored territory was both dangerous and burdensome. They had to come up with a plan if they were going to continue their journey."

He stopped to take a bite and have some wine. "There's a fascinating twist to the de Soto story that historians claim is fiction. Get ready for this." Harry watched Rudy pause to wait for a reaction that didn't happen. She merely stared out the window between bites.

"Some distance from the water, de Soto's men built a fortress in a clearing in the woods. Inside they dug a tunnel and a huge underground vault, where they hid the treasure. They cleverly concealed its entrance and left a small contingency of soldiers to guard the fort while the rest journeyed on. De Soto planned to return in a few months, recover his treasure, and liaise with a galleon heading to Spain. But he never came back. Two years after leaving Savannah, he died. Do you know what that means?"

Marcie looked up at him. "It means I have to go. Thanks for lunch and the history lesson, but I've wasted enough time with you. I only agreed to come because—" she paused, and everyone listening held their collective breaths "—because I wanted to know about that secret society my aunt belonged to. Instead, I got a lesson in Georgia history."

"I got enthused and went way off topic," he admitted in a rare moment of self-criticism. "Give me thirty more minutes and you'll understand. I promise it'll be worth your while."

With a surreptitious glance Harry's way, she told Rudy to keep going. As a busboy cleared the dishes, he poured his third glass of wine, noted that she'd barely touched hers, and accepted her refusal of a refill.

CHAPTER THIRTY-FIVE

"In a nutshell, de Soto brought a vast treasure to Savannah and left with nothing. The few soldiers at the fort stayed for over a year before giving up. They dispersed— some intermarried with the indigenous people, others headed for Florida, hoping their ship still lay at anchor there, and the deserted fort in a forest eventually was forgotten."

"How do you know all this if nobody believes it's true?"

"Because there's a record. It's the only thing that tells what really happened to the treasure, and it's been held by the Castile family for hundreds of years, Marcie. *Your* family."

That book! The book I took from my aunt's house— is that what he's talking about?

"Are you saying a book exists that goes back to the days of de Soto?"

Pleased that she finally seemed interested, Rudy replied, "Yes. It's a chronicle—like a diary, but about just one subject. When we had lunch the other day, I told you about the Order of the Red Serpent. Do you remember?"

"Not much, thanks to you," she muttered.

She was surprised when he apologized before

continuing. When de Soto never returned, five of his guards took wives and established homesteads in the area. After Oglethorpe arrived in 1732, their descendants married the English settlers.

One was a Spanish woman whose ancestor had been in de Soto's party. She belonged to a secret society called *Orden de la Serpiente Roja*, or the Order of the Red Serpent. The name came from legendary red snakes that lived in the underground vault and guarded the treasure. Their venom was so powerful that one bite was instantly fatal. Upon her death, her husband, Amos Castile, took her place as one of the five members of the Order.

"You must have assumed by now that Amos Castile is your ancestor, the first in a long line of Castile family members who swore to protect the treasure. In exchange, the guardians were granted vast wealth—every member of the Order is entitled to 'support' any time they wish. It comes in the form of a one-kilo gold bar worth over fifty thousand dollars."

Marcie asked, "If members can take the gold whenever they want, how can any gold still be there after hundreds of years? There must have been a hell of a lot."

"That's right, but far more remains. The members aren't greedy; they take some for financial security or to buy something they want, but most respect the ultimate goal to protect the hoard. When one dies, the Grand Master of the Order must retrieve any gold bars that have not been converted into cash. That keeps nosy relatives and neighbors from finding something nobody can explain. For instance, your aunt had taken support over many years, but it appears she never converted the bars to cash. Before the receiver invited you to come, Finn Perryman went to the house to find them, but he couldn't."

"How would you convert an expensive gold bar into cash? Wouldn't people ask a lot of questions?"

"Your aunt had a coded document. Do you know what I'm talking about? Did you find it?"

"Yes," she admitted. That was news to Rudy, and he made a mental note to get it.

154

"That sheet explains how to sell the gold. A shop in New Orleans buys it for cash. He cheats us on the conversion, but you can't sell a one-kilo bar with Spanish markings just anywhere. He asks no questions, and the process is simple. Gold in, a hell of a lot of cash out. That's how it's been done for the past two hundred years."

Marcie looked at her watch, surprised at the time. Despite her hatred for the man, Rudy's story fascinated her. Tales about her family, long-kept secrets and a hidden treasure trove under the protection of a mysterious cult her aunt belonged to made her wish she could stay longer. They'd been here almost three hours, and except for Harry, who'd moved from a table to the bar and sat nursing a Coke, the place was empty.

"I have to go. It's late, and my clerk has to leave soon."

"Of course." He signaled for a check and said, "I've been candid with you today, and I've revealed secrets I'm forbidden to mention to anyone who isn't part of the Order. The honor of serving is passed down through the generations. A Spaniard who was your ancestor was one of the five men who founded our society, and you're next in line, Marcie. You have to join. It'll mean financial freedom, but it carries a grave responsibility. I know you've been speaking with the ghost hunter Landry Drake and also with a private investigator. I trust you haven't revealed anything I told you. I warned you once, but you're still working with them. Cut the ties now. Don't ever talk to Landry Drake again. Am I clear?"

Teeth clenched, she looked into his face. "Yes, Rudy, and let *me* be clear. I'm under no obligation to do a damn thing you say. Two weeks ago I'd almost forgotten Aunt Dixie existed. She died, I got a call, and now you say I have to join some kind of hocus-pocus mystery cult because it's my turn. Well, I've got news for you. No. Not just no, but hell no. I won't join, I won't stop working with Landry Drake, and you've piqued my interest. Now I intend to find out exactly what Aunt Dixie was mixed up in." She stood, adding, "I can find my own way back.

Thanks for the lunch." She walked out the door, leaving Rudy at the table.

Surprised at the abrupt exit, Harry threw a twenty on the bar and hurried out after her, but by the time he reached the parking lot, she was nowhere in sight. He drove to her apartment in Tybee Beach and then to her shop, where he waited until the clerk locked up at six. He checked in with Landry and returned to Savannah to wait.

Late that evening Marcie called Landry. She was at the Castile mansion, and she sounded exhausted and afraid. He said he was sending Harry to help her and that he would return to Savannah first thing tomorrow. The audio feed they'd gotten during Marcie's lunch with Rudy had convinced Landry he needed to see this case through.

Inside her aunt's house, Harry found Marcie in a familiar place—the upstairs hallway—hugging her knees to her chest. She'd been crying, and her voice trembled as she asked him to sit on the floor with her.

"I lost you at the restaurant," he said. "You disappeared before I could get outside."

"Everything happened so quickly. His stories fascinated me, but then he began giving me orders, and it pissed me off. I forgot you were even there. I'm sorry, but I had to get away."

"How did you get here?"

"I ran, and then I just wandered around aimlessly. When I stopped to look around, I was standing in front of the house. I had no place to go, and somehow it seemed right to be here, so I used my key and came inside. I wasn't afraid anymore; by then I was so exhausted I would have accepted just about anything. I came up here and collapsed on the floor. And I called out to my aunt.

"And did she appear?"

Marcie nodded. "Down there in front of the mirror."

"She spoke to you?"

"Sort of. The scratching record sound started, and then I heard, 'Marcie, it's me. Marcie, it's me. Marcie, it's me.' I knew then it *was* her, and I got the feeling she's trying to help me."

"I'm going down the hall. Don't run away," he said with a smile, walking to the mirror. He'd gone over every square inch earlier, but he took time to look again. Everything appeared the same as before.

When he returned, she said, "You heard Rudy warn me not to talk to you and Landry again. They're going to force me to join the Order because I'm next in line. I'm mixed up in something scary. You heard him—it's a cult guarding an ancient secret. I don't want anything to do with it, but I'm afraid I don't have a choice."

"Landry will be here tomorrow," Harry said. "He'll have a plan by the time he arrives, trust me. For now, I'll take you home so you can rest."

CHAPTER THIRTY-SIX

Harry called Marcie the next morning at nine, but she didn't answer. She'd been exhausted when he dropped her off, and he thought she might still be sleeping. Harry had accompanied her upstairs and searched her apartment before letting her in. She showed him a .22 pistol she kept in a nightstand drawer, and Harry said it might not kill an intruder, but it was better than nothing at all.

When Harry picked Landry up at the Savannah airport at ten, they went back to Tybee. Marcie still wasn't answering the phone, and they drove to her store, where the clerk advised them Marcie was supposed to open at nine but hadn't.

After knocking on Marcie's door, they went to the leasing office. Harry flashed his badge, and the manager let them in, waiting in her front room until they looked through the place. He recognized Landry and wondered if this was part of a show. He smiled. *Maybe I'll be on TV.*

The gun was in the drawer, the bed was mussed, and damp towels hung on a shower rod. Harry called her cellphone and followed its ring to the kitchen counter next to a half-full glass of orange juice and a billfold containing a little cash, Marcie's credit cards and driver's license. Nothing seemed out of place except for Marcie. "Where could she have gone?" Landry wondered aloud.

After he locked up, the manager said, "Mr. Drake, something happened this morning that might interest you. Someone broke into Miss Epperson's car. I'll show you." He led them downstairs to where the car sat in the first-floor garage, the passenger window smashed.

He said, "I guess her car has glass sensor alarms, because around seven the horn began honking. If that kind of thing goes on for a while, it really upsets the tenants, and my night guy started getting calls. He opened the hood and disabled the horn."

"Do you have cameras down here?" Landry asked, and the man pointed to one mounted high in a corner. They went back to the office, the manager retrieved the video on his computer, and they watched Marcie come into the garage at 7:07 a.m., dressed in a sweatshirt and shorts and barefooted. The horn was honking incessantly, and she must have come down to see if it was hers. She walked to the car, saw the broken window but failed to notice a figure dressed in black who emerged from behind a post.

They heard her cry for help as he clamped a cloth over her face. In moments she lay limp in his arms, and he carried her out of camera range. Seconds later a car came into view—a red Maserati that passed directly beneath the camera, giving a clear shot of the driver and his unconscious passenger. Rudy Falco had abducted Marcie.

Harry called the police, and they met in her apartment. Tybee is a small place, kidnapping is a big deal, and the cops were there in under five minutes. Harry told them about the time he'd spent with Marcie yesterday, ending with his walking through the apartment before leaving her. Thirty minutes later an APB went out for Rudy Falco, his bright red Maserati, and a kidnapped girl.

Leaving Harry in Savannah to continue the investigation, Landry went back to New Orleans, since there was nothing he could do until she resurfaced. Harry promised to give him frequent updates as he heard from the police.

CHAPTER THIRTY-SEVEN

Fletcher bided his time, stifling his curiosity about the third floor. For some reason, his boss was lying about it. He said they stored relics and memorabilia up there. That would make sense, given that it was a very large room, but why was the basement filled with exactly the same thing stored neatly on metal shelves, each one bar-coded and cataloged for easy access?

Rob claimed the historical society's board met up on the third floor, so why did they conduct their regular monthly meeting yesterday—and every other month—in the conference room on the second floor? Fletcher knew the board members—wealthy people all, the cream of Savannah's business and society whose names were on hospital and university buildings. It seemed unlikely these people attended other meetings—secret ones held in a locked room late at night during a rainstorm. None of it made sense, but Rob was as regular a guy as Fletcher knew. He was great to work for, highly intelligent, typically even-tempered, and perfectly suited to run a historical society and small museum. What secrets would a guy like Rob be keeping?

Fletcher's patience paid off on Thursday. Rob left early to go with his family to the coast for a long weekend in a beachfront condo. "Call if you need anything," Rob said as usual, but Fletcher never called because nothing ever came up, and this time Fletcher wouldn't get caught because the boss would be gone.

The minutes ticked by slowly for Fletcher, who could hardly wait to lock up at five. At last he said goodbye to Bex and Rob's assistant, thanked the last museum visitors for coming, and turned the deadbolt. His heart racing, Fletcher shut off the lights on the main floor and went upstairs to Rob's office. He walked to the closet door, grabbed the knob and turned, but nothing happened. The door was locked.

Except for a few secure areas, most of the door hardware at the Parsonage was antique. This lock required a skeleton key, and Fletcher had a hunch where it would be. In Rob's middle desk drawer lay three of the old-fashioned keys, one labeled "Closet." In seconds he had the key to the hallway door.

As he closed Rob's office door behind him, the tiny light on a camera mounted high in a corner changed from red to green. It recorded the moment Fletcher entered, and when movement in the room stopped, so did it.

Fletcher climbed the narrow stairs, reached a door at the top and opened it. The room was dark, and he used his phone to locate the light switches. Flames from the faux tapers in the chandelier flickered and danced, casting eerie shadows on the walls and revealing the true enormity of the room. It was large, but so was the table that occupied most of the space. Chairs were pushed back against the walls except at one end, where four were arranged close by a tall wooden chair at the head. Shoe prints in the dust revealed a lot of traffic, and he followed the trail to several doors, behind which were storage closets. One was filled with black silk sashes and scarlet robes in various sizes. Another contained an ancient sword—Spanish, Fletcher decided after a brief look—and a tall candlestick that held a long black taper.

Behind another door lay a small janitor's closet. There were mops and brooms and buckets, an old-fashioned two-basin sink, a worktable and shelves stacked with cleaning supplies. Fletcher turned away, then whirled around when he heard a rustling noise. He listened for a moment, heard it again, and moved toward the back of the narrow room where the sound came from. He heard several muffled squeals, bent down to look on a low shelf, and found six white mice in a wire cage. When he picked it up, the squealing intensified, and he heard another sound—a soft scratch like a fingernail drawn down a chalkboard. Barely discernible one moment, it seemed to respond to the squeals of the rodents, growing more intense as they cried.

Curious, Fletcher moved things around on the shelf and discovered another cage, this one covered by a light cloth. Beside it lay a pair of heavy work gloves, the fingers reinforced with leather strips. He'd have missed the cage had it not been for that odd sound coming from it. The closet was too dark to see what was inside, so he carried it to the worktable. When he directed the beam of his light into the cage, he cried out in alarm.

"Beautiful, isn't it?"

The voice came from the doorway behind him. Already spooked, Fletcher cursed as he lost his balance and fell backwards, landing on his back on the rough floorboards. He looked up, saw a face he recognized, and cried, "What in hell's going on? What are you doing here?"

"It's my responsibility to feed the snake."

CHAPTER THIRTY-EIGHT

"Time's up."

As my hand remains in the serpent's cage, the words enter my head, but my body and my mind are so tense that I cannot register their meaning. The man I despise releases his grip on my arm and raises the trapdoor that has held it immobile. I am free to remove my hand, he says, but I know the horror will end only when it is out of the cage. Once I begin to slide my hand away, the serpent has one last opportunity to caress my skin with its razor-sharp fangs—to inject poison into my veins that will quickly and decisively end the Ritual of the Envenoming.

Shall I jerk out my arm as quickly as possible, challenging the snake to see who can act the fastest? If I remove it slowly, sliding it past the snake's scaly body and giving it ample time to act, will it strike before my hand is out?

The terror that overwhelmed me has become a dull resignation that I cannot change the inevitable. So far the snake has spared me, and if that is the outcome, it doesn't matter how quickly I remove my hand. I pull it back slowly, carefully, as it watches, then raises its evil head to stare into my eyes. Its mouth is wide open, and the forked tongue darts in and out, but it has retracted its fangs. Unless it plans a final surprise assault, the ritual is over. At last only my fingers remain inside. The man beside me holds the trapdoor, ready to close it when my hand is out. In a sweeping move, the snake suddenly rears up and prepares to strike, and my moment of reckoning is at hand.

CHAPTER THIRTY-NINE

Back at the office in New Orleans, Landry called Jim Parsons, a veteran agent in the FBI's New Orleans field office with whom Landry had worked on other cases. The bureau employed some of the best minds in the country and used powerful computer programs to gather information on subjects like domestic terrorism, narcotics cartels and human trafficking. If he could get to the right people, Landry had a hunch this computer superpower could decipher Marcie's coded sheet.

As these things sometimes happen, Parsons had a friend who had a friend, and soon the coded sheet went via email to a DC agent. Although he had no guarantees when or if he'd get a reply, the answer came quickly.

Just two days later Agent Parsons called to say they'd cracked the code. He drove from his lakeside office to meet Landry at the studio in the French Quarter and began by saying, "Certain aspects of this coded document pertain to an open investigation. You're a TV personality—a paranormal investigator. Ordinarily that would have stopped any further communication, but I've known you for several years, and I'm authorized to reveal the answer to the code after you sign this nondisclosure agreement. Landry signed, and Jim Parsons said, "Everything's off the record. Everything. Understood?" Landry nodded.

The FBI agent passed over another piece of paper, the translation of the complex symbols on the coded sheet Marcie found. It contained several paragraphs of text, mostly instructions—the proper way to wear a robe and sash; words to be repeated during rituals called Initiation and Envenoming; election of a Grand Master; attributes a candidate should possess; titles—Guardian of the Vault and Keeper of the Serpent—and responsibilities that each job carried; and the method of succession after a member's demise.

Another section listed the name and address of a shop in the French Quarter along with a certain phrase that would identify oneself to the proprietor. He would then answer with another phrase, and some sort of business transaction would occur.

An odd section covered the care and feeding of a reptile. Live food—mice, rats and the like—was preferred, although pet food or eggs would suffice in a pinch. There was a sentence about safe handling of venomous snakes and a reference to special gloves worn to avoid being bitten during the feeding process.

Agent Parsons said, "This is a set of instructions, but for whom? You said the girl found this note in an old house along with an amulet in the shape of a snake curled around a sword. Sounds like a cult, with robes and rituals and guardians and a serpent."

Landry asked which part of the letter interested the FBI, and Parsons pointed to the name and address.

Nigel Meriwether. Vieux Carré Rarities. 544 Burgundy Street, New Orleans.

"Have you ever heard of him or the store?" he asked. Landry, who lived only a few blocks from that address, said he didn't recall ever passing by the place.

"This guy's been on our radar for a couple of years. We think he's a fence for stolen rarities and a money launderer for drug cartels. You'd be amazed how much sales and income he reports each year from that tiny little storefront, and the IRS thinks there's a lot more that happens under the table. Nigel Meriwether doesn't seem to care much about provenance or authenticity; he just peddles his wares to unsuspecting buyers, especially wealthy foreign tourists. The agents working this case are hoping what's written on this paper—the phrase to use when you go to his shop, and what happens next—might help us nail him."

Parsons concluded by saying that FBI agents in Savannah would be interviewing Marcie Epperson to hear exactly how and where she found the document.

"She's missing," Landry advised. "She was kidnapped two days ago from her apartment on Tybee Island. Harry and I were there shortly after it happened. We watched the video and identified the kidnapper from the car he was driving. Far as I know, they're both still missing."

The agent said he'd check with the FBI office in Savannah to see if the local authorities had called in the bureau. With a final warning to keep the information to himself, the meeting broke up.

CHAPTER FORTY

At his ophthalmologist's suggestion, Finn Perryman made an appointment at the world-famous Cole Clinic in Ohio. He had no immediate family—only nieces and nephews who cared as little about him as he did them—so he enlisted Fielding, his trusted second-in-command, to travel with him. He ruled out a commercial flight, which would have meant changing planes in Atlanta, and chartered a King Air that made the flight from Savannah to Cleveland in under three hours.

He spent half a day at the institute, undergoing exam after exam conducted by specialists in ailments and diseases of the eye. In the wrap-up session, the physicians agreed his was a severe case and told Finn he might have to live with his blindness. Only time would tell. Meanwhile he should start getting accustomed to a world of absolute darkness.

Despondent over the consensus opinion, he snapped at Fielding over every little thing during the trip back. To make matters worse, the minute they landed, she got a call from the bank's vice president, a mousy little man Fielding detested, and with whom she'd left the examiners. They were in a snit over assets, he said, and despite it being after seven p.m., they insisted on seeing Mr. Perryman tonight.

She waved to the night guard in the lobby, guided her boss to the elevator, and led him down the hall to his office. She thought Finn seemed nervous, which seemed odd since he'd fought with examiners a hundred times in his life. Perhaps the blindness made him vulnerable.

When she flew to Ohio with Perryman, Fielding had left the senior vice president to babysit the examiners. Now he sat perched on the edge of a couch outside Finn's office, looking nervous as hell.

"We have a problem, sir," the man clucked as they went into Finn's office, his irritating, effeminate voice bothering the exhausted bank president more than usual. "It's the examiners, sir. They've brought up the asset base again. The gold, Mr. Perryman. They insist on auditing it. They want to go see it for themselves."

"Dammit, can't I be gone for one single day without everything falling apart? We've dealt with this issue before. Tell them to go to hell. So the bank keeps its assets in gold. Nothing wrong with that." He paused, imagining how the scrawny man in front of him must be fretting. "But then you wouldn't have said that to them, would you?"

The meek little man cowered. "No, sir, but it wasn't like that. They want to go to Atlanta and count the gold bars. They're asking you to tell them where the ingots came from in the first place. It seems a reasonable request..."

Finn sighed dramatically. "Maybe to you it does. I'll deal with this tomorrow. I've had a long day, and I'm going home for a drink and some solitude."

"But, sir, they're waiting downstairs. When I told them your flight arrival, they decided to stay. They demand to speak to you tonight."

"You had no business telling them when I'd return or promising that I'd come by the bank at this hour. Go down there and tell the bastards I went home instead. This can wait until tomorrow."

Someone cleared his voice. Finn looked up, realizing his door was open. "Actually the bastards would like a word tonight, Mr. Perryman," the lead examiner said. "If it isn't too much trouble, that is."

While Fielding waited impatiently outside the conference room, Finn spent the better part of an hour answering questions he'd answered a dozen times before. The gold was in storage at Mercantile Guaranty in Atlanta. It was in the form of one-kilo bars. There were six hundred and fifty, totaling just over forty-one million dollars, and that made up the bank's capital base. Finn claimed not to know where the bars originated, saying when it became legal for Americans to own gold again in the 1970s, his grandfather had transferred the gold to the bank in exchange for stock. Where he got it wasn't relevant. All that mattered was that the gold was real, and examiners over the years had confirmed that detail. Wearily he asked if it was necessary to go through this exercise yet another time.

They said it was, and Finn agreed to their suggestion so he could go home to bed. An officer of Mercantile Guaranty Bank would physically count the gold bars, and he or she would select one random ingot to bring to Savannah for the examiners to see. The sooner this happened, the faster they would wrap up the examination and leave Finn's premises, the lead examiner promised. This was the final item on their agenda.

"I can make it very fast. Tomorrow morning I'll have Fielding drive me to Atlanta, and we'll bring a bar here," Finn said, but the examiner refused. He wanted an independent person—a representative of the custodial bank to do it.

Finn went home with the weight of the world on his shoulders, skipped his cocktail and dinner, fussed with his housekeeper as she helped him undress, and went straight to bed. He slept fitfully, his head spinning with nightmares featuring Rudy Falco, Marcie Epperson, his blindness, a mountain of gold bars, and a sinister red serpent with its head reared and its venomous fangs bared.

CHAPTER FORTY-ONE

Fletcher rose slowly from where he'd fallen, rubbing the hip that took the brunt of his fall. He dusted himself off and stood to confront the person who'd spoken to him.

"I know you. You own a flower shop, right? When we have events for museum patrons, you've done flower arrangements for the tables. I'm Fletcher. Fletcher Skorza. I work for Rob."

The attractive thirty-something African-American girl smiled. "I've seen you around here. I'm Abby Wright. Nice to meet you. What are you doing up here? No one's allowed up here except…"

"Except who? What is this place? Rob said it's where the board meets, but I know better. There are robes and a sword in the closet. And what about that snake? What the hell goes on up here?"

Caught off guard, Abby struggled to extricate herself from his relentless questions without revealing secrets. Of course Fletcher was baffled—who wouldn't be, stumbling upon the odd vestments and ceremonial things, even finding the serpent itself. That created a big issue— Abby believed the other things could be explained away by someone more glib than she, but the snake and her comment that it was her turn to feed it would be harder to deal with.

She had to get away from here without making things worse. Another member of the Order could deal with Fletcher, whatever that entailed. "Um, I'm really sorry this happened, but I can't tell you anything about it. I'm sure Rob warned you not to come here, right?"

He nodded.

"Then you shouldn't have come, and you have to leave. I can't tell you anything, and if you're smart, you'll forget everything about this place and what you saw. I'll forget I caught you, and everything will be fine."

Her bizarre comments made him even more curious. "What's the snake for? Why do people have to feed it? Who comes up here? Who wears those robes?"

She shook her head and walked toward the closet that held the serpent. "I warned you, and I hope you remember that. Just turn and go, please. For your own good. I'm begging you."

"*For my own good?* Is that a threat?"

"It's a warning, not a threat. I'm simply warning you. You wouldn't believe..." She stopped herself, entered the janitor's closet, and closed the door. Fletcher stood his ground, waiting as the seconds ticked slowly by until she emerged.

"Did you feed the snake? That's what the mice are for, right?"

She stared at him a moment as a single tear ran down her cheek. "I have to go now. So do you. Please, I'm begging you. Please don't get me in trouble. Or yourself. You have no idea what you've stumbled upon. You really have no idea." With that, she turned and left.

Fletcher poked his head back into the closet. Everything was in its place as he first saw it, and he was certain if he looked inside the mouse cage, there'd be at least one less than before. The snake was quiet, presumably enjoying its dinner. His mind raced with questions as he turned off the lights and went down the stairs to replace the key in Rob's closet.

An unobtrusive wall clock ticked off the seconds as its hidden camera sensed the room was still and stopped recording.

CHAPTER FORTY-TWO

On Monday morning Fletcher arrived at work determined to find answers. He couldn't stop thinking about the upstairs room with candles flickering and a red serpent awaiting its dinner. It was eerie and almost supernatural. Then Abby came, her words confusing him more. And she appeared scared for both of them.

He lost a little sleep Friday night, but Saturday and Sunday were bright, sunny reminders that Fletcher lived in the twenty-first century, and that the Parsonage was just an old house. Whatever secrets lay within its walls could be explained. Two people knew—Abby and his boss—but she had cautioned him to forget everything he saw, and Rob wasn't himself these days.

How bad could it be? A Satanic cult, maybe? No, because Rob wasn't exactly the type to conjure up Satan. Neither was Abby. She was as quiet and nice as a flower shop owner should be. This was about something that was none of his business. Yet he had to know, if only to stop the constant questions that kept him from work and sleep.

When he heard Rob arrive, Fletcher mustered up his courage, walked quickly down the hall before he could talk himself out of it, and rapped lightly on the doorframe.

"Hi, Fletcher," Rob said, glancing up and then back

at his laptop. "Come on in. Close the door behind you and take a chair."

Close the door? That never happened. He sat across the desk from his boss and asked how the weekend with family went.

"Short. I came back Saturday afternoon."

"Wow, that's too bad. Did someone in the family get sick?"

Rob looked directly into Fletcher's eyes. "Why couldn't you leave well enough alone? The third floor's off-limits. Always has been. You've been here over eight years, and I had big plans for you. In a few years I'd retire; you'd take over and run CCHIP and the museum the way I did. We clicked on so many levels, and I couldn't have asked for a better right-hand man."

Alarmed, Fletcher said, "Why are you talking about me in the past tense? Are you firing me?"

"Trust is the foundation upon which every relationship is built. Only one place in the building was off-limits, and when I was out of town, you came into my office, rummaged through my desk to find the closet key, and found the one that unlocked the door. Why, Fletcher? Explain to me why you broke my trust?"

There must be a camera in here. "Because of the muddy footprints. People go up to the third floor at night, and I wondered why. That's all, Rob. That's all there was to it. Please don't fire me over something like that. I promise…"

"Stop it, Fletcher. I don't want promises. The damage has been done, and you've gone too far to rectify things. I just wish you'd thought before you did something so stupid."

What the hell is he talking about? Gone too far? Doing something stupid? All I did was go upstairs. The mice and the snake were weird, but I'm about to lose my job. For what? What did I stumble upon that's got him so upset?

"Rob, I don't understand what's going on, and I'm sure you don't intend to tell me. I'll admit my curiosity got

180

the best of me. Whatever goes on upstairs is none of my business. I swear I'll never mention it."

"Were you surprised when Abby showed up?"

I figured she called him after I left. "No, uh…well, yes, I was. She said…I'm sure you know what she told me. Rob, I love my job, and there hasn't been a single issue in eight years. Please forgive me for overstepping my bounds. I'm sorry, and it won't happen again."

Rob shook his head. "Your mind will never erase what you saw. It's a chance we can't take."

"What is it, Rob? What goes on up there? If it's some kind of secret society you're involved in, I'll understand."

His boss looked at him without speaking, and there remained nothing more Fletcher could do. Faced with the reality that a simple misdeed had cost him his career, he said, "I'll go clean out my office." He turned to go, looked over his shoulder, and saw the expression on Rob's face. *He doesn't want this to happen any more than I do, but it's not his decision to make. Whatever's going on up there, it's a really big deal, and it involves other people.*

He was emptying his bookshelves into boxes when Bexley arrived for work. She listened in shock as Fletcher told her the truth—he was fired for pilfering Rob's key and going to the third floor. He told her it looked like a place where rituals were held, complete with robes, a sword and candlestick, and a fearsome reptile kept in a closet. Bizarrely, a florist named Abby Wright had come to feed the snake and caught him there. Apparently he'd uncovered a huge secret, and "they" couldn't take a chance on his staying.

"I think Rob's involved in a cult of snake worshippers—several people, from the sets of muddy footprints. I don't know what goes on upstairs, but what I saw cost me my career, and I intend to find out why."

Stunned, Bex peppered Fletcher with questions for which he had no answers. He told her goodbye and suggested she go to the boss and plead for her own job. As someone who knew Fletcher's daily tasks and routine, Rob would be foolish to let her go, and hopefully he wouldn't retaliate against her simply for being Fletcher's intern.

"I don't want to work here without you," she said, but he urged her to stay on. She was perfect for her job, and she might be able to learn more about whatever was going on upstairs. That made sense to Bex, and she agreed to go see the boss.

Fletcher left the Parsonage and drove down to River Street. He walked into Abby Wright's flower shop and watched her smile turn to panic once she realized who he was. "What are you doing here? You shouldn't have come..."

"Nice to see you too. I just got fired because I went up to the third floor. Up there where the snake is, remember? Rob wouldn't give me answers, but he did say *we* can't take the chance. Who's *we*, Abby? What happens on the third floor? What kind of ceremony goes on there? Somebody's going to level with me. Eight years of my life just went down the drain for...for some stupid secret I uncovered. It's a snake cult, right?"

Her phone rang. Turning her back to Fletcher, she answered, and he heard her say, "He's here," and at the end, "Okay. I won't. I'll call you back."

"Who was that?"

"You have to leave. I'm sorry you lost your job, but you knew not to go up there. Take responsibility for your actions and accept the consequences. You don't understand..."

"Easy for you to say, isn't it? I damned sure don't understand, and yes, I accept responsibility. Just tell me what I threw away my career for. Was that Rob on the phone? What are you people up to? If you don't give me answers, I promise you I'll spend every waking moment finding out what's going on at the Parsonage. You can tell your friends—whoever the hell they are—what I said." He walked to the counter and wrote down a number. "Call me if you want to talk." He slammed the door so hard the front windows rattled.

Amy called the person back who rang a few

minutes earlier and said, "We have a problem. He's hell-bent on finding out what's going on."

"I was afraid of that when Rob told me what happened," Rudy Falco said. "Now he must be eliminated."

A shiver ran down her spine. "Eliminated? What...what the hell does that mean?"

"It means exactly what you think. We've never had a snoop in our midst before, and he must be dealt with. There's too much at stake."

"You're out of your mind! You can't do that!" she cried, but he'd already disconnected.

CHAPTER FORTY-THREE

As she watched him carry out the last box, Bex could hardly contain her anger. How could a valued second-in-command, a PhD whose only error was curiosity, get fired? Having interned under him, she knew Fletcher's value to the CCHIP team, and his abrupt dismissal was as curious as the business about the third floor.

She composed herself, went to Rob's office, said Fletcher had broken the news to her, and asked if she still had a job. Although still a student, Bex's superior intelligence and abilities made her invaluable, and Rob knew it. He concocted a story about the firing being over a security breach. It was unfortunate but unavoidable under the circumstances. Since employment issues were confidential, he could say nothing more.

"Should I leave too?"

"Not unless you feel you must. You're an asset to the society. We can use your help through the summer and even after school starts if you can work part time."

Bex had planned to quit over her boss's termination, but as Rob spun a tale she didn't believe, she changed her mind. If she stayed, she might be able to vindicate Fletcher, maybe even convince the boss to change his mind.

"I love working here, Mr. Taylor," she replied. "I'd

be happy to stay on."

Taylor looked past her and waved someone in. Bex turned to see a familiar face—a person she'd never met but whose ghost-hunting escapades on TV were among her favorites. He was standing in the doorway. "Landry Drake!" she cried, rushing over to shake his hand. "I'm Bex—Bexley Wolf. It's a privilege to meet you. I love your shows."

Clearly less impressed than his young intern, Rob remained behind his desk. "May I help you, Mr. Drake?" he asked, a hint of irritation in his voice. "We're in the middle of something…"

"I'm sorry. I didn't mean to interrupt. There was no one downstairs, and I heard voices…"

"What do you want?" His sharp tone surprised Bex. She hadn't seen this side of him and figured he was still angry after the situation with Fletcher's firing.

"I'm looking for information, and someone steered me to the historical society. I've been told you have the oldest burial records for Savannah's cemeteries. If it's not too much trouble, I'd like to look at them."

"Who told you to come here?"

Puzzled by his curt attitude, Landry said, "A custodian at Bonaventure Cemetery. I asked for a plot map, and he said the older records were stored here. Is there a problem?"

"No. Whose records do you want to see?"

Given the man's attitude, Landry decided to keep that to himself. "I'd just like to look through the older ones. I'm doing research on early Savannah history."

Rob knew exactly what Landry was after. His fellow members of the Order had been rightly concerned when Dixie Castile's niece had brought the ghost hunter and a private investigator to Savannah. Rudy was supposed to be handling things, but instead he'd screwed everything up by kidnapping Marcie Epperson and disappearing. Now it was up to him to stop Landry.

With a forced cordiality, he said, "The custodian

was technically correct. We have the records, but they're not available to the public. They're stored in our archives. It's not as simple as finding a library book on a shelf. Bonaventure Cemetery—or Evergreen, as it was called in the nineteenth century—is a huge place. There are thousands of burials beginning in the eighteen forties. Many of those records are on brittle old sheets, and we don't allow the public to access them."

Bex hadn't heard that rule before, but she knew a way to help the famous ghost hunter. "I can do it, Mr. Taylor! I know where they are; Dr. S asked me to sort and catalog them last month. I'm sure we can find what he wants to see."

Rob's face turned beet-red. He snapped at Bex and said she had work to do, but his protestations failed. She wondered what was wrong, but Landry smelled a rat.

"I get the feeling you don't want me to see the records," he said, and Rob snapped, "We're busy, that's all. Bex, help Mr. Drake with what he wants, and do it quickly. You have work to do." He sat, turned away, and began shuffling papers on his desk.

Bex guided Landry to a large room down the hall. Originally the master bedroom, today it contained row after row of steel shelves loaded with boxes. "It's Bonaventure Cemetery you want, correct?" she asked, and Landry asked if there was another.

"Yes, the first one is Old Cemetery, later called Colonial Park. It's across the street from here. It closed about the time Bonaventure opened."

That was news to Landry, and he suggested they look at both.

She led him to a computer station crammed into a corner and sat down. "What's the family name?"

"Castile. The most recent is Dixie Castile, who died not long ago."

"The town librarian. I knew her," Bex said. "She comes from an old Savannah family, and I have a hunch you're going to find the Castiles in both cemeteries."

When Landry asked why, she explained the Old

187

Cemetery was closed to burials in 1853. Evergreen Cemetery opened in 1846, and interments continued there to this day.

Bex found a reference number, took a large box from a shelf, and brought it to a worktable. "These are early records from Bonaventure, the newer cemetery," she said. "They date from 1846 until around 1950 or so. Later records are kept at the cemetery office."

A map showed the Castile family plot, which had a mausoleum containing six bodies. Seven other family members were interred in the grounds of the plot. Bex made a quick call to the cemetery manager and learned Dixie Castile would be next, her service was set for Saturday, and she'd be laid to rest in the crypt beside her father, Noah.

"What about the older cemetery?" Landry asked, and she returned to the workstation. Moments later she brought another box to him. A yellow, folded sheet of paper lay atop a stack of brittle records. "This is the Old Cemetery's plot map," she said, unfolding it on the table. Landry examined the sheet; it was a grid laid out in blocks with numbered burial spots that corresponded to handwritten names on side panels. There were hundreds of them, each meticulously entered by some clerk long ago. It took Bex no time to find seven Castiles buried not in a dedicated family plot like the one in Bonaventure Cemetery, but interred alongside each other close by other old Savannah families.

"Amos Castile died first, in 1762, then his wife, Maria, and then came Joshua Castile, probably his son, who died in 1798. Joshua's wife, Naomi, is buried beside him. Corinne Castile is next. She died in 1802 and so did an infant—Baby Girl Castile—who's buried with her. Nathan, Corinne's husband, died in 1838. He was the last Castile interred in the Old Cemetery." She offered to photocopy the map, and he accepted.

"You've been a big help," Landry said. "I'm glad you were able to access the information so easily. By the way, is your boss always this cordial to people wanting information? For a man who runs a historical society, he certainly has an unpleasant attitude."

Concerned about her job, she wondered how much to tell a bona fide ghost hunter who hadn't revealed his motives. She decided to go for it, since she was simply an intern, after all. She hadn't lost a career like Fletcher Skorza.

"Mr. Taylor's not usually like that. He's always friendly and cordial, but lately he's been different. He snapped at Dr. S and me the other day, and this morning he fired him for going upstairs to the third floor."

"He fired him for *that*? What's up there?"

"I have no idea. It's off-limits to everyone, even my boss even though he's second-in-command here. Was, I guess I should say. He saw muddy footprints downstairs the other morning that indicated several people came here during the storm. He followed them to a locked doorway that goes to the top floor, and his curiosity got the best of him. He went to Mr. Taylor's office and got the key and went upstairs. He told me about finding bizarre stuff—robes and ritual things and a red snake in a cage. He got the idea they were performing some kind of ceremony up there. He said a florist named Abby caught him when she came to feed the snake."

CHAPTER FORTY-FOUR

Intrigued, Landry told Bex he'd like to meet Fletcher, she called him, and thirty minutes later he and Landry sat in a Starbucks near Forsyth Park.

Fletcher introduced himself as a big fan of Landry's *Bayou Hauntings* television series and said he looked forward to the new *Mysterious America* episodes. "Is that why you're in Savannah?" he asked.

"Does the name Marcie Epperson ring a bell?"

"I don't think so. Should I know her?"

"How about Dixie Castile?"

"Absolutely," Skorza replied. "She was the town librarian from when I was a kid until a few years ago. She died recently, I heard. She also comes from one of Savannah's oldest families. Bex may have told you I'm into Georgia history. It's always fascinated me, and the Castiles go way back. The family home sits on Calhoun Square."

Without going into detail, Landry explained that he'd come to Savannah because Dixie Castile's niece, Marcie, who inherited the family home, experienced paranormal events there.

"Like what?" Fletcher said, hoping to hear a story. "Savannah has a reputation for being a haunted city. Are there ghosts in the Castile mansion?"

He was disappointed when Landry wouldn't discuss specifics. Maybe someday, he said, but right now he needed information, and Fletcher asked how he could help.

Landry described meeting Rob Taylor. "He clearly didn't want me nosing around the cemetery records, and it pissed him off when Bex agreed to help me look through them. She said he acted strangely—any idea what's up with him?"

"Why he would fire his number two man after eight years, you mean? I went into his office and took a key out of the box, but I've done that same thing in the past. Things have come up where we needed to get into a locked area when Rob wasn't there. So it wasn't about 'stealing' the key. It was about going to the forbidden floor."

"Bex said you found ritual things and even a live snake. What do you make of it?"

"I've given it a lot of thought. What could be so important—so secret that I'd get fired for seeing it? And I think I know the answer, as far-fetched as it may be. I think it's the current iteration of a centuries-old ritual. How much Rob knows, I can't say, but he's involved enough to be the gatekeeper of a secret room at the top of a two-hundred-year-old mansion built by James Oglethorpe in 1750."

———

Bex was getting the grilling of her life. "What did he want to know?" Rob asked for the third time. "Exactly what did he want to see in the records?"

Her voice trembled. First her boss and now her. *What's wrong with him?* She wondered. "He...he didn't say. He wanted to see information about Bonaventure Cemetery—the Castile graves. I...I helped him locate them on the map."

"What else did you tell him? There are cameras in the building, you know. Everything in here is recorded. Voices, movements, everything. Don't lie to me!"

She knew there were cameras—the first floor was a museum, after all—and signs here and there informed visitors they were under surveillance. But she also knew the single camera in the archives room where they'd been didn't work. Racks of shelving ran from floor to ceiling, each filled to capacity. She'd noticed the dusty, ancient camera stuck on a wall near the door and followed its cord down to an outlet. The camera hadn't been plugged in the entire time she'd been here.

"Mr. Taylor," she said, "I enjoy working here, but you're starting to freak me out. I didn't show Mr. Drake anything I shouldn't have. I can't think of anything in the archives we wouldn't allow him to see anyway, but you act as if I've done something wrong. What's going on?"

He slumped in his chair, removed his glasses, and rubbed his temples. "I'm sorry. I'm getting paranoid, I guess. When your boss violated an order and I had to terminate him, I lost a good friend. I've worked with him for years..." He stopped and looked up as if just realizing she was still in the room. "That's all, Bex. I'm sorry I went off like that. It's not about you, and you didn't do anything wrong. Go on back to work. Close the door on the way out, please."

He looked out the window for some time. It was a beautiful summer day, the trees swayed in a light breeze, and puffy white clouds hung in an azure sky. Rob saw none of that; it was a dark, forbidding time. People had held things together for many, many years—since long before he became a member—but pieces were starting to erode now. The tapestry was beginning to unravel, and suddenly a nationally recognized paranormal investigator was on the scene, wanting to know about the Castiles. It had been a mistake for Marcie Epperson to bring him to town, but she didn't know. Finn Perryman could have stopped it, but now it appeared things were on the verge of falling like a string of dominoes.

As much as he disliked doing it, he called Rudy. As Grand Master of the Order, he had to be told about the peril they faced.

CHAPTER FORTY-FIVE

FBI Agent Jim Parsons parked his unmarked black sedan on St. Louis Street, just around the corner from Vieux Carré Rarities on Burgundy. Dressed in chinos and a sport jacket, he looked like an affluent French Quarter tourist pausing to look in the shop window crammed with ancient leather-bound books, a set of silver goblets, American coins from the early eighteen hundreds, and ornately carved walking sticks, along with a hodgepodge of other antiques and relics.

The little store was crammed with furniture and showcases, and Agent Parsons had to weave through them to reach a dusty counter in the back. A bell sat next to a sign that said "Ring for Service," and when he rang it, a wizened old man emerged from behind a curtain. He looked up at the agent and in a pronounced British accent said, "How may I be of service?"

"A lady from Nottingham suggested I stop by."

Hearing the phrase from a stranger surprised the old man. In a thick Yorkshire brogue he asked, "An' who might you be?"

"Is that important? A lady from Nottingham…"

"Aye, aye, I heard you, but I'm accustomed t'…well, t' seeing acquaintances and longtime clients. Who would you be?"

"Is that a problem?"

The old man chuckled. "You're an impertinent one, aren't you? All right then. It's too rainy in Nottingham for me these days. There you go. Now show me what you brought."

The Nottingham phrase was all Parsons knew, so he went to plan B and flipped out his badge. "Agent Jim Parsons, FBI, Mr. Meriwether. What was it you expected me to show you?"

The man cackled and coughed. "Aye, you're impertinent, all right. Who told you to mention the lady from Nottingham?"

"Marcie Epperson."

"Never heard of her."

"How about Dixie Castile?"

"Nope. Run along, Mr. FBI man. You have no business here."

The shopkeeper was right. Parsons had run this line as far as he could, learning only that after using the code phrase and getting a reply, he was supposed to show something to the old man.

"We're investigating a case in Savannah. That's where your name came up."

"Do tell. Savannah. Heard it's a nice place, but I've never been there."

"You do business with people from there—people who use the Nottingham phrase when they come in here."

Unfazed, the old man sighed. "I do business with customers from all over the world. People love t' browse my store when they come to New Orleans. I'm sure some of them came from Savannah, but I really don't recall offhand. Nice t' hear people in Savannah are talking about me though. Tell 'em hello if you see 'em." With a wheezy laugh, he turned and walked back through the curtain, leaving Parsons by himself in the little shop.

Once the agent left, Nigel Meriwether placed a call to the Cotton Exchange Bank in Savannah. When he got

Finn Perryman on the line, he told him about the visit. "He knew the code words, and he said he got them from Marcie Epperson, whoever that is, but he also mentioned Dixie Castile's name. I've been assisting you and your friends for years without a hitch, Mr. Perryman, and it seems you have a leak in the system somewhere. I won't take a fall for you, so I suggest you plug the leak immediately."

It's Dixie's damned niece, Finn thought. *Somehow she decoded her aunt's instruction sheet. But how could it have happened, and what do I do about it?* It was just one more thing on top of everything else, but that minor problem put him over the top. He should notify Rudy about the FBI's visit to the New Orleans shop, but he didn't feel like helping anymore.

Finn sat in the darkness of his world, his hands on the arms of his comfortable chair, recalling how recently he'd stared at the river from the window just behind him. The river was still there, although Finn doubted he'd ever see it again. Problems that had been solvable irritations seemed monumental when one couldn't see. He couldn't look around his office, focus on this memento or that plaque, and conjure up fond memories that would replace the pesky problems. Now everything in life was negative, and it seemed things were coming at him from a hundred different directions. He wanted to stop Rudy Falco, but how could a blind man stop anyone? He couldn't even get home by himself, or fix a drink, or do anything other people did.

His phone rang, and he listened for several minutes, asked a few questions, and signed off. Rudy had called a meeting of the Order two nights from now—a Ritual of the Envenoming with Marcie Epperson as the candidate. How Rudy secured her cooperation so quickly was a mystery—he refused to say anything more about her—but he asked that Finn serve as Grand Master for the ceremony. Even without sight it would be simple, as Finn had presided other times. When he asked why, Rudy said he wanted to be the one who held Marcie's hand. That was typical for one's sponsor—the person who revealed the secrets to the initiate—so it made sense.

The grandfather clock in Finn's hallway chimed nine, and he decided to call it a day. He felt his way from chair to table to wall, moving slowly through the room and the hall and his bedroom. He ran his hands over the bed, grateful that his housekeeper had turned it down. He made it into the bathroom, cursed when he bumped a water glass and sent it crashing to the floor, and fumbled around until he found another. He opened the medicine cabinet and slowly ran his fingers along the rows of bottles that kept an old man functioning. If only there were a pill for blindness, he wouldn't be in this situation, but he had made peace with things now, and he was confident he'd made the right decision.

The large bottle at the very end contained hydrocodone left over from a recent dental surgery. He hadn't needed much then, but he kept it around in case something else came up. *Well,* he mused to himself, *I'd say something has.* He unscrewed the cap, filled the water glass, and took capsule after capsule until they were gone.

That should do it. He shuffled back to his bed, fluffed the pillow, and lay on the covers, fully dressed. He'd rather be found in his street clothes than his pajamas. As the release of sleep crept through the world of darkness he inhabited, Finn Perryman relaxed and allowed it to happen.

CHAPTER FORTY-SIX

Two days after his abrupt termination, Fletcher got a surprising phone call from his old boss. Apologizing, he said he'd reacted in anger over Fletcher's trespass, but he realized that was wrong. "If you can forgive my actions, I'd like you to come back," he added.

In a perfect world, Fletcher would already have accepted another position with a higher salary and better benefits, but the reality was he hadn't even looked. Being assistant director at the historical society was his dream job, and Fletcher wanted it back. He accepted his boss's apology and returned.

He knew from meeting Landry that Bexley would still be there, and he dived right back into projects he'd been working on forty-eight hours earlier. Rob seemed his old self, and not only did the misstep seem to be forgotten, Rob even offered to take him upstairs and explain everything. It was the least he could do, the man said apologetically, and Fletcher accepted without hesitation.

On the next day—a Friday—Fletcher locked the doors at five when staff and visitors departed. He joined Rob in the director's office. "Sit down," Rob said. "Let's have a cocktail while I tell you a story that may surprise you. Then we'll take a tour upstairs." He went to the kitchen, brought back an ice bucket, and fixed two Scotch and waters. Rob took the chair next to Fletcher's, they clinked glasses, and he said, "You know more Georgia history than anybody. You've heard of the Order of the Red Serpent, I'm sure."

"Of course. I mentioned it to Bex just the other day. It's one of Georgia's oldest legends." He took a drink, started thinking about Rob's statement, and said, "You're not going to tell me the Order still exists, are you? That's impossible…"

"Is it? You were up there the other day. Think about what you saw. Think about what Abby Wright told you." He sat back, smiled, and watched Fletcher's expression change as he recalled things one by one.

Fletcher trembled with excitement. What little he knew about the Order came from history books or legends, but what he saw with his own eyes—the robes, a Spanish sword and candlestick, and the serpent itself—seemed to indicate the Order was alive and well, and right under his nose.

"Does…I mean, does it exist?"

"Absolutely," Rob confirmed, "and its purpose over the years hasn't changed. Do you recall what that purpose is?"

"According to legend, members of the Order are guardians of Hernando de Soto's treasure. But that's not possible…"

Rob reached for his Scotch. "Finish your drink, and let's take a walk. I'll show you a living legend and explain everything."

In a few minutes Rob got the key, and they went upstairs. He flipped the switch, and the old chandeliers flickered to life, casting dim shadows about the room. He opened the door to what he called the Robe Room, explaining that the members wore robes for meetings and special ceremonies.

"Who are the members?"

"I'm one, and at the moment there are three others. In my twenty years as a member, there have been as many as seven and as few as four, like today."

"I can't believe you're a member of the Order of the Red Serpent. That blows my mind. I've known you for eight years—hell, my office is just below this room—and I had no idea this all existed. How did you become a member?"

"It's passed down generationally. My father was a member, as was his."

"Abby Wright caught me up here. She's one too?"

"That's right. We take turns feeding the snake, as she told you. The other members are regular folks, people you'd see on the street and never imagine belonged to the Order."

The information seemed to be coming faster than Fletcher could process it. He felt himself becoming light-headed and grabbed a chair back for support. "How do you..." He paused, struggling to put words together. "How do you become a member?"

"You take an oath, and then you participate in something called the Ritual of the Envenoming. The serpent chooses our members."

The room began to sway. What? What did he say? The serpent does what? "I don't...understand. I...what's happening..."

As Fletcher collapsed to the floor, Rob said, "Believe me, you'll understand everything sooner than you imagined."

CHAPTER FORTY-SEVEN

The death of the bank president had nothing to do with the ongoing examination of Cotton Exchange Bank. When a messenger from Atlanta brought the gold bar, the lead examiner compared it to photographs taken the last time an audit team saw one. A letter from the Guaranty Mercantile Bank confirmed there were six hundred and forty-nine more just like this one, all belonging to Cotton Exchange Bank.

"Where in the world did the Perrymans get this?" one of the auditors asked as she turned the bar over and over, marveling at its weight and beauty. "These have been authenticated by a gold dealer in the past, right?"

"Completely. Years ago Dillon Gage certified them as genuine and said they're identical to treasure recovered from shipwrecks. Spanish galleons carried these back in the 1500s. There's no law against keeping all your assets in precious metals, but I'm sure we all agree on one thing—there's no other bank in the United States that does this. But your question is valid—how did the Perryman family get hold of so many of them? And unfortunately, it's not a question we can ask."

Another examiner tossed out an idea. There might not be a law against a bank keeping its assets in gold, but maybe they could find out where it came from. What if they called the state archaeology people? He'd read about their work at Native American sites; maybe they'd be interested in looking at a trove of sixteenth-century Spanish gold.

"Great idea," the leader said, reaching for his cellphone. He called his boss, who agreed the enigma of the Cotton Exchange Bank's assets needed to be solved. With Finn Perryman no longer around to object, maybe they could make it happen. Two hours later the boss called back to report how excited the state archaeologist was to see the cache.

Upon Finn's death, Fielding had become president after a hastily convened meeting of the board of directors. She was irascible and curt even with them, but no one knew the bank better than she did. So it was she whom the audit team summoned to the conference room. She strode in, confident that they were ready to present the final report and head back to Atlanta, but instead came the stunning revelation that the controversial gold bars once again were a bone of contention.

"We don't question their authenticity or value," the lead man explained. "What we'd like to know is their provenance. They're Spanish, Ms. Fielding, and they're identical to sixteenth-century ingots recovered from shipwrecks. I realize Mr. Perryman's no longer able to answer questions, but do you know where his family got them?"

"We've been through this before," she snapped. "I have no idea, nor does it matter. The gold is real, and it's worth what we claim it is, period. End of story."

"Not this time, I'm afraid. You're correct that the state banking commission has no right to question the provenance, but we notified the state archaeologist. He wants to see the bars and can be in Atlanta tomorrow morning. We just need you to call Mercantile Guaranty and authorize him to examine them."

"You're way out of bounds doing that, and I refuse to allow him to see the gold." She doubted she'd win, but by God she intended to fight these bureaucrats just as her boss would have done.

"I understand your reticence," the examiner said, "but I think over the years we have always accommodated Mr. Perryman's requests to accept the gold. The courier from Mercantile Guaranty who brought the gold bar is gone, and in the interest of security, we don't want him to bring more bars here. The archaeologist is willing to meet at the bank in Atlanta and examine them there, so they never have to leave the premises."

"Absolutely not. This is outrageous!"

The examiner played his hole card. "With all respect, there's nothing outrageous about our request. If you refuse, the banking commissioner is prepared to place Cotton Exchange Bank into temporary receivership. During that time, you may neither take deposits nor make loans, so your customers will experience some inconvenience. The receiver will be someone appointed from our offices in Atlanta, and he or she will run the bank."

Fielding exploded in rage. "Are you serious? Our bank is solvent, and our asset base is solid, and you know it. I don't know what you think you're doing…"

"What we're doing, ma'am, is allowing you to choose between receivership and allowing the state archaeologist to figure out where the Perryman family's forty million dollars in gold came from. It's up to you."

"How much time do I have?"

He looked at his watch. "It's three p.m. You can let me know tomorrow morning at eight."

The woman stormed out of the room, slamming the door behind her. With Finn Perryman gone, she didn't know what to do. His family deposited the gold back in the seventies, when after decades it became legal again for Americans to own it.

Were the examiners on a fishing expedition, or did they know something? Maybe Finn's family stole the gold. Or it was bought with drug money. Or they were in the Mafia. Whatever the reason, she couldn't allow a receiver to take over the bank, because receiverships were the kiss of death. She'd been president for seven days, and by God she wouldn't preside over its demise.

Fielding walked back into the conference room. "Prepare the letter and I'll sign it," she said. "There's nothing wrong with our assets, and you know it. You people have tried time and again to cast doubt on Mr. Perryman's family's unconventional assets, but they're as legal as cash."

The lead examiner said he'd have the letter for her in the morning. She went back upstairs, remembering something Finn had told her long ago. If it ever came down to a pissing contest with the regulators, he could convert the gold to cash in a matter of days.

Now that she might be facing that very issue, she wished he'd told her how.

CHAPTER FORTY-EIGHT

As the members donned their ceremonial robes on the top floor of the Parsonage, they saw the Grand Master's tall chair was empty. On the table in front of it rested the sword and candlestick, ready for tonight's ceremony, and from the seat to the Grand Master's right, Rudy convened the meeting.

Abby intended to challenge Rudy the moment the meeting started. She had never trusted him, and his casual suggestion that Fletcher Skorza be eliminated was dangerous and irrational. Many controversial and illegal things happened within these walls, but Rudy had suggested killing an outsider.

She'd considered talking to Rob Taylor before the meeting, but decided to wait. She'd make her case and hope he agreed. Before she could speak, Rudy called for a moment of silence to remember Finn Perryman, whose housekeeper had found him dead in bed yesterday morning.

Rudy sat in silence, considering the perfection of Finn's demise. The others felt sorry for Finn, and whether he recovered from blindness or not, they wouldn't have let Rudy permanently replace him as Grand Master. Now he'd get what he wanted, because Abby and Rob were weak.

"It was a blessing for Finn to go," Abby said. "After

losing his sight, he was a broken man. He's in a better place." She regretted that statement the moment it came out of her mouth, because she believed nothing of the kind. Given the things this group had done over the years, God—if there was such a thing—would never allow them into His kingdom.

"We need to talk about something," she continued. "After Fletcher came to my shop, you said he had to be eliminated. I can't believe you said those words. It's insane to think…"

With a smile, Rudy held up a hand to shush her. "I changed my mind," he said, announcing the Ritual of the Envenoming would commence. The members shifted expectantly in their chairs; this was the Order's most nightmarish and sobering ceremony, a rite in which a life hung in the balance as a reptile—the fabled Red Serpent—decided the initiate's fate.

Rudy announced, "Tonight we have something truly special. Perhaps this has happened in the centuries our Order has existed, but I'm not aware of it. Tonight we have two candidates for initiation."

Two? That surprised Abby. She thought Marcie Epperson was the initiate as the heir of Dixie Castile, but how could there be another? Finn Perryman had been gone just one day, and he had no heirs. His lineage died with him, so his successor would be an outsider, chosen unanimously by the membership after consideration and planning. None of that had happened.

"What are you talking about?" Abby asked.

"I'm talking about Fletcher Skorza. Our beloved Grand Master's demise offered a perfect solution to it. Rob, why don't you fill Abby in on our plans?"

Rob said, "I warned Fletcher never to come up here, but he rifled through my desk, found a key, and did it anyway, and I fired him. But after he came to your store, Rudy and I talked. Fletcher has a PhD in history, and he knows about the Order, but when he saw our meeting room and the serpent, he didn't connect it. Regardless, the word Rudy used—elimination—was what must happen. I don't like it either, Abby, but we can't allow an outsider to know the things he saw here. He has to be stopped."

Rudy interrupted. "As Grand Master, I have decided to let the serpent decide if Fletcher should become one of us. Now that Finn's position is open, it makes perfect sense."

Rob shook his head. "No. This isn't right. Presenting someone for initiation takes a unanimous vote. I thought we were going to…" He paused. The words didn't come as easily for him as for Rudy.

Rudy smiled. "Kill him. You thought I was going to bring him here, explain everything, and then kill him. That was my original plan, but it's not up to us. What if the snake decides he should be part of our little group?"

"We should have voted, because he's an outsider and not a direct descendant. You arbitrarily picked Fletcher Skorza just like you made yourself Grand Master, and I say we stop right now and take a vote. What if he passes the initiation and then refuses to join? Or he goes public with our secrets? It's too risky."

"Au contraire, my friend. I made the decision, and I'll live with it. I can't go back at this point anyway; Fletcher is already awaiting his turn. His initiation is going to happen, and that's it. If the serpent selects him, but he refuses to abide by our oaths, then I'll kill him myself. We've done enough talking; it's time to begin."

CHAPTER FORTY-NINE

After twelve years waiting, tonight Rudy got what he'd been waiting for. According to the rules, the group unanimously selected a leader, but Rudy hadn't followed the rules. He'd appointed himself Grand Master, just as he'd singlehandedly chosen Fletcher to replace Finn, decisions that required a vote. His aggressive, overbearing personality got him what he wanted, and neither of the others challenged him.

"Prepare for the Summons," Rudy commanded. Abby went to the light switch, plunging the cavernous room into darkness, and returned. The three members sat at the near end of the table, their faces and robes shimmering as flames from gas lamps along the walls and a taper in the tall candlestick provided the only illumination. The eerie effect left the far half of the room bathed in darkness, and Rudy began the ceremony by raising the beautiful old sword high in the air and reciting an incantation in Spanish.

Rudy stood, said more words, and within moments there were murmurs in the silent room.

"He comes," first one, then another said. Only after they all saw their guest did they say the words in unison. "He comes."

A commanding figure swayed in the shadows

behind the Grand Master's seat. He wore a *capacete*—a metal helmet with a crest and a flat brim. A faceplate shielded his features, and full plate armor protected his upper body. The guest of honor was a formidable conquistador, fearsome to behold even as a transparent phantom. He would have ruled with an iron fist, leading his men for thousands of miles, conquering new territory, and amassing a vast hoard of treasure.

Rudy said, "As the sponsor of our first candidate, I'll fetch Marcie Epperson. Abby, prepare the table." He walked to the stairs and left.

Abby went to the janitorial closet and returned with the wire cage that held the red serpent. When she set it on the table, the beautiful cold-blooded creature reared its head and moved it about as if taking in its surroundings. It looked at each member in turn, pausing a moment as if measuring their loyalties. Then it settled in to wait, its body undulating and pulsating in anticipation.

Once Rudy was out of earshot, Rob said, "Marcie Epperson is one thing, but we can't initiate the other one. Rudy broke the rules and put us in a dangerous situation. We've always gotten the candidate's approval before the ceremony. There's no telling what he'll do afterwards."

"Maybe the guy agreed," Abby said. "As much as I dislike Rudy and his autocratic methods, I'm willing to give him the benefit of the doubt. And remember this— Fletcher Skorza is already a threat. Not only has he been in this room, he also saw the serpent. Revealing any of that would cause us irreparable damage. I agree with Rudy; it has to be this way."

They heard footfalls on the stairs, and in a moment a dazed girl stumbled into the room, her arms supported by Rudy Falco. He steered her to the table and said, "Let the ritual begin."

The mysterious dream that had haunted Marcie's nights began to unfold once again, although this time the nightmare had become real. Through her drug-induced haze, she beheld things she'd seen in the dream. There stood the ethereal figure—the ancient man in the helmet who watched everything. On the table six inches from her face sat the cage.

In his dual role as sponsor of the initiate, Rudy said, "She is prepared, so let us proceed." Rudy pushed her into a kneel, and for the first time she could see the snake. With the effects of the drug starting to wear off, she cried out in alarm and tried to move back. But it was time.

Rudy called on Rob to raise the trapdoor. "Now," he said, and in one swift movement the small door went up, and Rudy forced Marcie's hand inside. In morbid fascination, the people around the table gathered closer, craning their necks to see inside the dark box where the reptile waited.

Because of their concentration, and because the far end of the room lay in darkness, none of them noticed movement there. It began as a swirling vortex that took on the form of a human body. As it became a transparent shadow like the conquistador beside Marcie, this ghost also observed the ceremony.

Then a scratching sound filled the room—*Ka-chee. Ka-chee. Ka-chee.*—a noise like a scratchy needle on a vinyl record.

Let her go. Let her go. Let her go. Unearthly whispers startled those captivated by the ancient ritual. Maintaining a steady grip on Marcie's arm, Rudy watched the ethereal figure glide closer. "Dixie Castile," he said when its face transformed from a dark shadow to one he knew well. "Leave this room. You have no place here."

Still in a stupor, Marcie looked up at the sound of her aunt's name. The spirit said, *Be still. Be still. Be still.* Understanding those words were meant for her, Marcie forced herself to remain calm. The watchers purred as the serpent slithered across her palm, each scale sending shock waves of fear through Marcie. She glanced at her aunt's spirit, and the sense of dread disappeared, leaving her feeling peace and resignation. This situation was beyond her control, the sedative was wearing off, and regardless of the outcome, this horror would soon be part of her past.

Marcie realized she could no longer feel the snake's

skin, and she dared to look inside the cage. The creature had retreated to a corner. It stared in her direction, its beady, evil eyes boring into hers with an intensity that caused her to flinch. At the twitch of her fingers, the serpent became interested once again, and it moved its head so close she could feel the flick-flick of its revolting forked tongue against her skin.

"End this if you must," she whispered, and the others gasped as she closed her fingers around its strangely beautiful red scales while it slid effortlessly through them. Rudy lifted his arm into the air, and she knew from her dream what would be next. He struck the box hard, and the reptile sprang forward in alarm, looked at Marcie, and opened its horrid mouth to reveal the razor-sharp fangs that were its means of passing judgment. But instead of striking, it retreated to the back of its cage.

Marcie was waking up as the drugs wore off, and she wondered how much longer she must endure this horror. She knew there was a time limit, and mercifully, it happened.

"Time's up," someone said, and Rudy—the man she despised who held her arm immobile so the snake could have its way—released his grip. He put his hand on the trapdoor and whispered, "You may remove your hand slowly or quickly, but choose carefully. The snake can move at lightning speed."

Marcie remembered this part of her dream. Here in the world of reality, the snake reared its head and opened its mouth in what looked like a satanic grin. Its fangs shone like pearls as she jerked her hand out. Rudy slammed down the door as the serpent struck. Two fangs were embedded in the wooden door, and Marcie escaped with no time to spare. The other man—Rob, although she didn't know his name—opened the door, grasped the snake by its neck, and carefully pulled its fangs from the wood. He threw it back inside and slammed the door.

Rudy swept her into his arms and carried her to a nearby couch while the others remained seated at the table. Alert, she listened to them talk; they weren't surprised, because each of them had avoided being bitten by the snake or else they would be dead. But they remain concerned about Marcie's loyalty, and they wondered if she might betray them.

Alert now, Marcie lay still and watched. She saw the phantom—her aunt's spirit—glide across the room and hover near her, and heard Rudy speak. His words tore at her gut.

"Bring in the next candidate."

Oh my God, they have another captive. They're going to run this horror show all over again.

CHAPTER FIFTY

Marcie lay on the couch, hoping no one saw her trembling hands. Rudy waited while the other man opened a door and brought the next candidate in. His hands were bound behind his back, and he shuffled and stumbled just as she had.

Sitting in the tall chair, Rudy ran the show. He called out the man's name—Fletcher Skorza—and asked, "Rob, is he prepared?" He nodded, and Rudy said, "Then let us proceed."

Rob pushed the candidate to his knees; inches from his face the serpent waited in its cage. He struggled and cried out, and Rudy again asked if the candidate was prepared. Marcie wondered that too; she'd been pretty looped when Rudy had pushed her hand into the cage. This man Fletcher was resisting, and she wondered if he knew he must stop if he had a chance to survive.

She gasped as she watched. Now Fletcher's hand was inside the box, and Rob held his arm in a viselike grip, but he continued to struggle. *You mustn't,* she whispered as the snake slowly raised itself to watch the commotion. As the fingers twitched and moved, the red serpent opened its mouth wide. The robed people around the table were fixated like Romans waiting for lions to slaughter the gladiators.

There was a collective gasp as the snake dove toward Fletcher's hand, but its fangs weren't extended, and the result was a caress and not a fatal bite.

"Be still," Rob said to the victim. "If you can outlast him for five minutes, this will be over."

"Let. Me. Go." Fletcher's teeth were clenched as he raised his left hand to break away from Rob's grip. Everyone in the room realized something was very wrong—either the candidate's sedation had worn off early, or the dose was insufficient. Either way, he seemed in control of his faculties, and Marcie found herself rooting for him while the members around the table drew back in alarm.

With his hand still inside, he made a sudden, sweeping move and lifted the snake's cage off the table, swung it through the air, and slammed it into Rob Taylor's left temple. He fell backwards and released Fletcher's arm. Fletcher opened the trapdoor with his free hand, but Rudy flew across the table, knocking both Fletcher and the cage to the floor and landing hard on them. Now three men lay in a heap, fighting and pushing to extricate themselves as the stunned reptile surveyed the situation and made a choice.

The ghost of Dixie Castile swept in front of Marcie, protecting her as she sprang from the couch and distanced herself from the fracas. Abby scrambled up on a chair and screamed, "Be careful of the snake! It's loose!" Their fracas forgotten, the men separated and tried to get away, but they were too late. The snake found the closest and dug its ivory fangs into the soft flesh of a man's arm. Deadly venom coursed through his veins, instantly attacking the nervous system.

Fletcher sprang across the room and grabbed the serpent just behind its head. Rudy rose from the floor, trying to think how to contain the damage, while Fletcher's boss writhed in pain for a few seconds before going rigid on the floor. Moments later the venom attacked his heart, and Rob was dead.

The snake's mouth gaped, and its fangs were fully extended, but Fletcher's grip on its neck immobilized it. "Put it back in here," Rudy commanded as he picked up the cage, set it on the table, and opened the door.

"I don't think so." Fletcher looked at Marcie. "You. Who are you?"

"Marcie. Marcie Epperson. I'm the other initiate." She pointed at Rudy, who waited for an opportunity to take Fletcher out. "He drugged me…"

"Come on!" Fletcher grabbed her hand, flew to the stairway, and pushed her ahead. As Rudy sprinted to the stairs, he threw the serpent at him. Rudy sidestepped to avoid it, lost his balance and fell, hitting his head against the table as he went down. Screams echoed as the serpent slithered away. When Rudy looked up a moment later, Fletcher and Marcie were gone.

CHAPTER FIFTY-ONE

"We have to get away," Marcie cried as they fled through Calhoun Square, dressed in red robes, looking like two singers fleeing choir practice. "Is there a police station around here?"

"I don't know, and what good would it do? By the time the cops went to the Parsonage, everyone would be gone. These people know what they're doing, and no one's going to believe our story. There must be someone we can call—someone who can help us."

"Landry Drake! He and this ex-cop have been in town, helping me. I'll call him..." She immediately realized the absurdity of that statement. Here she stood barefooted, wearing a red robe and nothing else. Her phone and wallet were in her apartment, where she'd left them when Rudy kidnapped her.

Fletcher was in the same fix; his clothes and phone were gone too. Rob had drugged him at the Parsonage, restrained him with duct tape, and locked him in an upstairs closet. Tonight he'd been drugged, but like Marcie, his sedative had worn off during the ceremony.

"My apartment's not far from here," he said. "I'll get you something to wear so we're not walking around in robes."

She considered finding Landry top priority, because every minute counted. She said, "He's been staying at the Azalea Inn, but he could have left by now. Let's go find out; we can walk there in five minutes."

At almost two in the morning, they climbed the stairs to the front porch of the quaint yellow B&B. The emergency phone number on the door was of no help. They could see a long hallway through the front door's glass panes, a couple of lamps were lit, but at this time of night no one was up. Just as Fletcher was ready to knock, she recalled Landry saying Harry's room was off the patio.

They walked around the side of the house and opened a wrought-iron gate that, unbeknownst to them, was alarmed. By the time they got to the pool area behind the inn, a woman in a bathrobe stood on the back porch of the house next door, wielding a shotgun and demanding to know what they were doing on private property.

Marcie said they were in trouble and needed help. They were looking for Landry Drake and Harry Kanter. The woman—Teresa, the innkeeper who lived in the house next door—confirmed the men were still there, but added, "You can't disturb my guests at this time of night. If you know them, why didn't you call them?"

"We were kidnapped, and they took our phones. This is much bigger than we can explain," Fletcher said. "Harry Kanter's an ex-policeman, and we need his help."

"Stay right there and don't move a muscle," Teresa ordered, taking her phone from her robe pocket. She speed-dialed a number, waited a moment, and said there were people outside who wanted to talk to Harry.

She pointed to a door opposite the pool, said it was Harry's and that he'd be out soon. Moments later he came outside with a pistol stuck in the waistband of his shorts. They told him what had happened, he called Landry, and they all gathered in Harry's room.

"We have to call the police," Harry said. "You witnessed a murder, the perps have a decent head start, and time's wasting." He placed the call, spoke with a detective, and agreed to bring them to the station.

Fletcher said, "I feel a little odd going around in a robe. How about we stop by my condo? It's on the way downtown."

At that hour, everything was quiet at Fletcher's place. It appeared no one was around, the lights were off, and there were no cars parked at the curb. While Harry held his weapon, Fletcher led them to the entryway, dug his fingers into the dirt of a flower pot that held a sad-looking ficus, and pulled out a small plastic bag with a key inside.

"For emergency use only," he said as he unlocked the door. Harry waved them back, stepped inside, and did a quick walkthrough before allowing them in and dead bolting the door. Keeping the lights off, Harry and Landry waited in the living room while Fletcher dressed, rummaged through his closet, and found clothes for Marcie—a white cotton shirt and gym shorts with a drawstring waist. Flip-flops finished off the ensemble, and he left her to dress.

They were talking quietly when they heard a knock, light enough not to arouse the neighbors across the entryway, but urgent. Harry drew his pistol, pointed it at the door, and waited.

"Fletcher, Fletcher, open up. We need to talk." The words were low and muffled, but he recognized the voice. Marcie emerged from the bedroom, gasped when she saw the weapon pointed at the door, and whispered, "What's going on?"

Fletcher whispered, "Rudy's at the door."

She cringed. "Oh, my God. Does he know we're in here?"

Harry shushed them. The knock came again; they watched the doorknob move to the left and right and heard a shove against the door, then another. Through opaque curtains on a side window, they watched a shadow pause to try the locked window. It moved away, but they heard the tinkle of glass breaking in the bedroom.

"Call 9-1-1!" Harry whispered as he drew his revolver, stepped into the room, and shouted, "Drop the gun or I'll shoot!"

As the wailing sound of sirens grew louder, things escalated in seconds—a muffled scream, the sound of furniture breaking and a gunshot. Landry sprinted through the door and yelled, "Harry!" as another shot rang out. Unsure what to do, Marcie and Fletcher paused before hearing Landry cry, "Run! Get out now!"

They ran outdoors as three police cars careened around the corner and squealed to a stop. Suddenly the quiet street was ablaze with flashing red and blue lights, dying sirens and the crackling of police radios. They gave a sergeant a ten-second summary, and he led four cops inside, leaving one behind with them.

"I hope they're all right," Fletcher said, but there was little time to wonder. In a flash the cops seemed to be everywhere. They flew out the front door, running right and left, going to neighboring homes and knocking on doors. Porch lights came on, sleepy homeowners responded to frantic doorbells and knocks, and with sirens screaming, two more police cruisers and an ambulance roared down Abercorn Street and screeched to a halt. The sergeant issued quick instructions to the new arrivals, who ran to help the other officers as paramedics carried a gurney into the house.

"Who's hurt?" Marcie asked the sergeant, who said all he knew was the perpetrator got away. That left them wondering which of their friends needed an ambulance. And hoping it wasn't both.

CHAPTER FIFTY-TWO

When she saw Landry emerge into the yard, Marcie cried, "Landry, over here! Thank God you're all right. Is Harry hurt?"

"He's been shot. He and Rudy scuffled, and Rudy fired his gun. When I went in, I saw Rudy crawling out the window and Harry on the floor. The cops are doing a house-to-house search for Rudy now."

Landry walked over as the paramedics brought out the gurney and prepared to load it into the ambulance. "You'll be fine," he said. "You just aren't dodging bullets as fast as you used to."

Harry laughed. "Asshole got me in the shoulder, dammit. You know, I spent decades as a cop without taking a bullet. Now that I'm retired, I should be relaxing. But I made a bad decision, and that was to hang around with the likes of you. Take it from me, a guy can get in big trouble working for Landry Drake."

Landry laughed and squeezed Harry's hand. He got the name of the hospital and said he'd be there shortly, but Harry didn't want that. "It's almost dawn," he said. "Go get some sleep and come see me later. Sounds like I'll be in surgery for a while anyway, so don't waste time. I'll call you when I'm in a room."

With Rudy on the run, Landry was concerned about Marcie and Fletcher. They'd seen what Rudy did during the initiations and could testify against him, so Landry suggested a safe place to lie low. After taking her statement, a Savannah cop took Marcie to Tybee Island and waited in her apartment while she changed clothes, got her phone and wallet, and packed for a few days away. She also grabbed the two old books she'd found at her aunt's house, thinking there would be time to show them to Landry. Before leaving, she called her store clerk, arranged for her to work the next few days, and the policeman tailed her as she drove her car back to Savannah, dropping off when he saw her safely inside the Azalea Inn, the place Landry had picked for his short-term hideaway.

When the police heard Fletcher say there was a dead body on the top floor of the same building where he had his office, they took him to the Parsonage before allowing him to join the others at the B&B. Four cops stood on the porch as he entered a code on the front-door keypad. They went in first, clearing the building before bringing him inside. He took them to Rob's office, got the skeleton key from the desk, and opened the closet. The key box stood wide open, and the one he needed wasn't there, although he found his clothes, wallet, keys and phone in a pile at the back.

He took them to the door in the hallway that led upstairs. It was locked, but a cop's swift kicks destroyed its panels. They sidled through, ascended with weapons drawn, and called to Fletcher moments later. He entered the room, shocked at what he didn't see. In just a few hours, it had undergone a total transformation. As chaotic as everything had been earlier, he wondered how Rudy and Abby had managed to clean everything and dispose of a body so quickly. Abby didn't seem like the conspiratorial type, but by now Fletcher knew not to trust anything about these people. The cops doubted Rudy had singlehandedly toted off Rob's corpse, and that meant she'd helped him.

Fletcher took them to the closets. The one that held scarlet robes now contained a few empty hangers. The next was crammed with boxes, but the candlestick and sword used in the ceremony were gone. And the janitor's closet was just that—rags, solvents and cleaning solutions, mops, brooms and an old Hoover. No cages, no mice and no red serpent. Everything had been sanitized.

The cops taped off the spot on the floor where Fletcher claimed Rob's corpse had been and called for a forensics team. They searched every inch of the room but found nothing to indicate the bizarre ritualistic conclave Fletcher and Marcie had described.

Fletcher had learned about hidden cameras when he got fired, but he had no idea if there was an outside monitoring service. He'd never heard of one, but that made sense since he didn't know about the cameras. One place the video might be captured was Rob's laptop. He led the police to Rob's office, where the computer always sat on his desk. They weren't supposed to take work laptops out of the building, but Rob's was gone.

Fletcher's car sat where he'd left it, and several officers stayed behind while a squad car followed him back to his condo, only to find it still teeming with crime scene investigators. They allowed him to pack a suitcase and get his personal laptop, said they wouldn't be much longer, and promised to lock up when they left. The squad car followed him until he safely reached the B&B and joined the others.

The search for two missing people—perpetrators, if Fletcher's story was accurate—was in full swing. Police went to Abby Wright's home but found no one there, nor would she show up at the flower shop that day. They staked out both places but doubted she planned to return anytime soon. According to the doorman at Rudy Falco's building, he had not been home all night, and his Maserati was not in the garage. Cops easily located the fancy red sports car parked on the street a few blocks from the Parsonage. The two people Fletcher and Marcie had accused of murder had vanished.

Back at the Azalea Inn, Landry declined the Savannah police department's offer of protection, knowing it would be hard to spare three men, and instead he hired off-duty cops to provide round-the-clock security. As an additional precaution, they moved Marcie's and Fletcher's vehicles away from the house to a downtown lot.

Landry rented rooms for Fletcher and Marcie, and now his bunch occupied half of the inn. Having no other bookings for the next three nights, Teresa shut off reservations and gave them the run of the house. She looked forward to watching them work, and she refreshed coffee and soft drinks as Landry set up his laptop in the front sitting room, established a link to the office in New Orleans, and reported in to Cate and Henri.

Afterwards he called to check on Harry at the hospital but learned he'd already been released. That was all he could get from the tight-lipped nurse, who claimed HIPAA regulations prohibited giving out information.

Landry called Harry's cell but got voicemail, and ten minutes later he walked in, wearing a sling on his left arm. The wound wasn't as serious as the medics first thought; the bullet had gouged into the flesh just below the shoulder. A few inches higher and he'd be looking at a joint replacement, but instead he'd wear the sling for a few days and be sore as hell for a few more.

The group assembled in the sitting room and started to work. The sooner they helped the police solve this mystery, the faster Rudy and Abby would be behind bars.

CHAPTER FIFTY-THREE

At the Azalea Inn that evening, Teresa fixed a scrumptious pot roast with fingerling potatoes and carrots and homemade biscuits served with jam and honey. As they ate in the dining room, Landry pointed out the mural that depicted Hernando de Soto's treasure, and they discussed how it might be connected with the Order of the Red Serpent. Exhausted after a stressful twenty-four hours, Marcie and Fletcher declined after-dinner drinks in favor of an early bedtime and went to their rooms.

Later as she lay in bed, Marcie could hear every step Landry took in the room above hers. She was dog-tired but couldn't sleep until the house was quiet. At last it happened, and she drifted off into a dreamless state of exhaustion.

Which lasted until precisely two twenty-three in the morning.

Ka-chee. Ka-chee. Ka-chee.

She sat upright in bed, thinking that familiar scratchy sound had been part of a dream. Once it stopped, she waited a minute, then snuggled back under the covers.

Ka-chee. Ka-chee. Ka-chee.

Come here. Come here. Come here.

Marcie became aware of a subtle movement over in

a corner. She rose and gasped as the wraith—the spirit from her aunt's mansion—hovered in the air. She could see through its robe to the window behind, where illumination from a streetlamp outside filtered through. As before, the figure's face was a swirl of clouds, and this time when it raised its hand, she anticipated it. Instead of pointing, the bony finger curled and moved.

Come back. Come back. Come back.

"Aunt Dixie, is that you?" she whispered. "What do you want? What are you telling me?"

At the moment the specter disappeared, Marcie knew what she must do. She rose, quietly dressed, and slipped into the hall. She paused, saw flickers of light coming from the front room where the TV was, and knew the security guard would not see her go through the backyard. Careful not to make a sound, she cracked the door, sidled through it, and closed it gently. She went past the pool and crept through a garden on the side of the house, knowing cameras were picking up her movement but also knowing she'd be gone before the guard realized it.

Marcie made the short walk to Calhoun Square in less than ten minutes, passing no one else and seeing no cars at this time of night. Although the specter of the old mansion looming in the darkness was as eerie and sinister as a horror flick, she felt a sense of peace. Aunt Dixie wanted her to come here, and she had to learn the meaning of her inheritance.

She reached for the key but found the door unlocked. Wondering who had carelessly failed to secure it, she stepped inside, walked without fear up the stairs, and waited in the hallway. When she heard a faint noise from a nearby bedroom, she went inside.

"Aunt Dixie, here I am. Why did you bring me here?"

A rustling sound came from the darkness. "Sorry to disappoint you, Marcie."

Realizing she'd made a huge error, she turned to run, but Rudy's fingers clamped down hard on her arm. As she struggled to loosen his grip, she looked in his face and saw that cocky, disgusting grin. "I've been waiting for you. I knew you'd come here eventually," he said. She raised her knee to give him a groin punch, but he stepped aside and backhanded her, knocking her to the floor and leaving her dazed.

"It's useless to fight me," he said as he stood over her. "I wanted you that first day we met, and you gave yourself to me…"

"You drugged me, you rapist bastard."

"I'm sorry you weren't mentally alert enough to enjoy it, but trust me, your body seemed to be having a great time." He grinned again, and she kicked at his shin. "This could have been so easy. My mission was to ensure you'd join the Order, and all you had to do was agree. You'd have been privy to unimaginable secrets and joined an elite group with a noble goal."

"What goal? To kill people? How many people has the Order killed, Rudy? In however long it's been around, how many people died? How many did you kill personally?"

"It's been around nearly five hundred years, and I've never killed anyone. The serpent selects our members…"

"Bullshit! You stick an innocent person's hand inside a cage with a poisonous reptile and wait for it to strike based on their suitability to join some cult? Are the rest of your members as insane as you are?"

He merely smiled. "I came to your aunt's house after you and Fletcher got away from the Parsonage. I hid here and waited, knowing eventually greed or curiosity would bring you back. You couldn't stay away, and I'm happy to see you've finally arrived."

"I'll never join your Order, if that's what this is about…"

"Sadly, I think you've managed to destroy the Order. Abby Wright and I are the only ones left, unless we count you and Fletcher, who technically passed the initiation. So you've both already joined, and there's no going back. Right now I have something planned for you.

You missed all the fun last time, but you're wide awake now, so take off your clothes."

She scooted away on her butt. "No! No, I'm not doing that!"

"Want to make a bet?" he said, pointing to a nearby table where a wire cage sat in the gloom. "I brought a friend with me. If you won't cooperate, then maybe we'll redo your initiation ritual. As obstinate as you've been, I'm not sure you're fit to serve as a member. Maybe the snake will change its mind this time." He shook the cage hard, and the startled reptile coiled and struck at the wire.

"No!" She struggled for an idea—anything that would stop this madness. "I passed the initiation once, and I'm a member now, just like you. Don't—"

"Then get your damn clothes off."

She started to stand up, and he offered a hand, but she refused. She unbuttoned her shirt and unzipped her shorts, letting them both drop to the floor. "Getting a good look?" she snapped as he ogled her body.

"It's not like I haven't seen it before. You may not remember much of our afternoon delight, but I do."

"You disgusting pig. Is rape the only way you get sex? I can't imagine anyone doing it with you voluntarily."

"Very funny. Now strip down and shut up. We have things to do."

CHAPTER FIFTY-FOUR

Suppressing a shiver as she reached behind her and unhooked her bra, Marcie let it fall and said, "Will it feel more normal if you give me a hundred bucks? Isn't that how sickos like you get laid?"

"You should have been a comedian. Now take off the panties."

A muffled noise arose from somewhere in the house, but Rudy, caught up in the striptease, missed it. He also missed a cloudy wisp arising from the floor behind him. With her thumbs in the waistband of her underwear, Marcie saw the smoky figure and stopped what she was doing.

"Aunt Dixie's come to rescue me," she whispered, her mouth agape as she watched the ethereal tendrils of smoke swirl faster and faster, rising higher with each frenzied rotation.

"In your dreams. Aunt Dixie's dead and gone." Irritated at what he took for a delaying tactic, Rudy took a step toward her and snapped, "I'll tear the damn things off myself."

A noise—the sound of someone running—came from the hallway. Rudy whirled and saw the phantom just as Landry and Harry burst into the room.

"Thank God!" Marcie cried, covering her breasts as Rudy lunged for the wire cage. He reached the table, unhooked the trapdoor, and threw the box to the floor.

"Snake!" Marcie screamed as the red serpent sprang from its cage, slithering across the floor at lightning speed toward Landry and Harry. Harry drew his weapon, Rudy made a run for the open doorway, and Landry leaped on his back. Twisting and turning, they fell to the floor in a heap.

While Landry and Rudy wrestled, Harry tried shooting the snake, but the reptile was too quick. Although not a fighter, Landry was in decent physical shape and was ten years younger. Rudy carried more weight, but much of it was flab from his hedonistic lifestyle. As punches flew, Landry heard Marcie cry, "Oh my God!" and wondered if the snake was coming for them. The fight ended seconds later when Landry landed a sucker punch that put Rudy out cold.

Looking for the snake, he scrambled to his feet. Harry's arms were wrapped protectively around a half-naked Marcie while a bizarre scene unfolded. As the ethereal figure—a woman, by its attire—swirled lightly around the serpent, it responded by raising its head high into the air and swaying with the phantom in a macabre dance. A spectral hand reached down and caressed the snake's head as it crawled up, wrapping its scaly body around a ghostly arm. At that moment the spirit floated across the room and stood before Marcie.

"Aunt Dixie, I see you," she said, putting on her shirt and shorts as a face appeared through the haze. The spirit smiled at her niece but whirled around as Rudy sprang to his feet and ran out of the room. The ghost vanished, and seconds later, screams arose from somewhere downstairs. They ran into the hall and looked over the railing to see Rudy lying on the foyer's parquet floor, surrounded by a tornado of smoke and screaming as Dixie Castile's hands plucked at his face, hair and skin.

The moment they reached the bottom of the stairs, the spirit of Dixie Castile flew toward the ceiling and hovered twenty feet above Rudy, who lay spread-eagled on the floor, bleeding from his wounds and barely conscious.

Look. At. Me. The words burst in a crescendo of noise, echoing through the house with an unearthly, unnerving racket.

Rudy didn't move, and as Landry went toward the staircase, the ghost raised its arm and pointed at him. *Stay!*

Look! At! Me! Another cacophony of hellish words and sounds so awful Landry, Harry and Marcie held their ears against the noise.

"Don't kill him!" Marcie shouted. "Aunt Dixie, don't kill him! Let the police handle it."

The specter turned its head toward Marcie, nodded, and smiled. It floated gently back to the upstairs hall, and Marcie followed it into the bedroom as Harry and Landry checked on Rudy.

Harry drew his pistol, then holstered it as they realized Rudy couldn't run away this time. Moaning and sobbing, he writhed in pain from dozens of painful punctures that ripped his clothing and his flesh.

Landry retrieved his phone and dialed 9-1-1.

CHAPTER FIFTY-FIVE

The downstairs foyer at the Castile mansion teemed with activity. Radios crackled as EMTs tended to Rudy after moving him to a nearby couch. Two Savannah policemen sat with Landry, Harry and Marcie, to get a picture of what had happened to the injured man.

Before the police arrived, the three agreed they'd explain everything, as strange as it would sound. The time had come to reveal the mysterious activities of the Order of the Red Serpent.

Marcie explained how her dead aunt's spirit had awoken her with a summons to return to the mansion. When she came, she found Rudy Falco, the fugitive who had raped her before and intended to do so again. Landry began explaining about the cult and the red serpent, but one of the officers stopped him, took his partner aside, and whispered, "What the hell's going on here? These people are talking about ghosts and cults and a red serpent. Are they psychos or on drugs or what?"

"Do you know who the younger guy is?" the other cop asked.

"Yeah. Landry Drake. That's the name he gave us, right? What about him?"

"You don't recognize that name?"

He didn't, and his partner asked if he watched much TV. None, as it turned out. The cop was a gamer and said he didn't need television for drama. He got enough in real life.

Once his partner explained, it made sense that he'd be at a scene where a phantom had attacked a person who belonged to a cult with a red snake. Maybe not sense, but at least it fit the pattern for the well-known, respected ghost hunter.

The paramedics wheeled Rudy out to the ambulance and took him to the hospital. A police officer followed; since Marcie had accused him of rape, they would bring Rudy to the police station after he was discharged to get his statement and decide whether charges would be brought against him.

Soon the cops finished interrogating Marcie, Landry and Harry. An already unbelievable story got more outlandish with every new revelation, and the officers quickly realized whatever had happened here was beyond their pay grade. They asked the three of them to go to the station, where a detective would interview them.

At the station, Harry asked about Rudy, and the detective said he'd been treated and released from the hospital. He was in the building, giving a statement to another officer.

"Is he going to be charged?" Landry asked, and the cop said that depended on what they learned during the interrogation and what Marcie might add.

"Earlier you accused Mr. Falco of murder, although we found no evidence and no body. Now you're accusing him of rape. You say it happened several days ago. Why didn't you report it at the time, when a physician could have examined you?"

His callous comment shocked Marcie, who wondered if this was how rape victims always felt. "You don't believe me, do you? Do you think I'd make something like this up?"

"We take rape allegations seriously, Miss Epperson. When a victim doesn't call the police, it raises questions.

Your latest claim is that Mr. Falco was about to rape you again. Did he have a weapon? If not, why didn't you just run away?"

"He hit me. He knocked me to the floor..."

The detective asked if Marcie had a vendetta against Rudy, commenting, "So many unprovable accusations does muddy the waters."

"Goddammit, is this how you people treat victims? No wonder women feel powerless after being raped."

Landry added, "She was raped by this guy, Detective, and your words and your tone sound like you believe the perp and not the victim."

He stood. "If you'd like to give a statement, I'll arrange another officer to take it. It'll save you a trip back if you decide to press this rape allegation. You'll need to explain your relationship with Mr. Falco, how you met, all that kind of thing. For the record, Mr. Drake, my job isn't to believe one side or the other in a case. My job is to get the facts, and like I said, Miss Epperson's allegations— including the alleged rape—raise a lot more questions..."

"Dammit, Landry, all this asshole can say is my 'alleged rape.' Let's get out of here. Oh, Officer, is it safe on the streets, or has Rudy already walked out a free man?"

He looked at Marcie evenly and said, "Mr. Falco's been released. We found nothing conclusive enough to charge him. He claims you've been stalking him, Miss Epperson, and that you made up the rape charge. He doesn't know why, and he's a prominent citizen..."

"Wealthy too," Landry interjected dryly. "Don't forget wealthy. I bet he has friends all over the place. Even here in the police department."

The detective's lips drew tight. "It's terrible if you were raped, Miss Epperson, but it's his word against yours. You never reported a rape, he didn't have a weapon, yet you didn't try to escape. With all due respect..."

Landry interrupted. "Detective, with all due respect, Rudy Falco's a criminal. He tried to kill Marcie—Harry Kanter and I were eyewitnesses. You can't discount that."

The detective nodded. "Yes, you described that to me earlier. He threw a poisonous snake on the floor, is that correct?"

"Yes, in order to kill Marcie."

"So you say. Let me cut to the chase, Mr. Drake. You're a well-known television personality. Your shows conjure up thoughts of the supernatural and provide countless hours of entertainment for your fans. But this is the real world, and as a police officer, I deal in facts. Presuming there was a snake—which our team did not find—you allege he intended to kill Miss Epperson with it. But that's supposition. He didn't state his intention, so your allegation has no basis in fact, correct?"

Landry admitted he was right, although Falco's intentions had been clear.

"So what happened to this vicious reptile?"

"We don't know. After Marcie convinced her aunt's ghost not to kill Rudy, it disappeared and so did the serpent. The cage is inside the house, but the snake vanished along with the ghost."

The veteran officer shook his head. "I'm sorry, folks. I'm a small-town cop, and as nice as you people are, nothing you told me makes any sense. Look at it from my side. Ghosts, disappearing snakes, mysterious cults…it looks to me like you're working on a TV show and trying to incriminate Rudy Falco as part of the plot. How about telling me what really happened to the victim—how he got all those pecks and bites on his body? He says he scared off a vicious dog that attacked him. Frankly, that story makes better sense than yours does. Now unless you need me for anything else, I have real cases to solve." He picked up his notebook and left the room.

"I get where he's coming from," Harry said as he and Landry returned to the mansion. "I was a jaded cop myself until you came along. If that guy ever experiences what I've seen with my own eyes, he'll believe too. To him it sounds like pure fiction, and we can all understand why. It may be real, but hell, Landry, you know how it is. A lot of people who can't get enough of your TV shows still believe they're fictitious."

"Understood. But it's unacceptable that because of me, because I'm a paranormal investigator, a madman—not just a rapist, but a murderer and a truly evil person—walked free. Rudy Falco belongs behind bars, and I intend to do everything I can to make it happen."

CHAPTER FIFTY-SIX

The mood at Cotton Exchange Bank in downtown Savannah was somber. Fielding had just received an email from the state banking commissioner that foretold the end of an era.

For years the Perryman family had managed to keep the gold bars from becoming a problem. The mood was different now, because the state banking commissioner disliked Finn personally and was irritated that the banker snubbed the system by keeping his $40 million asset base in gold bullion. Although technically legal, no other bank did it, and banking commissioners over the years had tried and failed to bring down the Perrymans. Since the 1970s, no one had figured out a way, but when he received the independent appraisal and saw pictures of the extraordinary one-kilo bars, the commissioner had had an epiphany and called the state archaeologist. That move was all it took.

Two days later Fielding, the irascible, unlikable former second-in-command, now sat in the president's chair in the tenth-floor office. Unlike Finn, she didn't own Cotton Exchange Bank, but the hefty salary and benefits allowed her a very comfortable lifestyle.

The bank examiners had finished up and left a few days before, the lead man saying they'd email their final report once it was approved by his boss in Atlanta. A few minutes earlier Fielding had gotten the email and found exactly what she expected—the usual caveats for too few loans and an asset base consisting of gold bullion.

The final paragraph of the letter bore the title ASSET SEIZURE and gave her a chill when she read it. Fielding was accustomed to handling problems; it was the primary thing she did for Finn Perryman. From personnel issues to customer interface to data hacks, there was nothing she couldn't solve—until now.

Damn those banking regulators! The sons of bitches had finally figured out a way to take Finn Perryman down, albeit posthumously. And it was clever—she gave them that. They'd gone to the state archaeologist, shown him detailed photographs and the appraisal that said the markings on the bars were sixteenth century and identical to bullion recovered from Spanish shipwrecks off the coasts of Georgia and Florida.

In a nutshell, they were historic artifacts, not simply gold bars, and Georgia law required the state to confiscate them, set a value, and work with the finder—not the current owner, but whoever first found them—to establish an equitable price the state would pay that person. The bank no longer owned the gold. Confiscated from the depository bank in Atlanta, it was now state property, and the banking commissioner allowed Fielding just seventy-two hours to come up with forty million dollars in cash or assets to replace the gold.

What would Finn do? And since he'd died without heirs, what would his executors—the people downstairs in this building—do? Did he have enough assets outside his bank stock to solve a forty-million-dollar problem?

He knew a way to convert the gold to cash...or so he'd said. But that secret had died along with the man. Damn the son of a bitch for dying. If he were alive, she could make him dance like a puppet on a string. She had the goods—she knew about his secret life as a member of some mystic cult. She'd snooped and pried after hours, getting enough scandalous material to keep her job secure for life. But when the bastard died, none of it mattered anymore.

For seventy-two hours Fielding fought the banking commissioner. She hired the state's top law firm, pressured state and federal senators and representatives, challenged the appraiser's determination about the gold being ancient, and pleaded for more time. Nothing worked, and when the time was up, the Cotton Exchange Bank, founded by Albion Perryman in 1826, closed its doors forever. It had been Savannah's oldest bank, and its demise would be the talk of the town for weeks.

CHAPTER FIFTY-SEVEN

Abby had never experienced such loneliness. Just days earlier she had reflected on her life and decided things couldn't be better. She didn't have a mate, but she was in no hurry either. Thirty-four, she owned a flower shop, spent free time with a few friends, and traveled a lot. Business was slow but steady, and her income from the shop didn't matter anyway. It was nothing compared to the benefits she got from belonging to the Order of the Red Serpent.

Six years ago her mother, Claudia, had learned she had stage IV pancreatic cancer. By the time the symptoms manifested—nausea, severe abdominal pain and vomiting—it was too late. Abby would never forget the night she learned her mother would die soon, because along with that tragic news came another revelation.

Her mother held Abby's hand tightly the night she revealed the secret society to which she belonged. Abby knew her mother's family had settled in Savannah long ago, but now she learned that the Macphees came over from England with James Oglethorpe in 1733, making her family one of the founders of the city. And her mother told her about a secret society—a mysterious, legendary pathway to a vast treasure hidden in the New World.

Her family became a part of it because her ancestor

Macphee, like four others on Oglethorpe's ship, married Spanish women—descendants of Spanish conquistadors—who belonged to a group called the *Orden de la Serpiente Roja*—the Order of the Red Serpent.

Responsibility for protecting the treasure passed down from one generation to the next. If a member died with no heir, a trusted friend would be elected unanimously by the others. A ritual would be performed, and the Order perpetuated.

"It's your familial obligation to stand for initiation," her mother had said. "You will join four others...people whose names I am sworn not to reveal. But you will know everything soon."

Claudia Wright died not long afterwards, and Abby learned there was much her mother had withheld. She submitted to a ritual that required the snake to pass judgment on her. She would never forget the terror when the serpent revealed its fangs and raised its head, but instead of striking, it retreated, and she became a member. She learned she'd never want for anything again, although she couldn't spend money freely for fear of raising suspicions.

She kept her flower shop and her friends, but she took long and frequent vacations. Those who knew her thought Abby visited relatives up North somewhere; they would have been astonished to learn she flew first class from Atlanta to New York or Miami and from there all over the globe. She held elite status on Emirates Airways and always chose their $40,000 first-class suite when flying to the Middle East. She stayed at the top hotels, ate in the finest restaurants, and even had a fling or two with exciting, wealthy strangers she met in casinos or rooftop bars. She had access to all the wealth she could imagine, but to the public she was Abby Wright, a florist in downtown Savannah.

Tonight she was Abby Wright, fugitive. After she and Rudy cleaned up the top floor of the Parsonage, she left him to deal with the serpent. The scarlet robes, candlestick and sword lay in the trunk of her car, and she'd released the field mice before leaving Savannah. She'd dump the robes sometime soon, but the ceremonial objects dated back to the 1500s, and Abby couldn't bring herself to throw them away. If the Order survived—which she doubted could happen now—they would be used once again. Same for the snake—like the members of the Order, it was a descendant of the original snake found in the place where the treasure lay hidden. There were others still there, but this one had become the ceremonial serpent used in the ritual, and Rudy had to keep it alive.

With the support money she'd received over the years, Abby could have flown anywhere and disappeared, but she was afraid. Rudy had ordered her to help him get rid of Rob Taylor's body after the ritual, and that made her an accessory. Since Marcie and Fletcher had escaped, the cops could already be looking for her. She'd seen enough movies to know if she used her credit card or passport, she'd create a trail that could lead them straight to her.

Rudy had ordered her to stay at home until he contacted her, but she couldn't rely on anything he said. On her own now, she packed a few things, paid cash to fill the car's gas tank, shut off her phone, and left.

Forty-five minutes later she arrived at her cousin's condo at Hilton Head Island. None of her acquaintances knew about this place, and her cousin, who lived in Michigan, only used it during the winter months. He'd left a key with her ages ago, and for the moment it was her safe haven.

Abby had one last detail to attend to before hunkering down. She drove ten miles to the nearest small town, Bluffton, going street by street until she found what she needed. She parked in shadows, took a screwdriver, and removed the license tag off a car sitting in the weeds beside an abandoned house. Five minutes later her car had a different tag. Anyone running tags on Hilton Head Island would be looking for her Georgia plate, not this South Carolina one. On the way back she stopped at a convenience store to buy food and beer. In the condo she turned on the news, popped a beer, and put a slice of pizza in the microwave.

A few minutes later she saw two pictures appear on the screen—hers and Rudy's—and she listened as the reporter called them persons of interest in a missing persons case. She ran to the bathroom, threw up, and came back, sitting in the dark and wondering what to do next.

CHAPTER FIFTY-EIGHT

Her stomach churning with fear, every few minutes Abby went to the window and peeked out. Everything seemed normal—a few cars driving by, the sound of people laughing nearby, the familiar logo of an Amazon delivery truck parked next to her car. But it was only a matter of time, because Marcie and Fletcher had seen the serpent kill Rob Taylor. By now they would have told the cops who else was there, and that was why she and Rudy were fugitives. The cops hadn't revealed everything; she knew they were looking for two murderers, not persons of interest in a disappearance. Perhaps she shouldn't have gone across the state line into South Carolina. What if that would make them search even harder—or worse, get the FBI involved? Maybe she'd made a huge mistake fleeing instead of turning herself in and helping the police build a case against Rudy. But what if they didn't believe her? She had been in the room when a man died, just like Rudy had been, and she'd done nothing to stop the snake except scream.

Who can I trust? Who can I call for help?

Eventually the answer came. Finn Perryman said Marcie had brought the ghost-hunter Landry Drake and a private investigator to Dixie's house. Rudy had exploded and argued with Finn about who would handle Landry.

Landry Drake was her solution. If anyone could help, surely it was he. It was worth a try because she had little time and nothing to lose. She'd gotten Marcie's cellphone number when Finn had tasked her with recruiting Marcie. Rudy had taken over instead, but she still had the number. She used the condo's landline phone and instantly got Marcie's voicemail, indicating her phone was turned off. Abby said she wanted to talk to Landry, left a callback number, and hoped this plan would work.

At the Azalea Inn, everyone had turned in early. Landry was watching a movie on his iPad when Marcie rapped softly on his door. "Landry, are you awake?" she whispered. He opened the door, and she told him Abby had called, adding she didn't trust Abby after what had happened.

"She sat at the table and watched Rudy force my hand into that snake's cage. She didn't make a move to stop it. In fact, she seemed mesmerized, like Rudy and the guy who died. I told the cops what she and Rudy did, but they didn't believe me. I don't want to help her, Landry. She's mixed up in all this big time, and she needs to pay just like Rudy does."

"Understood, but I just saw on the news that the cops are looking for her and Rudy. They didn't believe you before, but something's changed their minds, and I think the best thing might be to get her to turn herself in. That way you can give a statement, and they can decide how to deal with her."

Marcie agreed to listen to Harry. He could tell them more about why the cops called them "persons of interest." But it had to wait, because Harry was fast asleep. Earlier, complaining that his arm throbbed painfully, he'd taken pills to ease the pain and let him rest.

"We'll deal with this in the morning," Landry said. "Call Abby back and talk to her, but don't let her tell you where she is, because I don't want to withhold information from the cops. Just say we'll do what we can. I'll get with her tomorrow morning."

"I'll call her back, but don't look for any help from me," Marcie muttered. "She didn't raise a hand to stop Rudy. I could have been the one who died. So could Fletcher. She can go to hell for all I care."

When Abby heard Marcie's voice, she burst into tears and said, "You all are the only people I can turn to. When I saw my picture on TV, it scared me to death. I had to get away, and I—"

"Stop!" Marcie snapped. "Don't say anything more. If Landry can help, he will. We'll talk and get with you tomorrow."

"Is there a former cop with you? Finn told us Landry brought a private eye to Savannah with him. Maybe he'll know what I can do. I can come back if it'll help. I'm not that far away..."

"Stop it, dammit! Yes, an ex-cop's with us. Landry will call you tomorrow." She hung up and said she wished she'd told the bitch off.

Sunlight flooded the dining room at Azalea Inn as Teresa served up classic eggs Benedict, crispy bacon and toast with Georgia peach jam. Everyone tossed out opinions about Abby Wright and her situation. Fletcher and Marcie had seen the Order in session, and both agreed Rudy ran things while Rob and Abby took orders.

"But let's not forget Abby's as much a part of this as Rudy," Marcie added. "Because they did nothing, a man died."

Harry summed it up. Marcie and Fletcher had witnessed what Harry called murder by snakebite. Rob Taylor held Fletcher's hand inside the box, Fletcher freed the snake, and it bit Rob. A good lawyer might frame it as an accident, but the snake's purpose for being there was to either kill an initiate or let them live. It was as much a murder weapon as a pistol or a knife.

"Abby's best shot is to turn herself in, cooperate with the police, and help them nail Rudy Falco for kidnapping Marcie and attempting to murder her. I'd guess they'll charge her as an accessory, and she might have to do some time, but if Fletcher and Marcie testify Rudy was the mastermind, I'd bet on probation for her."

Marcie shook her head. "You do what you want, Fletcher. I can truthfully say Rudy called the shots, but that's it. I refuse to help her." Fletcher agreed, adding that Abby deserved no mercy. Rob either, but he had gotten his just reward from the serpent's fangs.

They moved to the sitting room, where Landry made the call and put it on speaker. Abby answered on the first ring, anxious to hear the plan, and Harry did most of the talking as he suggested how she surrender to the authorities.

"Do you have an attorney?" he asked, and she said she'd dated a criminal lawyer in Savannah whom she trusted.

"Call him and turn yourself in before the cops find you. If they locate you first, you'll end up in handcuffs charged with a felony, and it'll be too late to prove you're trying to help."

"I've never even had a traffic ticket," she sobbed. "I never asked to be part of this group. Nobody does. Marcie, you know I'm telling the truth. Rudy used drugs on you to bring you to the initiation."

"Not to mention raping and kidnapping me," Marcie snapped. "Thanks for your help, by the way. I watched you sit there. You didn't lift a finger to stop what was happening. How many times have you watched that ritual? How many people have you watched die from snakebite? Was it exciting?"

"I'm so, so sorry, Marcie, and I understand your anger. Rob was the first person I've ever seen die. I'm the newest member of the Order; I came in six years ago after my mother died, and I only went through one ritual besides Rob's, and that was my own. Finn Perryman was a member for a long time. Your aunt Dixie too. They would have witnessed Rob's initiation and Rudy's too. Your family started the whole thing, Marcie, and Dixie knew all the secrets."

Watching Marcie's face turn beet-red, Landry interceded. "Are you willing to do it like Harry suggested?

Will you surrender to the authorities?"

"I guess so. What other choice do I have? It's not like I'm going to flee to some desert island for the rest of my life. I'll call my lawyer friend.

The instructions were simple—come to the Azalea Inn and meet her attorney there. Then Harry would notify the Savannah police and her lawyer could accompany her to the station. She promised to be there within the hour, and when she arrived first, saying the lawyer would be along in half an hour, Landry seized the opportunity to grill her about the Order before he came.

CHAPTER FIFTY-NINE

Abby picked at a scrambled egg Teresa had prepared and washed it down with strong black coffee. After a long, lonely night in the condo, she was hungry but apprehensive at what lay ahead. Little time remained before she'd be taken into custody, and Landry wasted none of it. He wanted to know everything she could tell them about the Order.

"It exists to guard de Soto's treasure. He came to this area in 1540 with an army of men and two hundred horses laden with gold, silver and gems. His men buried the treasure in a huge vault…"

Landry put a hand on her arm. "And de Soto died without ever coming back to get it. Rudy gave Marcie the background earlier. In the interest of time, tell me how this fits with the Order as it exists today."

"Membership is passed down from one generation to the next. If a member dies with no heir, then the Order names a successor." She turned to Fletcher. "You were an exception. Rudy made himself Grand Master after Finn died, and he selected you without a vote. Rob and I didn't try to stop him; I don't know if we could have at that point. We pledge an oath to protect the secrets, and challenging Rudy might have blown everything sky-high."

"What do you get in return for protecting the secrets?" Landry asked.

"We get what the Order calls 'support.' The treasure is supposedly huge beyond imagination. I've never seen it—only the current Grand Master and a Castile family member know where it is. But it's definitely real; when any of us wants support, all we have to do is ask. We go to Finn's bank, and he hands over a one-kilo gold bar."

"What happens then?" Landry asked, and she explained an antiques dealer in the French Quarter would exchange the bar for cash. Lots of it—sixty thousand more or less, depending on the price of gold. He asks no questions, and we were told his family has been doing this for generations. You go in the store—"

Landry interrupted. "We know about the code phrase. Go on."

"How could you know that? Did you find Dixie's instruction sheet?"

"Marcie did, and I had it decoded." He glanced at his watch. "We're running out of time, Abby. Keep talking."

"After the ritual ceremony, new initiates learn that Marcie's ancestor Amos Castile came to Georgia on Oglethorpe's ship in 1732. That was two hundred years after de Soto's treasure went missing. Presumably others protected the cache before 1732, but by 1734 Amos was the protector. Nobody knows why the change happened, but ever since, Castiles have been Grand Masters of the Order."

Landry pressed for more information, asking exactly who knew where the treasure was hidden. Only the current Grand Master, she answered, adding that Finn Perryman's untimely death probably meant that Rudy had not received the secret. If that was true, then no person alive knew where the hoard lay.

Just then the front doorbell rang, and Teresa ushered in a man dressed in suit and tie. Abby ran to him and gave him a hug. There would be no more discussing the Order today. It was time for Abby to surrender to the authorities, and as they left, her attorney assured them she'd be back by the end of the day.

Marcie asked what was next, and Landry said he wanted to take a look around Colonial Park cemetery and the Castile family's graves.

"It might help if I came along," Fletcher said. "I've spent a good portion of the past eight years researching that cemetery and its residents. It's not a small place, and I'm familiar with most of it. I also have a theory—more like a hunch, I guess you'd say—about the Castiles. There's something you'll find interesting about their graves."

Landry agreed and asked if Harry and Marcie wanted to come too. He did, but Marcie declined, saying she was exhausted and preferred not to be out and about with Rudy's whereabouts unknown.

They drove to the cemetery and parked on Hull Street in front of the Parsonage. Fletcher wondered aloud if he still had a job there, and Landry bet him ten bucks the board of the historical society would appoint him director.

As Fletcher guided them to the Castile burial site, they walked along paths shaded by tall oak trees, limbs dripping with Spanish moss. They all felt uneasy, even the unflappable Landry, who never got graveyard jitters. Today he had goosebumps and the feeling that at any moment a spirit might rise from its grave. If any cemetery belonged in a horror movie, it was this one.

The deeper into the place they went, the older the markers and crypts were. Fletcher reminded them no burials had taken place here since 1853, and in the back of the cemetery they found hand-carved stones dating to the mid-1700s. The resting places of many people were lost as markers crumbled or vandals hauled them off. In much of the cemetery, only the plot map would reveal who was buried where. Landry took out the copy he'd made and attempted to link names to specific places.

According to the map, seven Castile family members had been buried together—six adults and a baby—but only four stones remained. They found Amos, the first Castile burial in 1762. Barely visible on the stone next to his was the inscription "Dearly Beloved" and his wife's name, Maria. Joshua and wife Naomi lay side by side, but a grassy area with no marker was where Nathan Castile had lain since 1838. Next to him was an obelisk with a lamb carved into the top. Two people were buried in this grave—Nathan's wife, Corinne, and the baby girl who died with her during childbirth.

Landry knelt to better examine the graves, rose, and wondered aloud why they were crowded up against someone else's old crypt. Fletcher agreed. He had visited this site without taking into account how the Castile graves lay nestled against someone else's crumbling mausoleum. "Why would Amos Castile's family pick this place?" he muttered to himself. "In 1762 the cemetery was still new; there would have been plenty of burial plots to choose from."

The stone crypt had fared less well against the elements than nearby ones constructed using granite. Missing blocks lay in the grass, the metal gate hung by a single rusting hinge, and thick tendrils of ivy were slowly engulfing the structure. Over time the family name etched in stone above the entrance had worn smooth, but something interesting caught Landry's eye—the carved image of a serpent in the middle.

"Keep in mind this cemetery closed in 1853," Fletcher said. "Many families paid for perpetual care, and others still live in the area. The city keeps it mowed and weeded, and that's why so many plots around here look decent. This family either died out long ago or moved away or doesn't care."

Landry pointed out this structure appeared to be much older than the rest. He took the map from Fletcher, looked at something, and said, "This crypt is different. It's drawn on the map as a blank square with the name La Guardia inside it. All the others have reference numbers that tie to the names listed on the side panels. Does this mean no one's buried in there?"

"I don't think so," Fletcher replied. "If you examine the map, you'll see this isn't the only place where you find blanks. Over the years I've spent many an hour trying to figure out why that is. The blank areas are always in the oldest part of the cemetery, and sometimes I've found stones that indicate a body is buried there, even though no name is associated with it on the map."

"Don't you think that's strange?"

"This is where my theory—my hunch—comes in. I think it has to do with when those burials happened. My so far unprovable theory is that this place was a burial ground long, long before the cemetery opened in 1750. I think those blanks represent deceased people whose names nobody remembers. This crypt is different—although no burials appear on the plot map, there is at least the family name La Guardia.

"Beginning in the 1500s, lots of Spanish families settled in what is now Georgia. Part of de Soto's treasure legend mentions his leaving a contingency of men to guard his fort. When he never returned, some of them went back to Florida and caught a ride home. Others stayed and intermarried with Indigenous people. Several other Spanish explorers came through here, and historians believe a decent number of soldiers decided to make the New World their home. When Oglethorpe came in 1732, he found many with Spanish surnames living here."

"What do you make of the snake carved in the stone above the entrance?" Landry asked. "Is this somehow linked to the Order of the Red Serpent?"

"Possibly. The Castile family is involved for sure, but I don't know if they have any connection with this crypt, or if their being buried next door is a coincidence."

"I don't believe in coincidences," Landry said, and he wanted to have a look inside. Fletcher warned him to be careful, because the decaying old structure seemed on the verge of collapse. When Landry pulled open the metal gate, the remaining hinge snapped, and it fell to the ground, narrowly missing Harry, who quipped, "Nice try, Landry. Nothing like having one arm in a sling and the other crushed by an iron gate."

Landry ducked and stepped through the doorway into a claustrophobic chamber about eight feet square. He

261

sneezed as his head brushed the ceiling, dislodging clouds of dust and grit. Pieces of broken stone lay strewn about the room, illuminated by rays of sun that filtered through cracks in the walls and ceiling.

Half-hidden in the dirt floor he saw a small rectangular stone tablet. He tried to pick it up, but it wouldn't budge. Kneeling in the dirt, he brushed away a layer of dust and saw words etched into the marker, too faint to read in the dim light. He pulled his phone from his back pocket and snapped several pictures, and when he went to return it, he lost his balance. Falling hard against a wall, he heard a low rumbling noise followed by shouts from outside.

"Landry! Landry, get out! Hurry!"

As he struggled to rise, a rock hit his shoulder; then another bounced off his knee. The wall beside him began to crumble; when he fell against it, he'd dislodged some stones, and now the ceiling began to shake. As he scrambled on hands and knees to the door, Harry grabbed one arm and Fletcher the other, and they pulled him free seconds before the crypt collapsed. The room where Landry had been was now a pile of rubble.

Hidden in a grove of trees fifty feet away, Rudy Falco watched Landry's narrow escape. Now the crypt would provide no answers. It would have been better if Landry had died in the collapse, but the ghost hunter couldn't have learned anything during the brief time he'd spent inside.

CHAPTER SIXTY

At the cemetery, a rueful Landry explained how he'd caused the collapse, then pulled out his phone and showed them the faint inscription etched on the rectangular stone.

Fletcher enlarged the picture as much as he could, but the faded letters were indecipherable. He sketched them on the back of the plot map:

L _ _ _U _ _ _ I _
M D _ C _ I
_ _ D R _ _ D _ _ _ A _ _ E R _ _ V E _ _ _ L L _

Landry asked if he had any idea what it meant.

"No, there just isn't enough. If we had the marker itself, I could possibly bring out more letters, but it's at the bottom of that pile. Some of those stones must weigh a couple of hundred pounds. It'll take a backhoe to remove them."

"Where could we get a backhoe?"

"Every working cemetery has one. They use them to open graves for burials. Most likely this one doesn't, since nobody's being buried here anymore, but the other graveyard in town, Bonaventure, has one. I'll call the cemetery director and see what I can find out." On the brief call, Fletcher ended up listening far more than talking.

He hung up, saying the call didn't go well. "About the only good thing is that I kept your name out of it. He's unhappy that someone trespassed inside a crypt, more upset that it's destroyed, and if he knew Landry Drake was the culprit, I think he'd have had a seizure."

"I suppose this means we aren't getting a backhoe."

"He never stopped talking long enough for me to ask. He mentioned vandalism and criminal trespass and said he's calling the cops. The cemetery department's office isn't far from here, and I suggest you disappear and leave the explaining to Harry and me. We'll meet you back at the inn."

Instead of the police, the director himself arrived minutes after Landry's departure. Much calmer than he'd been on the phone, he apologized for losing his temper. "You're with the historical society, for God's sake," he said to Fletcher. "I know you wouldn't deliberately destroy something like this. Tell me what happened."

Fletcher explained he was giving his friend Harry from Louisiana a tour of the cemetery. This old crypt had always interested him, and today he did something stupid. He shouldn't have gone inside, especially into a clearly unstable structure. He'd accidentally hit a wall and caused the collapse. "I can't tell you how sorry I am," he said, "and I'll pay for rebuilding it or demolishing it, whatever you decide."

It turned out the man was more interested in learning what had happened to Fletcher's missing boss, Rob Taylor, saying, "Rob and I have known each other since high school. Now he's gone missing and so have Abby Wright and Rudy Falco, who the cops call persons of interest. What's going on, Fletcher? Do the cops think Rob's dead? And do they think Abby and that Falco guy are involved? Abby's a friend; she's provided the flowers for countless burials here. She's a good person, and I can't imagine she has anything to do with Rob's disappearance. Rudy Falco I'm not so sure about. I've never met him, but I hear he's a pompous jerk with more money than sense. Do you know them? Any thoughts on if they're involved?"

I know them too well, and I'm as involved as they are, Fletcher thought. *It would blow your mind if I told you the truth.* "It's bizarre," he said. "Rob doesn't seem the kind of guy who'd just disappear. Abby's a merchant, like you said. And Rudy may be an ass, but could he and Abby have kidnapped Rob...or worse? I can't imagine that." Those three sentences were a pack of lies, and it surprised Fletcher how easily they came. He knew everything about Rob, including how the man died, but he couldn't say a word for fear of incriminating himself.

Fletcher changed the subject to the enigma of this crypt. It was older—perhaps far older—than the cemetery itself, and no one knew who built it or why it was incorporated into the graveyard when it began in 1750.

The director said, "On the very first plot map, this crypt bears the name La Guardia, a name that appears nowhere else in the records. It's like the family came, buried their dead, and departed, leaving no mark on Savannah history except on a cemetery map. Here's the bottom line—there's no family left to be upset about their crypt falling down, and no one who could give permission to rebuild it. I'll get my men to remove the debris, and we'll erect a small stone with the family name on it. You don't need to pay for anything, Fletcher. It'll take a two-man crew less than an hour to remove all this stuff."

"Do you mind if I come back when they do the work? No telling what they might uncover in a place as old as this. Something might turn up that the historical society would be interested in."

The director made a call and said, "The guys can be over here in an hour. I can't be here myself, but I'll talk to the crew chief. He's a good guy; just give him a heads-up if you want to see anything while they're working."

Fletcher and Harry left to meet Landry for lunch, and learned he'd gotten a call from Jim Parsons, the New Orleans FBI agent who visited the French Quarter store that converted gold into cash. Although Nigel Meriwether was

265

on a watch list, they had nothing concrete to prove either money laundering or fencing stolen property. Using the code words had prompted a coded response, but that alone wasn't grounds for opening an investigation. Unless something else developed, the FBI considered the matter closed.

They all returned to Bonaventure Cemetery and watched as two men removed what had been stone walls and a ceiling. "There's the marker!" Landry shouted as he signaled the backhoe operator to stop. He and Harry borrowed the workers' wheelbarrow and toted the stone to Harry's rental car.

When they returned, they found Fletcher on his knees, brushing away dirt while the backhoe operator and his helper sat under a nearby tree, waiting to continue.

Landry asked what he'd found, and Fletcher said the backhoe had uncovered a wooden platform that had formed part of the crypt's floor. He swept away more clods of earth, and a square shape took form. About four feet on each side, it was made of logs and sat squarely in the middle of the ruined structure. He ran his hands around each edge to see if he could get his fingers underneath, but it rested solidly in the earth.

Harry asked, "What do you think it is?" and Fletcher held a finger to his lips. For the moment, the workmen were talking and smoking cigarettes, and he hoped to find out what lay beneath the wooden square without getting them involved. He pulled and pried, but nothing worked. Fletcher asked the crew chief for a shovel.

A few minutes later the workers had cleared the dirt from all sides, and everyone saw that what appeared to be a wooden square actually was the top of a square box made of tree branches lashed together. It was too bulky to move, and the crew chief offered a wheelbarrow.

"Ain't ya gonna open it here?" the backhoe operator asked. "I want to see what's in it."

"No. I don't know what this is, and we have to be careful. We'll take it to the historical society to examine."

Grumbling under his breath, the worker went to his

266

truck and brought back a wheelbarrow. Fletcher asked Landry to take one side as he moved his fingers under the other. They tried to lift the heavy box out of the ground but couldn't.

"I can lift it with the backhoe," the man said. "You stay there and guide me." With a precision learned from years of practice, he carefully guided the blade into the earth and under the box, lifted it out, and put it on the ground beside the wheelbarrow.

While Harry watched, the four others each took a side, and on Fletcher's signal, they lifted the box. The moment they got it off the ground, its bottom collapsed, and a heavy square stone fell to the earth with a thud.

"The floor of the box rotted out after being buried all that time," Landry commented as the cemetery workers knelt beside Fletcher, who used a paintbrush to clean the surface of the stone.

"Look! Is that writing?" one of them said, pointing.

Long ago someone had chiseled a series of words into the surface that survived the ravages of time by being buried inside a box. Fletcher used his index finger to remove some remaining grit and brushed the stone again.

Sud. Setze cordeles. Del secret del governador està protegit per la guardia.

The backhoe operator looked closely and said, "Bunch of gibberish, if you ask me." Fletcher, Landry and Harry knew why—the crude markings, perhaps etched into this stone centuries earlier, were in some other language.

Now there were two stone inscriptions to decipher, one ravaged by time and the elements, and the other, protected by burial in a wooden box, with its words intact.

CHAPTER SIXTY-ONE

The larger of the two stones they found was too heavy to move indoors, and Fletcher put it in a garage where it would be protected from the elements. They toted the other stone—the small one Landry first saw—to an examination room next to Fletcher's office.

The woman who'd been Rob's assistant brought a note to Fletcher and said, "Mattie Hughes came by to see you earlier. Here's her number; she asked you call her when you returned." Fletcher told them Mrs. Hughes was an octogenarian society matron who was president of the historical society and technically his boss.

"Get out your ten bucks," Landry said. "She's going to ask you to become the director."

"Maybe it's something else entirely," he said, going down the hall to make the call. Ten minutes later he came back and handed Landry a ten-dollar bill.

Landry grinned and pocketed the money. "Congratulations, Mr. Director! First round of beers is on me. Right now, let's figure out what these two stones are trying to tell us."

"Okay, we'll tackle the big one first since the letters are all intact." He sent Landry to the garage to get a good picture of the markings.

CCHIP owned a sophisticated translation program that the staff used to decipher old documents. When Fletcher entered the words, the answer popped up instantly. He grinned and exclaimed, "The words are in Castilian. It predates modern Spanish by hundreds of years. Listen to the translation. This is interesting!"

La Guardia. Ordre de la Serp Vermella. Setze cordeles. Protegim allò que el governador va amagar.

The guardian. Order of the Red Serpent. Sixteen cordels. We protect what the governor hid.

Until now, they'd assumed the words La Guardia on the cemetery map were a name. But instead it was a title— the guardian who protected the governor's secret.

Landry asked what it meant.

"A cordel is an old Spanish unit of length." Fletcher's fingers clicked on the keyboard. "Sixteen cordeles would be around seven hundred yards or a little under half a mile. Let's pull up a map of Savannah." He printed a copy, took a drawing compass, and made a circle a half mile from the place they found the stone. Then he ticked landmarks that lay on the perimeter—Bay Street and the waterfront, old churches, houses and pubs, the Massie Heritage Center and two of Savannah's twenty-two historic squares, Whitefield and Calhoun.

Harry called it a daunting challenge that depended on the age of that stone. If it predated Oglethorpe's founding of Savannah, then none of the landmarks on the map mattered. The treasure could be anywhere.

"Oh, it predates the founding of Savannah, all right," Fletcher answered with a smile. "I have a hunch it's far, far older than that."

His cryptic comment unleashed a barrage of questions from Landry.

What's your hunch? I'm not ready to talk about it just yet. It's no secret—it's a work in progress, and I want my thoughts together before I toss out ideas.

The cemetery opened when? 1750, Fletcher replied.

When was Savannah founded? 1733, by James

Oglethorpe.

Who and what was here before that? This whole area was a dense forest. Oglethorpe would have found Indigenous peoples and descendants of the earlier Spanish explorers already here.

Who's the governor mentioned in the stone carving? Possibly de Soto. A few years before he came to Georgia, the king of Spain gave him the title governor of Cuba.

Could the Order of the Red Serpent be hundreds of years old? Fletcher shrugged. I doubt anyone can answer that. None of us knew the Order existed until Marcie Epperson called you.

Knock off the noncommittal stuff, Fletcher. This is just between us. You're the expert on Georgia history, and I want to know your opinion. Who put the stone in the cemetery, when did they do it, and why?

"Okay, you asked for it. I've always been one to think way, way out of the box. Like every history major in this state, I spent a lot of time learning not just about de Soto, but also about James Oglethorpe, and I think they both have roles in this mystery, even though they lived two hundred years apart.

"Let's talk it through. First is the question of whether the treasure ever existed. This is the easiest piece of the puzzle, because Abby Wright told us members of the Order can get 'support' any time they want, in the form of one-kilo gold bars worth over fifty thousand dollars. They simply go to the Cotton Exchange Bank, and Finn Perryman—who's now deceased—hands it over. Unquestionably those gold bars are part of the hoard, which means the treasure is real.

"Let's consider Perryman next. He passed out the gold, but I don't see him going into some underground vault to pick up one every time a member asks."

Harry suggested Perryman kept a small stash at the bank, replenishing it when necessary. "There must be a hell of a lot of gold bars," he added, "because Abby said that store in New Orleans has been converting them into cash for generations."

"Right," Fletcher agreed. "We've established that the treasure exists, and according to Abby, only the Grand Master and a member of the Castile family know where it's hidden. I guess that would have been Dixie Castile, who was Grand Master until she died, and Finn, who became Grand Master afterward. Wonder who passed the secret location along to him? Maybe a deathbed revelation from Dixie? Or perhaps the Order has another way to convey the secret. That's something we don't know.

"Back to this marker, this is pure supposition, but I'm inclined to think de Soto's men buried it at the time they built his fort and the hiding place for a vast hoard of loot."

Landry wasn't buying it. "It's been here since the mid-fifteen hundreds? That would mean the Order of the Red Serpent started when de Soto left. You just told us nobody knows when it started."

"Which means it could have started in the 1540s."

Harry said, "Why would de Soto's men reveal where the treasure was hidden by writing it on a stone? If you're going to reveal it anyway, why not just put the stone where the treasure's buried, as in 'x marks the spot'?"

"The words say sixteen cordeles—no directions, no explanation, nothing. Nobody could follow those words and find the treasure. It'll take more than that. Let's go inside and tackle the small stone."

As Fletcher snapped pictures from every angle, Harry asked how they'd ever learn what this one said. If those were words, too many letters were missing.

L _ _ _ U _ _ _ I _
M D _ C _ I
_ _ D R _ _ D _ _ _ A _ _ E R _ _ V E _ _ _ L L _

"Maybe we can make more letters appear," Fletcher said, bringing over a roll of aluminum foil and a damp sponge. He tore off a piece of foil, pressed it carefully down into every indentation, and rubbed the sponge over the foil. Amazed, they watched as the missing letters magically appeared.

LA GUARDIA
MDXCII
Ordre de la Serp Vermella

"How the hell did you learn that technique?" Landry asked, and Fletcher said people who did grave rubbings discovered it was safer for the old stones and did a better job of bringing out faint inscriptions.

"This stone was on top of the box that held the larger one. It's dated 1592 in Roman numerals, and all it says is the Guardian and Order of the Red Serpent. The bigger stone has what appears to be a clue to where something is hidden. Now we have to find out what that is."

Landry's phone dinged with a message from Teresa at the Azalea Inn. "Is Marcie with you? She said she was going to her room to rest, but she's not here."

"Crap! I got caught up in what we found and completely forgot about Marcie," he cried. "I have to find her!"

CHAPTER SIXTY-TWO

After the men left for the cemetery, Marcie and Teresa sat in the Azalea Inn's front room for almost an hour. Marcie's tale of the bizarre initiation ritual at a house just blocks from the inn was the strangest story Teresa had ever heard. Savannah's reputation as a haunted city attracted tourists, but to hear an eyewitness account of ghosts, a venomous serpent and a now-missing dead body was beyond belief.

After Marcie went to her bedroom for a rest, Teresa sat by herself, trying to process everything that had happened. She closed her eyes, but they popped open as her head gave a sharp jerk. *Must have fallen asleep,* she thought as she took the empty wineglasses into the kitchen.

Surprised to see Marcie's door standing open across the hall, she called her name. She called again from the back patio and went to the front porch, where the security guard sat in a rocking chair. He hadn't seen Marcie leave, but when Teresa checked the side yard's video camera, she watched her go out the back and through the gate. She texted Landry, and he replied they'd be there in five minutes.

Mentally and physically exhausted, Marcie had gone to her room, collapsing on the bed and immediately falling asleep. A dream began to play out in her mind—she was standing in the upstairs hallway at the Castile mansion, looking down the long corridor to the far end where the tall mirror hung in the darkness.

Ka-chee. Ka-chee. Ka-chee.

No! No, I don't want to do this!

Once again, the wraith appeared, floating lightly in front of the mirror. It beckoned to her.

Come here. Come here. Come here.

Marcie struggled, trying to resist the siren's call of the figure hanging in the air. At last she gave in. She took one step, then another and the next, until she was halfway down the hall. The picture of the old mansion disappeared when she heard a soft snap behind her and turned to see the Azalea Inn's side gate. She realized she was outside, she'd just come through the gate, and now she understood what she had to do.

Moving furtively to avoid the security guard, she turned on Abercorn Street and walked the short distance to her aunt Dixie's old house. She was surprised to see the front door standing wide open, but once she stepped inside, Marcie knew resolution was coming. She embraced it, because the time for resistance was over. Whatever her fate, it would happen in this house, and it would happen today.

Ka-chee. Ka-chee. Ka-chee.

Marcieeeeeeeeeee. A soft whisper that might be nothing at all. A voice from the grave beckoning her to come. She walked to the staircase but paused as she caught a glimpse of movement. She'd never seen the spirit on the ground floor, but now it floated lightly in a hallway that led to the back of the house.

Follow me.

The figure led her into the kitchen and approached a door, which swung open on its own. As it turned toward her, she saw the face of her aunt Dixie instead of a gray mist. With a smile, the wraith beckoned her down a flight

276

of rickety wooden stairs.

Marcie allowed her eyes to adjust in the dimly lit basement as scant light filtered through a dirty window at the top of a wall. Tools hung above a workbench, and a rusted push mower sat in a corner. Buckets and cans were strewn about, and a black potbelly stove stood in the middle of the plank floor.

The spirit was close enough for Marcie to touch—much nearer than ever before, she thought, but she felt no fear this time. Her aunt raised her hand and extended a finger toward the stairway. At the top the door slowly closed.

Look. Look. Look.

The figure knelt and pointed at the bottom of the old cast-iron stove, where Marcie found a metal handle behind one of its legs. She grasped it and tugged, but nothing happened. After another try, she looked at the figure, who nodded. So she pulled harder.

This time the stove and part of the wood floor on which it rested swung quietly to one side, revealing a square entrance framed with old timbers and a ladder that led down into the darkness.

Go there, the figure whispered.

Resigned to her fate, Marcie shrugged off a shiver and went down the ladder. Every step took her deeper into darkness, and by the time her foot touched solid ground, she couldn't see a thing.

She heard a noise off to one side—a slight scratching sound followed by the smell of sulfur. She followed the faint glow of a match as an unseen hand raised it to a lamp on a wall. The lamp flickered to life and illuminated the place where she stood. She looked around the dank cellar before she heard a familiar voice.

"Hello, Marcie. I figured with your aunt Dixie's help, it wouldn't take you long to find this place."

Marcie raised her hands defensively and thought, *Where am I? How is he here, and why would my aunt put me in danger?*

BILL THOMPSON

A fleeting thought crossed her mind as he approached.

Until I inherited my aunt's house, we had no contact for years. Maybe that pissed her off, and this is her revenge.

CHAPTER SIXTY-THREE

Landry and Harry rushed to the Azalea Inn, leaving Fletcher to search the Parsonage in case she'd gone there. The security guard and Teresa were in the dining room, and she revealed what little she knew. The front camera of the house had captured Marcie sneaking past the guard and turning north on Abercorn Street. All the venues important to this case—her aunt's house, the Parsonage and the Old Cemetery—lay in that direction, and Landry knew he'd have to go one by one until they found her.

"She looks like she's in a trance," Harry said as he ran the video footage from the side yard in slow motion. "Look at her face—it's like she's sleepwalking. But as soon as she goes through the gate, she wakes up. Do you see that?"

Landry nodded and said they couldn't waste another moment. They knew she wasn't at the cemetery, and Fletcher was at the Parsonage, so he and Harry drove to the Castile mansion, thinking the ghost might have summoned her back.

Worried when he found the front door open, Landry stepped inside and called Marcie's name but heard no response. Harry searched the ground floor while Landry flew up the stairs, shouting her name from the upstairs hallway. The old house was silent, but only for a moment.

Help her. Help her. Help her.

He watched the apparition coalesce in the darkness at the far end of the hall, and immediately—as if it also realized time was precious—the figure floated toward him. He backed away and watched it glide toward the staircase, turn, and beckon him to follow. The phantom guided Landry to the kitchen, pointed to the basement door, and spoke to them.

Marcieeeeeeeeee. Go there. Help her.

Landry flew down the stairs with an injured Harry stumbling behind. When they saw the hole in the floor, Landry told Harry to stay put, since he couldn't navigate a ladder with his arm in a sling. Landry scampered down into a damp, musty room, long and narrow and extending into blackness. A lantern hanging on the wall yielded scant light, but it was all he had. He carried it with him into the gloom.

"What do you see down there?" Harry yelled into the opening, but the answer was muffled and indistinct. Landry had already entered a tunnel carved into the earth. His shoulders brushed against the sides, and he bent his head to avoid hitting the ceiling. After a few feet, he came to a sharp right turn where dim light filtered from around the corner. Wary of danger, he cautiously eased his head around. Seeing no one, he stepped into a room that might have been twenty feet square, but its dimensions were hard to determine because of the sheer amount of things the chamber contained.

Dancing flames from torches that hung in wall sconces made a roomful of gold and silver appear to come alive. Urns, golden chalices, swords and shields and armor lay strewn about the floor. Wooden chests were stacked along a wall; where some had rotted, a cascade of glittering jewels spilled out. Ingots of gold and silver reflected the flickers from the torches, creating a dazzling light show that defied imagination.

This is the realm of fantasy, Landry thought. The sheer enormity and beauty of the objects was more than he could comprehend—it was the fabled lost treasure of Hernando de Soto. His mind racing with questions, he forgot everything but the splendor before him.

The first inkling that someone was behind him was the hard steel of a gun barrel in his lower back.

"It's beautiful, isn't it? Did you ever think you'd see something so incredible?"

He recognized the voice at once. "Are you holding a gun on me? What's going on?" He began to turn around and heard, "Don't do it! Walk straight ahead and don't do anything stupid. I don't want to shoot you, so don't make me."

Landry swung around. "*You* shoot *me*? What's going on? I don't...I don't understand. Why would you shoot me? You pretended to help us. What have you done with Marcie?"

Fletcher Skorza held a .38 pistol. "I know you don't understand because you don't know the whole story. I'm not your enemy. Rudy Falco is."

"That's hard to believe, since you're the one holding a gun on me. If you're not my enemy, then what the hell are you doing?"

"We don't have much time—it may already be too late for Marcie. You must promise you'll never reveal this room exists. I've spent my life researching de Soto's treasure, and yesterday I used the words on the stone to find it. Sixteen cordeles from here is the cemetery where we found the stone, Landry. All it took was a computer program to pinpoint every landmark sixteen cordeles away. This place is sacred, and the treasure must be revealed in its own time and with proper dignity. There's nothing on earth like it…"

"Fletcher, help me out here. Nothing's more important than finding Marcie. Do you know where she is? Does Rudy have her?"

"First you must promise never to tell anyone about this room."

"Sure. Anything. Where's Marcie?"

"She's behind that wall of ingots." He pointed to gold bars stacked four feet high. Landry sprinted across the room, finding Marcie lying on the dirt floor with her mouth, wrists and ankles taped. Her eyes darted about frantically as he gingerly removed the tape.

"We have to get out of here!" she whispered. "He's not far away. He'll kill us!"

"He's not going to kill us. When did you find out about him?"

"Rudy? I knew about him from the minute I met him."

Fletcher stepped into view, still holding the pistol. "Landry isn't talking about Rudy."

"Fletcher? Why do you have a gun? I don't understand."

"This doesn't involve either of you. Sometimes you make a deal with the devil to get the things you want. This is the most incredible discovery in American history, and by God, it's going to be *my* discovery. I'll reveal it when I'm ready."

From the tunnel entrance across the room, Rudy emerged, wearing a sardonic grin and brandishing his own weapon. "Well, well, look who the cat dragged in. Fletcher, I didn't give you enough credit. I didn't know you had the balls to own a gun. Whatever you think you're doing, it's over. I'll take over from here. You're way out of your league; drop the gun before you shoot your foot off."

"You drop the gun, Rudy. I'm not going to let you have this treasure. It belongs to the people…"

"How noble of you. But you're mistaken. This doesn't belong to the people. It belongs to the Order—the guardians who have protected this place for five hundred years. Abby and I are the last ones, and soon it'll just be me. This treasure is rightfully mine."

"Mine too, don't forget. And Marcie's. Both of us went through the initiation, hands in the cage, everything. We're members just like you, and we outnumber you two to one. Three, if Abby Wright were here to vote. I think she'd agree your time's up, and I came here to stop you.

You're going to prison…"

"Not me, pal." He pulled the trigger, and Fletcher fell to the ground. That instant an army of dust devils arose from the floor, gyrating upward as they formed into cylindrical shapes. They were all around the chamber, and several whirled madly around Rudy.

As the cloudy shapes tightened their circle, Rudy lashed out, but his arms passed easily through the misty forms and seemed to heighten their frenzy. Marcie and Landry sat on the floor beside Fletcher, watching mystified as each of the swirling clouds became an ethereal figure. As bodies coalesced, colorful clothing appeared, along with facial features—beards, a mouthful of snaggly teeth, fancy hairdos and jewelry. Their clothes revealed the span of time covered by these phantoms, and despite their differences, they all seemed hell-bent on stopping Rudy. Spirits from every corner moved to the center to join the ones encircling Rudy, and the furious whirlwind tore the pistol from his hand. He covered his face and fell to his knees, screaming.

"There's my aunt!" Marcie cried, pointing to the figure they'd seen upstairs in the mansion. She floated across the room and hovered near her niece.

Ka-chee. Ka-chee. Ka-chee.

Amidst pandemonium in a room where spirits far outnumbered the living, the scratchy sound reverberated above the din.

You're safe, child.

"Thank you," Marcie murmured. "Thank you, Aunt Dixie."

The spirit smiled.

CHAPTER SIXTY-FOUR

Landry sprang across the room, dove into the whirling vortex, and grabbed Rudy's pistol from the floor. Rudy remained on his knees, crying for mercy, and the phantoms began to withdraw—first a few, then more, until they encircled him from a distance.

Landry ran back to Marcie and saw Fletcher standing beside her, apparently unhurt. They watched the spirits open the circle and allow Marcie's aunt Dixie to sweep inside. On her arm, coiled around the hazy sleeve of her garment, was the symbol of the Order of the Red Serpent.

RISE!

Marcie stifled a scream as her aunt's spirit shouted the word that shook the walls around them. Her voice was always quiet and even, but now she demanded obedience. The other spirits wailed in unison until the cavern echoed with that one word.

RISE!

Stunned by the jarring discord, Rudy obeyed the command. Once upright, he looked at the ghost for the first time, and he saw the serpent coiled around its arm.

"Oh, no you don't!" Rudy shouted, turning to run. The phantoms tightened the circle as Dixie Castile's ghost screamed.

LOOK AT ME!

As hard as he tried to move, Rudy's feet were firmly planted on the ground. He raised his head, and the figure dove toward him, her eyes flashing with the brightest light any of them had ever seen. She stopped only when her face was inches from his.

"My eyes! My eyes!" he screamed. "What have you done? God, the pain. I can't see! I can't see!" He collapsed on the ground, clawing at his face and moaning.

The wraith moved closer to Rudy as the serpent slowly uncoiled itself from the phantom's arm and dropped lightly onto Rudy's chest. Although intense pain like lightning bolts shot through his brain and he could see nothing, he felt the creature hit his body and knew what was coming.

"No, please don't do this! Help me! Somebody, help me!"

Instantly the phantoms vanished, and the cavern was still. Marcie, Landry and Fletcher stepped back as Rudy flailed about, arousing the venomous reptile that slithered up his chest. Simultaneously mesmerized and horrified, they watched it dodge his blows and reach his collar. Landry took a step forward, but Marcie pulled him back, crying, "Don't go there, or you'll die too!"

When Rudy rolled over, the snake found something to hang on to—the soft flesh of Rudy's left cheek. With its forked tongue extended, it raised its awful head, bared its fangs, and struck.

His wails of pain revealed the agony he experienced as the venom coursed through his system. Seconds later he lay still, breathing lightly, as the poison entered his heart. In moments everything would shut down.

"Catch the snake!" Landry yelled. "We need proof!" They backed the reptile into a corner, where it reared its head and prepared to attack. Its fangs glistened in the flickering light, and Fletcher shouted, "Stay back! It can jump five feet." As they watched helplessly, the creature found a crevice between the wall and floor and slithered through it.

"We've lost it!" Landry shouted, but Marcie spoke in calm, even words.

"Aunt Dixie, you're the only one who can help us now."

The spectral figure of Dixie Castile instantly appeared where the snake had been. It murmured soft whispers that might have been words, and the reptile emerged from its safe place. She lowered her ghostly arm, and once again the red serpent moved up and coiled contentedly around it. The ghost drifted toward the tunnel that led to the outside, disappearing into the darkness. They raced after her and found the wire cage a few feet up the tunnel with the serpent locked inside.

"Thank you once again," Marcie murmured, and a rustle of wind in a corridor with no draft provided her answer.

CHAPTER SIXTY-FIVE

Although the Azalea Inn's owner had been privy to many of their meetings in her front room, today Landry requested privacy. Abby Wright had just returned from the police station, and there was much to discuss about the chamber they'd discovered—a room that Landry had pledged to keep secret.

Earlier, when Landry had carried the snake's cage into the house, Teresa blew her top, insisting that creature wasn't coming in. He promised it would only be for a few hours; they had some decisions to make, after which he'd take it away. Reluctantly agreeing, she said if the damn thing got loose, he was responsible for catching it. She pulled the ancient pocket doors shut and left them.

It had been a relief to see Fletcher rise unhurt from the cavern floor. Although Rudy's shot had missed, he had wisely hit the deck and lain still as if dead. After the melee that ended with Rudy's death, Marcie, Fletcher and Landry had joined an anxious Harry, who had waited in the basement.

Fletcher apologized for holding a gun on them, saying, "I took my father's old pistol to stop Rudy. I didn't know if he was watching, and I held it on you so he'd think I was on his side. Like Rudy said, I probably would have shot myself; I just hoped he would believe me long enough to capture him."

As her lawyer promised, Abby had returned after only a few hours. Landry and Harry were curious to know what had happened, while Marcie and Fletcher remained upset that she hadn't tried to help them during the initiation.

Abby had spent an hour with her attorney explaining she was a person of interest because Fletcher Skorza informed the police about a bizarre ritual that ended in murder. However, when officers accompanied him to the scene, there were no clues—no snake, no body, no ritual paraphernalia or robes—nothing but an empty room atop the local historical society's building.

She nodded when her lawyer asked if the ritual actually occurred. She'd run away because she was scared—afraid of Rudy, afraid of other things, and terrified she'd be arrested if she stayed. When Abby began to talk about Rob's death, the lawyer cut her off. He didn't want to hear anything about it.

Landry said, "So your own lawyer didn't want to hear about your involvement with a dead body?"

"He said his job was to keep me out of jail, not to determine my guilt or innocence. He told the policemen they could talk to me only with him in the room. She described sitting across a desk from two officers as they fired questions about what had happened on the top floor of the Parsonage. With Rudy missing, no corpse and a lawyer in the room, the cops stopped short of making direct accusations. "I told the police I didn't do anything wrong, but they kept hammering me with the same questions. Trying to get me to change my story. Finally my lawyer said it was over. The police wanted to keep me overnight, saying I had fled once before, but he wouldn't go for it. He said either charge her with something now or let her go. And here I am."

The casual way in which she admitted withholding evidence rankled Marcie. "You lied to protect yourself. Don't forget you're talking to Fletcher and me—the ones who were victims that night. Rob too, but he was no victim because he was a member. You can claim to be an innocent bystander, but you didn't stop Rudy and Rob from cramming our hands into a snake's cage. We might have died, and Rob Taylor did die. You're an accessory to murder, Abby, even though you and the lawyer neglected to mention that part to the cops. Speaking of murder, where's Rob's body? Floating out in the ocean by now?"

Fletcher added, "Either you come clean with the police, or Marcie and I will go down and do it for you. Two eyewitnesses will be enough to keep you in jail until they find Rob's corpse."

She begged them to stay out of it. She pled a flimsy case, that she was helpless to challenge Rudy's demands. That she'd panicked when she watched their hands in the cage. That while Rob lay dead on the floor, Rudy made her help remove the robes, the sword and candlestick, the snake and mice.

"Please don't do this to me," she sobbed. "I understand if you hate me enough to want me behind bars, but I'm begging you to let me go back to my life. I was weak; I obeyed Rudy, even though I knew what we were doing was wrong. No matter what you decide, I'll tell you everything I know about the Order. I can explain how the Castile family fits into all this. I can give you the sword and candlestick used in the ritual; they're in the trunk of my car. You hold my future in your hands. Please don't do this."

"We're not doing anything," Marcie said evenly. "You're an adult responsible for your actions. If you tell the police everything, maybe they'll lay it all on Rudy and give you leniency. If I testified at your trial, I'd say Rudy had a dominant personality and he could make people do what he wanted. Hell, I did it myself. I let my guard down long enough that he drugged me. He's dead, and although that might help you, it doesn't change what you did. You committed crimes that night, and you have to confess and take your punishment. I agree with Fletcher. Either you go to the cops, or we will."

Head in hands, she remained seated until Landry

said, "Abby, we have things to talk about. Things that don't include you. You've gotten your ultimatum, so it's time for you to go. Give the sword and the candlestick to the police. They'll consider them as evidence."

She rose, pulled open the pocket doors, walked into the hallway, and turned. "I'm sorry. There's so much you still don't know, and I'm sorry for how things turned out. Good luck." She walked through the door, closing it softly behind her.

Incapacitated by his wounded arm, Harry had stayed topside and missed everything. Now he listened as they described a vast treasure, a procession of dozens of spirits, and Rudy's appropriate death by snakebite.

The phantoms fascinated everyone, and especially Fletcher, the historian. To Marcie he said, "They spanned the centuries, and I'll bet they're your ancestors—members of the family who still guard the treasure, even in death. Your aunt Dixie is the latest in a long line, and I think we saw them all."

Except for Harry, each of them watched a man die, and that meant they had to call the police. Landry had experienced the same thing another time—a homicide committed not by a live perpetrator but by a ghost. In this case, the murder weapon was a viper. The means of death could easily be proved—the venom would still be in his body—but the police would never believe that a phantom had dropped the reptile on Rudy so he would die. Could they end up being charged with murder?

"We have to get Rudy's body out of there before we call the cops," Fletcher said. "You swore you wouldn't reveal anything about that room."

"Yeah, when you had a gun on me and I was looking for Marcie," Landry snapped. "Listen, man. You have to get real. There's a dead body in that room, and it's a crime not to report it. I'm sorry about your treasure, but I'm calling the police."

"Before you do that, I have an idea," Marcie said. "It's a long shot, but maybe my aunt Dixie can help us."

Harry asked how, and she explained, then walked to

the front door. Concerned for her safety, Landry demanded to come along, but she refused, saying this was something she had to do alone, and she'd contact them when she could.

"One hour," Landry said. "If I don't hear from you by then, I'm calling the cops."

She nodded and left.

Harry wanted to follow her, but Landry said, "No. This is her riddle to solve. We have to let her do it by herself. I gave her a short window, and we'll see how it plays out."

CHAPTER SIXTY-SIX

The two old books Marcie had found at the Castile mansion lay on the coffee table. While they waited, Fletcher picked up the Bible and thumbed through it, muttering to himself as he skimmed page after page.

"Wow!

"I can't believe it!

"Amazing!"

"I give up," Landry said. "What's in there?"

"This Bible dates to the sixteenth century. It's written in Castilian, but the important part is the handwritten family tree in the front, like old Bibles sometimes have." He laid it open on the table so Landry and Harry could see.

"This answers a lot of my questions. The first name listed is Diego Sanchez 'La Guardia' and the year 1543. I have a hunch about his name. Look at the later ones." Several of them had the name "La Guardia" in quotations, but after a while the marks were no longer used.

"This man Diego Sanchez—I'll bet he was one of the men assigned to guard the treasure when de Soto left Savannah. He was one of the five who founded the Order of the Red Serpent. Someone appended the words La Guardia—the guardian—to his name. It wasn't a family name at first, but succeeding generations adopted it. They protected the treasure just like members are sworn to do today."

He flipped pages, looking for the period when Oglethorpe and the English arrived, and saw when the Castiles came on the scene. The Bible duly recorded Amos Castile's marriage to Maria La Guardia in 1734, two years after Oglethorpe founded Savannah.

"I'm certain Maria was a member of the Order, and when she died in 1751, he took her place. From then on, Castiles carried the tradition as one of the five families who belonged to the Order. It all makes perfect sense."

Rudy had told Marcie there was a book that chronicled the history of the Order, and as Fletcher opened the second book Marcie had brought from her aunt's house, he realized this was it. Like the Bible, it dated to the 1500s, and it began in Castilian, switching after a hundred years or so to Spanish, and eventually to English.

"Listen to this!" he exclaimed as he read some of the pages in English. "The Castile mansion was built on the original site of de Soto's fort. That's why the cavern's in the basement—it was a vault built inside the fortress to hide the treasure. Man, this book makes history come alive, doesn't it?"

Landry smiled at the man's enthusiasm. "The amulet!" he said. "Here's a description of that amulet with the red serpent and the sword. It was crafted from the treasure in 1592, the year those five guardians—the La Guardias—officially started the Order. We found Roman numerals with that date on the stone at the Old Cemetery. The amulet is always kept by whoever's the current Grand Master as a symbol of the Order's tie to de Soto himself.

"I can't read a lot of the Castilian, but I understand enough to know this book has immense historical value. The first parts of this are written by Hernando de Soto himself." He pointed to the bottom of a page. "Look. There's his signature."

Now Landry became as fascinated as Fletcher. They tossed out theories about how family members had passed down the two old books from generation to generation until they ended up with Dixie Castile and now Marcie.

The time had flown by. Almost an hour had passed without a word from Marcie, and Harry asked if Landry actually intended to notify the police about Rudy's demise. Once again Fletcher argued for moving the corpse out of the chamber so no one would find the treasure.

"We can't," Harry said. "You all didn't kill Rudy, and we have to try to convince the police of that. But if we move the body, we tamper with evidence. Instead of eyewitnesses to a homicide, we all become perpetrators in a crime. We can't make a bad thing worse."

As the final minutes ticked by before Marcie's deadline, Fletcher sat staring into space. A treasure trove of inestimable worth and historical significance lay hidden just blocks from where they sat. Fletcher knew it was the booty carried to Georgia by hundreds of de Soto's men, and that meant the state archaeologist and his team would be the ones to decide what would happen to it. Ditto for the two books Marcie had found. When translated and studied, he was certain they'd provide a fascinating look into five hundred years of Georgia history.

He wanted the books for the historical society's museum at the Parsonage. And if the treasure had to be revealed, he wanted it too. The artifacts belonged in Savannah, where they'd lain hidden for centuries, not in some museum in Atlanta or on a university campus.

It was premature to think of things like this. First they had to convince the police they weren't murderers. Instead, a ghost did it.

He wondered how on earth they'd accomplish that.

CHAPTER SIXTY-SEVEN

Alone in the dark, Marcie stood in the old house she'd hated as a child. Just days ago it would have terrified her to wait in the upstairs hallway, listening for a familiar scratching sound and faint words lingering in the air. This night was different—tonight she'd come willingly to give thanks to a phantom.

"Thank you, Aunt Dixie. You protected me and you saved my life." She spoke aloud, looking at the far end of the hall that lay quiet and bathed in shadows. "Now my friends want to call the police about Rudy. It means everyone will find out about the treasure…"

The air rustled as though someone had opened a window, but she was the only living soul in the house. At last the thing she'd been waiting for happened.

Ka-chee. Ka-chee. Ka-chee.

It was a sound that once sent chills down her spine, but tonight it meant her aunt had answered her.

Marcieeeeeeeeeee. Come here.

Marcie took a few steps down the long hallway as a figure morphed from vapor in the darkness ahead. A wisp of smoke at first, it twirled and whirled until it became the familiar spirit she had come to see. A few steps closer she could make out the stern face of Dixie Castile. Beckoning her to follow, it swept gracefully toward the staircase, then down through first-floor rooms into the basement.

They stood before the ancient potbelly stove that hid the entrance to the cavern, and the ghost showed Marcie that there was no need to involve the police now.

Now. Follow.

Marcie followed her aunt's specter back to the upstairs hallway until it stopped and turned to her.

Look there.

The figure's arm rose, and a finger extended toward the tall mirror hanging on the wall. Marcie walked into the gloom, standing mere inches from the specter as she touched the mirror.

"I don't understand. Why am I here?"

Move it.

She ran her fingers over the massive frame. The mirror was much taller than she—seven feet or more—and it was heavy. It was probably attached solidly to the wall behind it, and there was no way Marcie could move it.

"I don't know what you want me to do…"

Move it!

"Okay, okay. I'll try again." She extended her arms and grasped both sides of the frame, attempting to push it in one direction and then the other, but nothing happened. She gave the glass a hard shove, pulled on the bottom part of the frame, and tried lifting it. The massive mirror remained solidly in place.

"I give up, Aunt Dixie."

Look here.

The wraith pointed to the floor below the mirror. On hands and knees, Marcie looked but saw nothing unusual. Then her aunt's spirit floated so close that Marcie was enveloped in the gauzy wisps of its arms. She followed the finger until it touched the base molding along the wall until she saw an odd place—a piece of molding with cuts on the edges that no one would have suspected was different.

When she pressed on the one-inch-square panel, it popped out to reveal an old metal lever built into the wall behind it. She gripped the lever, pushed it down, and dodged as the mirror swung open on recessed hinges. Instead of being mounted on the wall, the mirror functioned as a door like that on a medicine cabinet, concealing a large recessed area as tall and wide as the mirror itself and extending into the old mansion's three-foot-deep walls.

It was the perfect hiding place for the "support" Dixie Castile had received from the Order of the Red Serpent over the years—support she took but rarely converted into cash. Stacked neatly at the bottom of the recessed cavity were twenty-two gold bars. Although they'd lain in place for years, they gleamed as bright as new.

When she saw the other thing hidden behind the mirror, Marcie stumbled backwards, her heart thumping wildly and her hands shaking as she moved to get away. Hanging on the wall above the ingots was the corpse of Rudy Falco. His wide-open, bulging eyes gave a glimpse into the terror he'd seen coming, and the black, rotted flesh of his left cheek marked the spot where the red serpent's fangs had struck.

"Why are you showing me this?" she shouted. "Everything was just fine until you died. I might have been poor, but my life was simple. Now I'm mixed up in murder and shootings, and I was raped and kidnapped...by him—" she pointed to the body hanging on the wall "—and now I know there's a vault below this house filled with treasure and snakes. I'm not strong enough to do this. I don't want any more dead bodies hanging behind mirrors. Or secret rituals on the top floor of the Parsonage. I can't do any more. I'm going home."

She had almost reached the stairs when a light breeze caressed her arm. She turned and looked to find the mirror closed and the hall quiet. A sense of peace swept over her until the phantom's words sent waves of fear through her body.

You. Can't. Leave.

CHAPTER SIXTY-EIGHT

One hour after she left, Marcie called Landry, insisting, "Don't call the police yet. Something big has happened. Come over here, and I'll explain." Convincing himself that another hour or two couldn't make things any worse, Landry agreed.

When she met them in the foyer, Landry thought she appeared more scared than ever, but she immediately began explaining. "Aunt Dixie helped us. Follow me, and I'll show you how."

They went into the basement and gathered around the potbelly stove as Marcie pulled the latch that moved it aside. Beneath it, where the square hole and a ladder had been, now there was packed earth. "Someone filled in the hole," Landry said.

"That's how Aunt Dixie helped us," Marcie replied, suddenly screaming, "Watch out!" as Landry fell to his knees to examine the soil. She gave him a hard jerk that knocked him backwards.

"What the hell? I'm trying to see how well-packed the soil is. I appreciate that your aunt thinks this helps, but it doesn't change anything. We still have to call the police, tell them to remove the dirt, and let them find the cavern."

"I don't think so. Watch this." Marcie picked up a

long stick lying nearby and jabbed it into what had been the hole. In the very place Landry had knelt seconds earlier, she poked the soil, and it appeared to come alive with undulating, writhing shapes.

He said, "Oh my God! What the hell is that?"

She pushed the stick down and levered up the shimmering red body of a snake. Beside it writhed others—too many to count. "There are dozens of them here in the dirt. My aunt showed them to me. She said the tunnel is completely filled in, and thousands of snakes are in in the cavern down below. They live in the hidden places down there, and they're the real protectors of the treasure. Members of the Order of the Red Serpent took on that responsibility long ago, but it's always been the reptiles that keep it safe."

Landry said filling in the tunnel was clever, but it didn't change anything. There was still a body in the cavern, and they still had to call the police.

"No!" she screamed. "No, you can't do that! This isn't your house, and this story isn't about you. It's *my* family and *my* destiny. Don't you understand that? I'm trapped here. I was initiated; I took my aunt's place at the table. I'm a member of the Order, and I'm bound by a solemn vow to protect the treasure. You have no right...you can't do this!"

She flew up the staircase, her footsteps echoing as she ran down the hall.

"We have to go with her," Harry shouted, but Landry stopped him.

"You guys wait in the car. Let me talk to her and see what's going on."

"Don't call the cops without talking to me first!" Fletcher pleaded as Landry headed for the stairs. "Marcie's right. We can't let them see what's in that cavern."

Landry shook his head at the fallacy of that statement and raced upstairs.

CHAPTER SIXTY-NINE

He found her in the room with the rocking horse, sitting on the side of the bed that had been hers during summer visits. "You shouldn't be here," she cried. "No one can help me now…"

"What happened?"

"I didn't tell you everything that happened with my aunt Dixie," she sobbed. "I have to assume my destiny. I'm trapped."

"I don't understand."

She led him into the hallway and pointed. "It's because of her. The cavern's not the only secret in this house. She revealed things to me…and now I can't leave."

The spirit of Dixie Castile drifted lightly in its usual spot down the hall in front of the tall mirror. Landry placed his phone on a plant stand and turned on its camera. "I'm going down there to talk to her. Come with me."

She pulled back for a moment, unsure if she should go on with this. If the ghost allowed her to show Landry what lay behind the mirror, he'd realize that their problem with Rudy Falco was solved. But would Aunt Dixie allow it?

She received her answer as they walked down the long corridor. The wraith moved toward them, blocking their way and holding out its hand.

Stop.

"I'm here to help your niece," he began. "I'm trying to protect her from people who want to hurt her."

Protect the treasure. The words came as a drawn-out whisper.

"Marcie says the cavern's been filled in. The serpents are protecting it now."

Protect it. Promise. Forever.

"I promise…"

The figure rose in a spiral of smoke, almost touching the ceiling before it dove and stopped in front of Marcie. Once again it raised its skeletal arm and pointed. *Not you. Marcieeeeeeeeeee.*

"I will, Aunt Dixie. I won't tell anyone…"

Protect it. Promise. Forever.

"I…I don't know what you want. I've already promised…"

Live here. Protect it.

Marcie looked at Landry, understanding now what the ghost's earlier words meant. "You said I couldn't leave. Do you mean you want me to live here? Is that what you're saying?"

A nod of the spirit's wispy head gave her the answer.

"I have a life…I mean, not a life, exactly, but I have an apartment. And a shop. It's not much, but it's all I have."

You. Have. Everything.

"What are you saying?"

I. Showed . You.

Landry didn't understand the words, because he didn't know what lay behind the mirror. Marcie didn't understand either; how could gold bars solve her problem? You couldn't spend a gold bar at the grocery store or the gas station.

Resigned to her destiny, she turned to her aunt's spirit. "I guess I could live here. Why not? What do I have to lose? I've never thanked you for giving me this house, and at first I was afraid to come here, but now I know better. I know you'll protect me, and I promise I'll protect the treasure. Yes, I'll live here. I'm not sure I can afford the upkeep, but I'll try. It's the least I can do for you…and for my family. For centuries you've dedicated your lives to protecting the treasure, and I'll carry on the tradition. Who knows? Maybe I'll get married and there will be another heir. If not, when it's my time to go, you can help me decide what happens next."

Dixie Castile smiled and pointed to Landry.

Now you.

Puzzled, Landry shrugged again and said, "What do you want from me?"

Protect the secret.

"I already told him that, Aunt Dixie. He's not going to tell about the treasure."

"Wait a minute, Marcie. We've helped you through all this. I was hoping after it was all over…"

Protect! The! Secret! As the ominous words resounded through the hall, the wraith spun madly in the air.

Never in his career as a paranormal investigator had Landry confronted a spirit that demanded the story not be told. From the outset, he'd promised Marcie he wouldn't act without her permission, but after all they'd been through, he expected she'd allow them to make it public. And that might have happened, except for the ghost that floated before them, who wasn't going to allow it.

Disjointed thoughts coursed through his mind. He'd invested time and effort into this story. The police should have already been called, and de Soto's treasure lay hidden two floors below. He could refuse the ghost…and Marcie. He could renege on his guarantee there would be no story without her permission, but he'd never broken a promise to get a story. Plus this was Marcie's house, and if she refused to cooperate, he couldn't shoot footage or interview her or reveal the treasure while the body remained down there with it.

When it came down to it, he'd given her his word. Without Marcie's permission, there would be no Castile ghost story. But this new promise would mean everything that had happened—the entire story about de Soto and Savannah—would never be revealed.

It's the right thing to do, he thought as he said, "I swear to you I will protect the secret."

Instantly the wraith turned and pointed at the mirror. *Show him.*

Marcie pulled aside the molding, tripped the lever, and watched his reaction as the mirror swung back.

"So this is what you meant about your aunt solving our problem with the cavern," he said, looking at Rudy's grotesque face leering at them. "Bastard got what he deserved, that's for sure."

She pointed to the stack of gold ingots below the corpse. "I think my aunt wants me to use those to pay my bills and live in the house. But I don't get it. You can't live on gold bars."

"I think you can, actually. There's this man in New Orleans…"

Landry's phone was still recording when he got back to it, but there would be no record of what had happened in the hallway. The video portion was a fuzzy haze, and the only sound was a constant hiss.

CHAPTER SEVENTY

Three weeks later a sensational mystery broke when a passing freighter noticed an eighty-foot Hatteras yacht named *Thanks a Million* adrift in the ocean thirty miles offshore from St. Augustine, Florida. When the Coast Guard arrived, they had already confirmed the boat belonged to a missing Savannah millionaire named Rudy Falco. With almost a full tank of diesel and well stocked with food and wine, the two-million-dollar yacht was drifting aimlessly with no one on board. A decomposing corpse found stuffed into a marine ice box below deck would be identified as Rob Taylor, another missing person who had been the head of the Coastal Center for Historic Preservation in Savannah.

Video footage revealed an odd scene--a woman boarding the yacht at Isle of Hope marina late at night with a tall candlestick in one hand and a sword in the other. Shortly afterwards the vessel departed. She was identified as a third missing Savannah resident, a local florist named Abby Wright.

Police and the Coast Guard speculated that Falco might already have been aboard that night, and they'd sailed away together. Both had been persons of interest in the death of Taylor, the man whose body was found on the vessel. Abby had spoken with police one time before disappearing, but Falco, the primary suspect, had not come forward.

From the evidence gathered, officers surmised Abby was a frequent visitor on *Thanks a Million*. DNA testing proved lipstick smudges on wineglasses and a toothbrush in the bathroom were hers, and women's clothing hung in a closet.

Did they fake their own disappearances? Was foul play involved, or were they living the good life on a Greek island or a Thai beach? If the latter, what were they living on? The bulk of Rudy's known wealth—upwards of forty million dollars—lay untouched in savings accounts at the now-defunct Cotton Exchange Bank. Authorities uncovered fifty million more in brokerage and bank accounts, and they put a hold on all Rudy's funds, but no one would ever make a claim for that money.

When they heard the news, Harry and Landry pieced together what they could. Instead of going to the police that night when Abby had left the Azalea Inn, she went to the marina. She was clearly familiar with the boat; she'd parked her car nearby and knew the keypad code to get on the dock.

Landry knew Rudy hadn't been on board, which meant Abby had the key to start the engine and the know-how to singlehandedly pilot an eighty-foot yacht, which was no mean feat. All signs pointed to Abby and Rudy having been involved in a relationship, and that she decided to vanish rather than face prosecution and possible time in prison.

In a locked compartment on the vessel, investigators found the sword, candlestick and a laptop with a CCHIP sticker on it. They tracked the device to the Coastal Center for Historic Preservation—CCHIP—where Rob Taylor had once been director. Police contacted Rob's successor Fletcher, who said it was Rob's and used a common work password to unlock it.

The one significant thing they discovered was video from the night of the ritual. Fletcher knew from experience that hidden cameras existed and Rob could see the output, and he easily located the files that held the audio/video recordings. At last everything Fletcher had told the police could be verified. Mesmerized, they watched the bizarre initiation rituals and saw Rob die from snakebite. Rudy's involvement was unmistakable—he'd been in charge of everything, and he'd abetted Rob's murder. In the unlikely event the missing pair surfaced someday, a warrant was issued for Rudy's arrest.

The whereabouts of Rudy Falco and Abby Wright would forever be an unsolved mystery.

CHAPTER SEVENTY-ONE

The little bell above the door tinkled as Marcie and Landry entered Vieux Carré Rarities in the French Quarter. Moving right and left through antique furniture, silver tea services, floor lamps and the like, they took a circuitous route to the back counter. They rang the bell, and the old proprietor emerged through a curtain.

"Is there something I can help you with?" he asked.

Marcie replied, "Are you Mr. Meriwether? A lady from Nottingham suggested I stop by."

He cackled and said, "That so? An' you are…?"

"I'm Marcie Epperson. Did you know my aunt Dixie Castile?"

"Doesn't ring a bell. Who's yer friend here?"

"Just a friend. Now if you don't mind, I'm in a hurry."

The old man coughed into his sleeve. "Yer the one who sent the FBI man here. He said 'twas you."

"I don't know what you're talking about. I told you something. Now you're supposed to reply."

He looked at Landry. "You an FBI man too?"

"No. Just a friend, like she said."

"Hmm. You look familiar. Have you been here before?"

"Never," Landry replied. "Now can we finish Marcie's transaction?"

"It's too rainy in Nottingham fer me these days," he replied. "Satisfied? Let's see what you brought."

She removed two ingots from a backpack and laid them on the counter. He gave them a quick glance and said, "Where do I send the money?"

Not knowing how to answer, Marcie glanced at Landry.

"Do you have your checkbook with you?" he asked, and she pulled it from the pack.

Landry asked, "Is a bank wire okay, or do you prefer another way?"

"Whatever you like. I can even give ye store credit if ye like shopping for antiques." He cackled again, which led to a coughing spell. When he recovered, he wrote down the bank information from her check and said the money would be deposited in a few days.

"Do I just leave the gold with you?" Marcie asked, and he looked into her eyes.

"Of course. Do ye not know anythin', girl? Didn't Dixie Castile tell ya what happens next? Go home and ask her. Now I have things to do…"

"She's dead," Marcie said, throwing an envelope on the counter. "Look at this. Did you give her this?"

He opened the envelope and watched thirty-five one-thousand-dollar bills flutter to the counter. "I don't know what yer askin'," he snapped.

"I'm asking if my aunt sold you a gold bar a long time ago and you paid her with these thousand-dollar bills."

"Curiosity's what gets folks in a heap o' trouble." He grinned and shuffled through the curtain.

Two days later an officer of Marcie's local bank on Tybee Island called her to advise her a significant wire transfer—just under $132,000—had come in that morning, and the funds were on hold for five days to ensure everything was kosher.

"This is a hefty deposit for our bank," he added.

"Were you expecting such a large sum?" He'd already looked up her account, noting it had never contained more than five thousand dollars, and officers at the bank were curious about the large wire.

It was none of his business, but Marcie was ready for him, because Landry had crafted an answer should the question arise. It was better to give a response than to leave them wondering. "My aunt died, and I was her only heir. The money's from an antique gallery in New Orleans that bought a lot of the furniture."

"Congratulations, Miss Epperson," he gushed. "I'm sorry about your aunt's passing, but what a nice gift she left you. And if you'd like to speak to a vice president about investing, the bank would be pleased to work with you."

She promised to give it thought, and he advised the bank was obliged to report any financial transactions over ten thousand dollars to the IRS. She assured him that would be no problem; Marcie intended to pay her taxes—there were enough gold bars left to tide her over for a lifetime.

She also intended to honor her family's commitment. After investigating Rudy's yacht, the police allowed Marcie to take the candlestick and sword, She and Fletcher were two fully initiated members of the Order and the historical society he directed occupied the Parsonage, where the third-floor ritual room was.

For the present, the Order of the Red Serpent would have just two members. But it would survive.

CHAPTER SEVENTY-TWO

Teresa watched as her guests hauled their belongings out the front door. She'd prepared one last breakfast—apple fritters, poached eggs and homemade hash—and everyone came for the farewell meal, including Fletcher and Marcie.

Disappointed to learn there would be no episode for the *Mysterious America* series, she told Landry there were far more ghost stories in Savannah besides this one. All he needed to do was call her, and a room would always be ready. A tear or two was shed as they hugged and thanked her for the hospitality and help she'd given each of them.

The unanimous decision among Landry, Fletcher, Harry, Marcie and the ghost of her aunt Dixie was that nothing could be gained by revealing the treasure now. The body that hung behind the mirror would remain there while those who knew him presumed he and Abby Wright had drowned in the open seas.

Over time Marcie would return to the antique shop in New Orleans now and then, dealing with Carson Meriwether, a nephew, after the old man's passing. She used the money to fix up the Castile mansion, which became a favorite venue on Savannah's holiday home tour. The ghost tour operators asked to put it on their lists too, but she refused to allow them inside, so they parked out front and told the tourists rumors about what was reputedly one of the city's most haunted houses.

Dixie Castile joined her niece for cocktails some evenings. The sound of a scratchy record would announce her arrival, floating in a corner or near the fireplace, and they'd talk. Dixie used her familiar rhyming cadence—*Look here. Look here. Look here.*—as she would point to one keepsake or another on a shelf.

The time and expense the Paranormal Network invested in the Savannah project wasn't wasted, Landry promised Cate and Henri. They had learned a fascinating story about a famous explorer, proved a fabled treasure existed, and discovered the origin of a mysterious secret society called the Order of the Red Serpent. Would the Order continue, with only two members—Marcie and Fletcher—to guard the treasure? Landry doubted the need; if anyone happened to discover the chamber under the Castile mansion, the red serpents would be La Guardia. Could they keep it a secret?

In his heart, Landry hoped so.

Author's Note

     Serpent is a novel. Although most of the places I mention exist, you won't find the Parsonage on Hull Street near the cemetery nor the Castile mansion on Abercorn Street, and the Cotton Exchange Bank isn't real.

     Hernando de Soto came to the Savannah area around 1540, along with an entourage of men and a trove of loot he gathered during his expeditions in La Florida. Somewhere that treasure trove went missing, and de Soto died without recovering it. There is no Order of the Red Serpent, although supposedly de Soto built a fort and left men to guard it while he continued his travels throughout what is now the southern United States.

     Savannah is a beautiful city filled with old mansions, ghostly legends, wonderful places to eat and drink, and some of the friendliest people anywhere. I enthusiastically recommend a visit, and if you go, be sure to stay at the Azalea Inn. Yes, the bed-and-breakfast exists, sitting on a tree-lined block just off Abercorn Street and a few blocks from Calhoun Square and Colonial Park Cemetery. Teresa Jacobson, the owner and innkeeper, is a delightful person who graciously gave me permission to weave her name and her inn into this story.

     Although most of what I depict inside the Azalea

Inn is fictional, several things are true and worth mentioning. The breakfasts each morning are tasty and creative, Teresa does a great job explaining the murals painted on every wall of the dining room...and the inn is haunted.

During our stay, my wife and I heard the sounds I describe in the book—a noise like a needle hitting an old vinyl record and a voice whispering commands three times in a row. Teresa hadn't heard them, nor had other guests mentioned it, but they made such an impression on me that they became part of this ghost story.

I hope you enjoyed Landry Drake's first adventure outside the state of Louisiana. Soon he'll find another spooky tale to investigate somewhere in Mysterious America!

Thank you!

Thanks for reading *Serpent.*

.

If you enjoyed it, I'd appreciate a review on Amazon.
Reviews are what allow other readers to find books they enjoy, so thanks in advance for your help.

Please join me on:
Facebook
http://on.fb.me/187NRRP
Twitter
@BThompsonBooks

All of my books are available in ebook or paperback format on Amazon or our website Billthompsonbooks.com

MAY WE OFFER YOU A FREE BOOK?

Bill Thompson's award-winning first novel,
***The Bethlehem Scroll*, can be yours free.**
Just go to
billthompsonbooks.com
and click
"Subscribe."
Once you're on the list, you'll receive advance notice of future book releases and our newsletter.

Made in the USA
Monee, IL
24 February 2024

54036006R00184